I0661730

Wrighting the Wrongs

THE WRONG MOVE

MAREN JENNER

ENTWINED PUBLISHING

The Wrong Move
ISBN # 978-1-80250-261-9
©Copyright Maren Jenner 2025
Cover Art by Kelly Martin ©Copyright September 2025
Interior text design by Entwined Publishing
Published by Entice, an Entwined Publishing imprint

Published in 2025 by Entwined Publishing, United Kingdom.

Entwined Publishing is a division of Totally Entwined Group Limited.

THE WRONG MOVE

Dedication

To all those who are hurting. It can be easy to hide behind your walls, but I hope you find the courage to move beyond them, to live your life to its fullest potential and find the strength to put yourself out there again.

Acknowledgements

Thank you to Totally Entwined for helping this story reach its full potential. I'd also like to thank Rebecca for her editing help. To my amazing beta readers Lindsay and Christine, I'd be lost without you! To all my friends and family — thank you for your support and encouragement.
Lastly, a big thanks to you, my readers, because this wouldn't be possible without you. A full list of trigger warnings for this and all my books is available on my website at marenjennerbooks.com.

Chapter One

Meg

Friday stretches before me, blank and empty. I scowl at the ceiling from where I sprawl on the bed, in the same position I've been in since I came home half an hour ago. I'd forced myself to go to my summer classes at Southern Michigan University this morning, despite just wanting to stay under the covers after the text I'd received.

Chad broke up with me.

The thought has been playing on repeat in my head since I read the message. I'd known the breakup was looming, but had expected him to at least tell me face to face. We'd been together for four months, after all. I deserve more than a text.

Another ripple of anger washes over me, and I huff then flop onto my side, yanking my extra pillow into my arms before hugging it to my chest. It's not that I'm heartbroken or anything. Chad and I had a good run and he was a fun guy, but he isn't the love of my life.

He'd been a stable presence for me after so many one-night stands and disappointing blind dates.

The only thing missing was the spark.

I let out a despondent sigh as I stare unseeingly at my wall, thinking of the one time I'd found that elusive spark, that connection. But he hadn't lasted, just like every other guy to date, starting with my dad taking off when I was ten. *Why do I even bother?*

I wish I could talk to someone. Ideally, my best friend Leah, but she's working at the campus library. And when she does come home, she'll probably hang out with her boyfriend. Not that I begrudge her that happiness, but it has made getting together with her more difficult.

If I were working today, I'd be able to vent to one of my coworkers, but I'm not close enough to call any of them out of the blue and dump all my problems on them. I'm sure they have more important things to do.

Picking up my phone, I scan my pathetically short list of contacts and one name catches my eye. Mom.

We haven't spoken much since Chad and I went to visit her a couple of months ago. Between that and the disaster of our family Spring Break trip earlier this year, I don't know that I want to call her. But the idea stabs me until I sigh and push her name.

She answers after a few short rings and I can hear my half-sisters screaming in the background. Georgina is eight and Naomi is six, more than old enough to listen when Mom tells them to quiet down. Yet the noise doesn't lessen.

"Hey, Mom."

"Meg, you'll have to speak up. The girls are at it again."

I hold my tongue against the snarky comment I want to make. Instead, I say, "I thought maybe we could catch up?"

She sighs and I can picture her pinching the bridge of her nose. "I don't have time for idle chitchat."

The words sting, but I try once more. "Well, maybe we could get together soon? Sounds like you could use a break." An old memory of the two of us pops into my head and I smile, remembering how things were. Before. "What about getting a pedicure? Like we used to?"

"Oh, that sounds lovely. I'm just not sure how I'd find the time..."

A glimmer of hope peeks through the black cloud hanging over my head. "I could stop by tomorrow afternoon?"

Several moments pass, then she says, "Okay. I'll take you up on that. Say one o'clock?"

A full smile stretches my lips. "Great, Mom. See you then."

The idea of reconnecting with my mom bolsters me, and I pop off the bed with renewed energy after I hang up. Time to tackle my laundry. Grabbing one of my earbuds from the nightstand, I shove it in my ear and connect my music from my phone. I leave my other ear free in case I run into one of my housemates. Shinedown blares in my head, and I find myself bobbing along to the heavy beat as I gather the clothes near my bed.

Balancing the full clothes basket on my hip, I sashay through the house to the laundry nook off the kitchen. When I lift the lid of the washing machine, I instantly wrinkle my nose at the musty, stale smell of clothes that have sat for way too long.

My housemates are pretty tidy overall. I've lived in the mini-suite with my best friend and cousin Leah since I started college. We each have our own bedroom with a shared sitting room and bathroom, but it's part of a larger house that we share with the four Wrighting brothers. We all make it a point to keep up the public spaces like the kitchen and main living room.

But we draw the line at taking care of each other's laundry. It's every person for themselves.

I start searching for clues as to who the clothes belong to. They're definitely men's clothes, based on the pair of khaki shorts on top. Steven, the oldest, is too responsible to forget he had laundry going, so I rule him out. I could see Shawn getting distracted by Leah, since they're together. Sebastian is out because this load has both whites and colors in it.

Then I spy a pair of black briefs with the word Jockey written across the waistband and I shake my head. Growing up with the Wrightings and sharing a house, not to mention a laundry area, I know most of the guys prefer boxers, or at least boxer briefs. Only one wears briefs — the youngest and closest to my twenty-two years.

Silas.

The name conjures an image of his stupidly handsome face as well as a complicated mix of emotions left over from our tangled history. The pair of underwear taunts me because I know just how good Silas looks in them. Or, better yet, in nothing at all.

Memories threaten to slip past my carefully constructed walls that are already fragile from my breakup. I grit my teeth, then set about pulling the damp clothes out of the wash machine. Annoyance flares within me as I toss them in a heap on the dryer. I mutter the entire time about how he's a grown-ass man who should be able to remember a simple thing like finishing his laundry.

Once I've replaced his clothes with my own and shut the lid, I listen to the washer fill as I run through my options. The clothes need to be washed again, so it's not like I could just throw them in the dryer. Not that I would anyway. Did that once for Steven and he got upset with me for drying his favorite silk shirt. I no longer wash or dry anyone else's clothes, just in case.

I could leave Silas' stuff there in a heap. It would serve him right, plus eventually he'd run out of clean clothes and come looking for his stuff. Right?

My gut twists, though, and I curl my lip as my conscience pokes me. I could at least text him. That would be the nicer thing to do.

But I know Silas and as soon as he read the text, he'd forget it. Despite his best intentions, he gets sidetracked easily. This isn't the first time this has happened. I stare at the wet heap of clothes and let out a resigned sigh. I guess I could take them up to Silas' room where he'll be sure to see them.

Then they'll also be out of my way and I don't have to smell them anymore.

An empty clothes basket sits on the shelf above the dryer so I toss his laundry into it, fighting a groan at the odor when I set the weighted basket on my hip. I make the trek upstairs into the guys' territory—a place I rarely venture.

The unspoken rule used to be that the upstairs belonged to the guys while the mini-suite downstairs was only for me and Lee. Although lately that line has been blurred. Shawn is a frequent guest of Leah's now that they've been dating for several months. On top of that, Sebastian's girlfriend Callie moved into his room.

But I still feel like I'm trespassing whenever I walk upstairs.

Plus, I prefer to keep my distance from Silas when I'm able. Once upon a time, I wished for all that distance to disappear, but that was before. That flame has long since died, buried in the rubble of secrets and resentment that has piled up ever since.

Silas' door sits almost closed as I reach the landing, a sure sign he's home. Since it's not shut completely, I stalk over and nudge it open with my toe —

Getting a full glimpse of a wide-eyed Silas wearing only a pair of his signature underwear.

My mouth goes dry at the sight of all that skin. He's always been the perfect eye candy — lean and muscular, fit from playing soccer, with sun-kissed skin from all his time outdoors. His unruly curls are damp and sticking every which way, the way they always do right after he's showered.

I want to run my fingers through them, to tame them. But I clench my free hand into a fist instead and work on finding my voice. "It wasn't closed," I explain. "I thought..."

His ever-present confidence snaps back into place and a smirk tips his lips as his amber eyes twinkle. "Nothing you haven't seen before."

The reminder only raises my hackles, and I pin him with my fiercest glare, unable to find a snarky retort.

"What's up?"

I drop the heavy basket of clothes onto the messy floor where it makes a dull thud. "Forget something?"

"Shit." He frowns. "How'd you know they're mine?"

I wrinkle my nose and dip my finger under the waistband of a pair of his Jockeys. "It wasn't rocket science."

His smirk grows into an infuriating smile as I drop the briefs back onto the pile. When I look at him once more, I can't help scanning his sculpted legs and the way the underwear hugs his trim hips. My mouth goes dry.

"See something you like?" He folds his arms, making his biceps stand out.

I know he's only doing it to taunt me and I retort the first thing that pops into my head. "Just because you have a nice package doesn't mean I want to open it."

He blinks as my words settle between us.

My cheeks feel like they're on fire. The anger I've been fighting seeps out of me, overtaken by embarrassment. "I-I mean..." I stammer, wishing I could fall through the floor and disappear forever. I drop my head with a quiet, "Fuck."

Normally I'd be able to own the compliment, raise my chin and stay defiant in the face of inflating his already-too-big ego. But not today. The walls I keep in place for interactions with him already feel flimsy in the wake of my breakup. I try to brace myself for whatever teasing comment Silas will come up with, hoping I'm strong enough today to handle him.

"Take off your shirt, and we'll call it even."

The outrageous request has my fight rushing back in and I snap my head up to meet his audacious gaze. He smirks, but a knowing reassurance rests in his eyes as he stares at me. As if he prodded me on purpose. I feel unsettled that he can still read me that well, even as a subtle warmth steals over me and I melt. Just a little. I know on some level he still cares and always will.

Because I feel exactly the same way.

Another moment passes as he holds my gaze. My heart stutters when a flash of longing appears in those amber orbs, then heat flares between us. Just because we've tried this and failed doesn't mean there's nothing here. Not that I'd admit that to him.

He clears his throat, then reaches for his jeans. "I need to get ready for work."

"Fine. I've got my own laundry to tend to." But I can't help lingering in the doorway, watching him button his pants. A wisp of desire grounds me to my spot, as I wish for what could have been.

Then Silas puts on his most charming smile and strides over. He's all smooth confidence, a walking sex magnet as he leans into my space and props his arm on the doorjamb above my head. I'm a solid five foot eight, and he's got a good six inches on me. My stomach flips as I inhale his familiar scent—sandalwood and oak.

I can't help staring at his perfect bare chest, then he clears his throat. I meet that intense gaze as he quirks a suggestive eyebrow.

"You wanna do me a favor?"

I feel my forehead crinkle as I narrow my eyes.

"Maybe you could pop those clothes back into the wash?" He tilts his head. "I'm sure I can find some way to repay you."

The arrogant tone is exactly what I need to free myself from his magnetic spell. "Fuck off, Silas." I toss my hair and walk down the hall without a backward glance.

* * * *

Silas

Saturday morning, I lounge in bed, replaying last night's dream about Meg. I don't remember much of it—her flashing dark eyes, the sassy toss of her black hair, the tempting smirk on her lips—but it's enough to make me ache. Not willing to follow those thoughts over that edge, I grab my phone, choosing a distraction instead.

I check all of my social media, then look through my email. A note from my doctor's office catches my eye and I bolt upright as my heart stutters. *My test results...*

A couple of weeks ago, we found out that my brother Sebastian has been diagnosed with autism. It came as a bit of a shock to our family, but it's also been an eye opener. Sebastian and I have never been extremely close, despite being the two youngest. He likes to keep people at arm's length, has a photographic memory, is incredibly smart, and is one of the most introverted people I know.

I'm his opposite in almost every way—outgoing, love physical touch, enjoy meeting new people, crave attention. I've never understood him.

But now I'm starting to.

He gave us all some basic reading material about autism and it's given me a new perspective on my brother. I feel like I'd never taken the time to get to know him before. The very idea sends guilt gnawing at me, and I vow not to waste that chance again.

Especially since he's helped me with my own journey. Along with the links about autism, he sent me a separate email, saying while he'd been researching his own diagnosis he'd found a lot about ADHD and I might want to check into it. I'd clicked the link and been sucked down a rabbit hole of information that explained so many things about myself.

I made an appointment the next day, was referred to a specialist for testing, and have been waiting for the results.

Which are finally here.

My chest is tight and doubts race through my head as I hover my finger over the email. What if I *don't* have ADHD? What if all of the times I've jumped into a rash decision or been called out for disrupting the class are just…me? Nerves rattle within me as I press my lips together and open the email.

Several moments later, I scan the official document and my shoulders relax when I see the diagnosis. I have ADHD. The knowledge settles into me, a missing piece clicking into place. There's a reason I don't always follow through with tasks or forget simple things — like finishing a load of laundry. I'm not stupid. I'm not broken.

I'm neurodivergent.

A weight lifts off my chest as I read through the rest of the recommendations. They'd like me to follow up with a cognitive therapist to help me adjust to the diagnosis and learn how my brain works. Medication is an option, if I choose that route. My head spins as I think of the possibilities, and I turn off my screen.

I think I'll start with coffee.

Downstairs, I round the corner into the kitchen where I almost bump into Leah who leans against the counter near the doorway. We share a smile. Callie sits on Sebastian's lap, the two of them cozy at the table and in their own little world. I catch myself before I shake my head, still having a hard time wrapping my mind around seeing them together. I guess opposites really do attract.

Meg leans on the counter near the almost empty coffee pot, her hand on her mug as she longingly watches the steady drip of the brewing java. I can't help grinning at the sight. She'd hook herself to an IV of the stuff if they'd let her.

I don't say a word as I stride up, reaching around her to grab my own mug out of the cupboard. Satisfaction courses through me when I hear her breath hitch, and I smile even wider when she snorts in annoyance. I love pushing Meg's buttons. Riling her up is one of my favorite things to do, and always has been.

Even before the tangled lines of our history knotted together into impossible strands neither one of us can sort out.

"You know there's a line, right?" she grunts.

I can't help smirking, knowing it'll irritate her even more. "I work at a coffee shop, Meg. I think I understand the concept."

Sebastian peers over at me, and I don't like how his eyes narrow. Something in his gaze makes me want to shift, as if he's piecing together the secret Meg and I have kept hidden for so long. But I'm used to feeling this way. At first, every glance had me wanting to spill my guts. I haven't, though, and here we are, two years later, the secret still intact.

Why would today be the day it all blows up?

I relax slightly as Sebastian turns back to Callie. My tension eases even more when I notice Meg sneaking peeks at me, and our moment in my room yesterday replays in my mind. I remember how that heat between us flared as I picture the longing in her dark eyes when I'd leaned above her on the doorjamb.

I'm waiting for another glance from her, and this time I meet her gaze, smirking again that I caught her. Her mouth tightens before she turns away.

Callie murmurs to Sebastian, who sucks in a sharp breath, and I turn my focus to them.

He stares right at me. "You two slept together, didn't you?"

I freeze at his smug tone, unable to move even when I feel Meg look at me again.

She calmly asks, "What?"

My teeth clench together so hard I feel like they might break. What tipped him off? My gaze shifts to

Callie and guilt flashes over her face before she ducks her head. She must've said something that connected the dots.

"You two slept together," Sebastian repeats. "That's what changed between you, isn't it?"

Fuck. Honestly, I'm surprised he'd never figured it out before, but did he have to blurt it out like that? He sounded so triumphant, like he'd figured out the final answer to Clue.

Leah stares at me, then Meg, before quietly asking, "Is that true?"

Meg's cheeks turn pink as she glances at me once more and bites her lip. I can read her perfectly. Neither of us wanted Lee to find out like this. She values honesty above everything else, and she's always been so protective of us brothers. For Meg and I to keep this from her will be a punch in the gut.

Meg promised to let me know if she ever found the right time to explain, to tell Lee the whole story, but it never came. Not once in the past two years. Now, here we are, caught in our web of secrets. Meg shifts and I know she's going to confirm it.

Resigned, I watch her dip her chin, admitting the truth.

The color drains from Leah's face, then she spins on her heel and rushes from the room. My stomach turns over, feeling sick that I hurt one of my best friends, but frustration and anger are right there too. Why couldn't Sebastian keep his mouth shut?

"Dammit," Meg mutters, turning to Sebastian with a glare. "That's not how we wanted her to find out. We were trying *not* to hurt her." And she storms after Lee.

I swipe a hand over my face. "Sebastian, for such a smart guy, you can be pretty dumb sometimes."

Then I stride out of the room, not waiting for a response. In the living room, I anxiously frown at the mostly closed door of the mini-suite, wondering if I should go in. I'm as much a part of this as Meg, had just as much a hand in hurting our friend, and if Lee is going to rake someone over the coals, it should be both of us.

Relief trickles through me when only murmured words reach my ears. Lee is like a sister to me. She's one of us, and we protect our own, even from our dumb mistakes. She rarely yells, even if it's deserved.

The rush of memories from my brief interlude with Meg crashes into me. We'd barely begun to explore the tension that had built for years, but our fledgling relationship couldn't handle the severity of the storm life threw our way.

I clench my fists as I shove the past aside, then stomp upstairs to my room. I hate feeling helpless, and rage at my inability to do anything simmers within me. My pillow catches my eye, and I let my anger flood out as I pound my fist into it several times over until I feel calmer.

We'd done so well—two whole years with no one the wiser. For Sebastian to just blow our cover like that…

My pillow gets another punch.

Chapter Two

Meg

I'd woken up this morning in a great mood after my sleepover with Leah and Callie last night, feeling optimistic and grateful for my friends. Only to have everything blow up in my face as Sebastian put together the pieces of the secret Silas and I had kept for two whole years.

I didn't even get a chance to explain to Leah. She had plans with Shawn, promised we'd talk later. But I couldn't miss the hurt in her eyes. Guilt lingers in my stomach, even though there's nothing more I can say at the moment. I've practiced the speech a thousand times at least, but it still hasn't left my lips.

I slept with Silas.

The words echo in my head, the memories a double-edged sword of beautiful, effervescent moments twined with hurt and pain. As each one darts through my mind, I wince at the slice of its sharp blade.

The alarm on my phone saves me from that torturous trip to the past, reminding me to get ready to go see Mom. She's not always the best listener, but I'm hoping today can be like it used to be.

Before my dad left. Before she threw herself into her new family.

It'll be just the two of us, and I can't shake the feeling that this will be the day we reconnect. I smile at the thought of catching her up on my life, telling her about Chad and my secret relationship with Silas. Maybe she'll have some advice for me.

If not, at least she'll finally hear what I want to say.

* * * *

The once-pristine white house is now a mere memory and my stomach turns over as I pull into the driveway where I grew up. The past whispers in my ear, remnants of fights between Mom and Dad, then the ghost of that final time he slammed the door before walking out for good.

I remind myself that if he hadn't left, I'd never have been so close to Lee. Never become friends with the Wrightings. Yet, the familiar well of loneliness aches within me as I picture my preteen self being shipped off to Leah's day after day while Mom searched to patch the hole in her life I wasn't big enough to fill.

Although it hasn't stopped me from trying.

With a determined grunt, I shut the door on the memories and step out of the car. The house may look like crap. Mom may have chosen to marry my deadbeat stepdad and have two unruly kids with him that he couldn't care less about. But she's still my mom, and she invited me here today.

I knock on the door, ignoring the peeling paint as I wait on the steps. Footsteps race behind the closed door, and I hear Mom yell for the kids to slow down. My lips twist in a wry smile as I try to remember a moment they haven't been wild in all the times I've visited. I fail, but I'm still smiling when she opens the door. I struggle to keep my lips tipped up as I take in the reality of her haggard, worn expression versus the lighter one that lives in my memory. "Hey, Mom."

She lifts one side of her mouth in a semblance of a happy expression. "Meg. I'm so glad you're here."

The relieved words buoy me and I lean in to give her a half-hug.

"It'll be so nice to have some time to myself."

Her statement sends my heart soaring as I think about us going out like I'd suggested. "Pedicures?"

She dips her chin, ushering me inside. "It was such a great idea. I decided to treat myself, since you offered to come over. You mentioned how much I needed a break, and I couldn't get that out of my mind." She pats my shoulder. "Thanks, Meg. I'll just go get my purse."

I can hardly believe that George will actually watch the kids while we go out—the only thing he watches is TV, here or at the bar. But I guess miracles do happen.

The kids race by, Georgina holding a doll above her head as Naomi screams for her to give it back. I glance around for George, but his usual chair is empty. *Maybe Mom hired a sitter?*

The girls nearly knock Mom over as they tear back down the hallway, but Mom just sidesteps them. I notice then that her lipstick is fresh, her hair pulled back in a tidy bun, and I see a glimmer of her old self. I can't wait to tell her everything that's been going on, to dish to her like I used to.

"Well," she says, slipping on her shoes. "I'll be back in a couple of hours. There should be some snacks in the cupboard if the girls get hungry, otherwise, I'll figure out something when I get home."

I frown as her words sink in. "Wait, what?"

She pats my cheek. "You're such a dear for volunteering to come over and give your mom a break. Hope they're not too rowdy for you."

Then she walks out of the door, leaving me standing in the entryway with my mouth open, knee-deep in smashed pieces of the hope I let myself feel. When will I ever learn?

* * * *

Three hours later, I'm surprised I have any hair left on my head. Sure, they're my half-siblings but they act like total nightmares. The only time they weren't yelling at one another is when they were screaming at me. I tried coloring, cleaning, even scrounged up some stuff for a craft, but nothing occupied them.

When Mom walks back in the door, appearing calm and rested, I can barely contain my anger. I try to explain how the day went but she interrupts me.

"They're kids, Meg. You were rambunctious too, and look how you turned out?" She brushes off my concerns about their behavior with a wave of her freshly manicured nails.

I grit my teeth at the realization that she got a mani too. But I don't say anything, knowing it would be a waste of breath.

"Darlings, come to Mama. I got you a present!" She walks past me without a second glance.

I stand there for a long moment, watching my half-sisters run to Mom. She thought of them while she was out, took the time to pick them up gifts. I know I'm twenty-two and I don't need presents, but she could at least say thank you. Or tell me goodbye.

"Bye," I mutter, one hand on the door. "You're welcome..." I might as well be talking to the wall.

I stew for the entire drive home, feeling more down by the minute. Once I've parked in my normal spot on the street, I turn off the car and slouch in my seat. Shawn's car isn't back in the driveway yet, meaning Lee also isn't home and I still have no one to talk to.

My mind conjures an image of the one pick-me-up that might help, and my mouth waters at the thought of my favorite coffee from Not Your Average Joe. The only trouble with going there is I might run into Silas. One more glance shows his car is still here — plus, he doesn't usually work Saturdays.

Why not? I deserve a treat, and a walk might do me good.

* * * *

Silas

My afternoon shift at Not Your Average Joe's is a welcome distraction. I'll be starting my internship at Dad's law office on Monday, so I'm changing my schedule to weekends only, beginning today.

Halfway through my shift, I see Meg coming down the sidewalk. It's not unusual for her to stop in on her way to or from study sessions or work. She's here often enough that I've memorized her standard order — a grande mochaccino with extra whip.

I give her my usual grin, meeting her eyes as she makes her way to the counter, but my expression falters at the weight in her gaze. She quickly tips her lips up, but the expression doesn't mask the heaviness emanating from her. I wonder if things didn't go well with Lee.

Before I can ask, a scowling middle-aged woman steps in front of me. "Excuse me, young man," she says in an entitled tone that sets my teeth on edge.

Meg blinks, and I lift a shoulder in a silent apology then focus on the customer. "What can I help you with?" I ask as nicely as I'm able.

I'd been looking forward to an easy order from Meg, maybe a little banter. Today has been filled with complicated coffees and overly particular customers. *Can't I catch a break?*

"I asked for a white mocha with four shots — two on the bottom and two on top. With almond milk, extra hot. And caramel drizzled inside the cup." She lifts the lid, a triumphant gleam in her eye. "This caramel is *on top* of the whip cream."

My face falls as I stare at the woman, unable to believe someone could be that picky. "And?"

"I said inside the cup, not on the whip cream."

I fight the urge to roll my eyes as I turn to my coworker who made the drink. She glowers out of sight of the customer, but I ask, "Did you put caramel inside the cup?" When she nods, I face the customer once more. "Our staff followed your instructions to put the caramel inside the cup as well, so it seems you just have a little bit extra caramel."

Why anyone would complain about that is beyond me, but it's the wrong thing to say. The lady's eyes narrow and she pins me with a glare so menacing that if looks could kill, I'd keel over.

"I did not ask for extra caramel —"

Meg steps up next to her, her mouth set in a determined line, but she doesn't say a word as she pulls out her wallet. I glance at her curiously, then try to focus on the customer.

The lady side-eyes her before continuing, "I specifically asked for caramel inside the cup. It's not that difficult of an instruction."

It's hard for me to bite my tongue, but Meg just slips a dollar bill into the tip jar and smiles sweetly at the woman. I suck in a breath at the feral edge to that smile, recognizing it from all of the times I've coaxed it out of her. This customer is in for it. A beam of satisfaction shoots through me, that Meg has my back.

Despite everything.

The woman freezes at the gesture, but her wrath is undeterred as she plops the drink onto the counter with enough force that liquid sloshes over the side. "The customer is always right, and I demand you remake my drink correctly. Unless that's too difficult for you."

Another dollar goes into the jar. Meg's expression doesn't change as the lady glares at her, and I have to fight to hold back my laughter.

Trying to compose myself, I tell the woman, "Ma'am, I'll have to get a manager because we didn't technically do anything wrong." I could remake the drink, but it's the principle.

"I am a paying customer," she screeches, making Meg slip another bill into the jar. The woman turns her furious expression on Meg and demands, "Just what do you think you are doing?"

"Oh," Meg says, all innocence. "I believe in treating people like human beings, so I'm making sure this man is well-compensated for dealing with an entitled customer like you."

"Excuse me?" she says, her eyes widening.

Meg waves a stack of dollar bills. "I've got plenty, and there's an ATM right around the corner. We could do this all day." She grins at me. "I'm sure he won't mind."

The woman sputters and stammers but no full words come out. Finally, she glares at me then the cup and mess of coffee on the counter. "Well? Aren't you going to fix this?"

"As I said, I'd have to get my manager since —"

Meg drops another bill into the jar, and the woman growls then huffs, "Never mind. I'll get my coffee elsewhere. Don't expect to see me in here again!" And she storms out.

A scattered round of applause sounds from the customers who had been watching the scene unfold. I quickly toss out the coffee in question then wipe the counter while Meg steps closer.

"Now," I say with a big smile, "that was something to see."

She grins. "I thought she was going to explode there for a second."

A pang of longing hits me at the easiness of this moment. I miss my friend, I miss how things used to be before life screwed us over. Before our fight. Before she walled herself off. The usual resentment and bitterness are gone, replaced by nostalgia, and it takes me a second to recover.

Clearing my throat, I ask, "So, um, your usual?"

"Yes, please."

"Coming right up." I make it myself, exactly as she likes, then wave her off when she offers her card. I get two free drinks per shift, so I'll take it out of that. "Nah, you deserve this. Thank you."

She lifts the lid to blow on the hot liquid, pursing her lips in a way that locks me in, unable to look away. "Mmm," she hums, smiling before licking a bit of whipped cream off her upper lip. "Thanks, Silas. It's

one thing for *me* to pick a fight with you. I've earned it."
With a sassy wink, she saunters away.

I shake my head, trying to clear the wisps of desire
clouding my mind. But my gaze is pulled back to her
retreating form and I watch until she's out of sight.

* * * *

Meg

I feel much lighter on my way home. My coffee is
delicious, and I can't help being proud of how I
defended Silas. I ignore the part of my heart calling
attention to the obvious interest I saw in his eyes before
I left today, and yesterday in his bedroom.

We're always dancing around that tension, but I
don't know if I can ever give into that pull again. It's
much easier keeping my walls in place. Safer, too.

These past two days have been enough of a downer
without opening myself to being hurt by him again. My
mind runs over everything that happened with my
mom, rewinding further to Lee's hurt expression this
morning. A weight sits on my chest, and I know it
won't lessen until she and I can actually talk.

So much for a pick-me-up.

At home, I busy myself by throwing my last load of
laundry into the dryer, then I tackle some reading for
school. My homework occupies me long enough for the
clothes to be dry when I check on them. I take the load
back to my room and have just started folding it when
a tap sounds on my door, followed by Leah calling my
name.

"Come in!" Hope and anxiety swirl within me. I'm
ready to get this over with but I'm not thrilled to dredge
up the past.

She walks inside, and I'm relieved at her easy smile. I remember a time not so long ago that her smile never met her eyes. But now, her spark is back.

"I thought we could actually talk," she says.

"Yes, please." I keep folding clothes as she shuts the door and plops on my bed, making herself at home. Her eager gaze tells me the ball is in my court. "So, I guess I should start at the beginning."

Leah knew about my crush on Silas, how I'd been closest to him out of all the Wrightings. He and I hung out in school too, being in the same grade, and I found myself craving his attention, loving how he made me feel seen.

We danced around that tension through high school, neither of us making the first move though there was plenty of flirting and banter. I'd told her all of it, but I've got some gaps to fill in. I take my time figuring out how to begin, knowing this is a painful period for her to talk about.

"It happened when everything was going down with you and Vance," I say, hoping to rip off the Band-Aid. "So I understand if you don't want—"

"I'm fine." Her firm tone and reassuring smile tell me it's true.

So I take a deep breath to brace myself for the sting of the past then dive in.

Leah had just broken up with her manipulative boyfriend, Vance. I'd been trying to support her, but it was also the week I'd taken my test to receive my medical assistant certification. She seemed okay overall, and the day came I would receive my results.

Everyone knew I was waiting and they were all anxious for me. Each ding of my phone had the guys looking at me expectantly, or Lee smiling in my direction. My own anticipation was heavy enough without adding theirs, so I escaped to Leah's tree house, needing a break from the added pressure.

A while later, Silas showed up with snacks and all the things for my favorite drink — vodka cranberry. He waited with me, sipping and chatting, an easy, flirtatious air between us. His presence calmed me and I was having so much fun with him that I didn't even notice at first when my phone dinged.

The next time I picked it up, I saw the notification. I met Silas' gorgeous eyes and held my breath as I reached out my hand. He took it, squeezing tight and not letting go as I opened the email.

When I saw that I'd passed, a slow smile spread over my lips as I met his gaze and nodded. He whooped and threw his arms around me, his oaky sandalwood scent a heady addition to the exciting moment. We clung to each other, but when he pulled back, his lips were right there.

I couldn't help myself.

He didn't resist when our lips met, and I felt like I could fly. Especially when he kissed me back. All my dreams were coming true — my longtime crush returning my attention, me getting my MA cert and taking the next step toward a nursing career.

The sparks dancing between us ignited into a firestorm of passion, and I clung to him as he eased me down onto the blanket on the tree-house floor. All I could see was him. My whole world narrowed to his every movement, his every noise, his every touch.

When he slid inside me, it had seemed like the next natural step.

"Nothing had ever felt so right…" I trail off, caught in the wistful haze of that perfect memory, then I realize I'm still holding a hoodie. I quickly finish folding it and put it on the pile.

"Oh, Meg," Leah says, her voice full of sympathy. "So what gives? Why didn't you tell us then?"

"Well, it all happened so fast, and we both decided it'd be better to tell you guys after things were official. If we went that route." I shrug, not liking Lee's concerned frown. "I couldn't even be upset about keeping it a secret. I was too busy walking on air."

We both chuckle, but I sober first to take a deep breath, steeling myself for what happened next. Leah's gaze drops to the comforter and I know she's bracing herself too.

"The next night was *the* party." We'd had a houseful. Friends invited friends, and soon the place overflowed with people and music. I smile wryly. "To be honest, I was surprised no one called us out because Silas couldn't keep his hands off me. I don't think he danced with anyone else all night."

But Leah had been flirting with other guys and Shawn had been pretending not to be jealous. Steven stayed in the corner with his friends, and Sebastian hid in his room.

On the floor, all I could see was Silas. Tension built between us until I could take no more. I dragged him to my room where we barely made it inside. We tumbled to the bed for another passionate interlude that felt far too short for what I wanted.

It was long enough for everything to change, though.

I set down the newly folded pants and sink onto the bed. "When we came out, the house was quiet and empty. I knew in my gut something was wrong."

Leah's gaze flicks to me, and she brushes a piece of hair back behind her ear. "I wondered where you'd gone..."

I know she could never bring herself to ask, since Leah rarely speaks of that night. I'd found out later in bits and pieces how Vance had showed up, pleading for Leah to take him back. She'd refused, and he'd backhanded her. A stupid move because Shawn was right there and ran after him with Steven on his heels while Leah stayed with Sebastian.

While Silas and I were sneaking around, my best friend had been abused. Right on our doorstep.

"I'm so sorry I wasn't there for you, Lee. You don't know how many times I've wished..."

She grabs my hand and shakes her head. "No, please don't feel guilty. Nothing would have changed if you'd been there. Vance is an asshole who seized the moment."

I know this, but it helps to hear her say it. We both fall quiet while I put away my clothes in my closet, needing to move and wanting to give Lee some space. She'll speak when she's ready to talk more.

Those days after the party were so difficult. Guilt haunted me, and I know Silas felt the same. He hadn't been there to help defend Leah or go after Vance with his brothers. Resentment built between us, but it didn't stop there. Neither did Vance.

"So..." Lee's voice brings me back, full of curiosity as she asks, "What ended things between you and Silas?"

"We were so new," I say quietly. "We weren't strong enough to stand together under the weight of everything life threw at us. I think we both felt guilty and resented that we weren't there for you. It built between us. Combined with the stress of the rest of Vance's aftermath?" I shake my head. "It's no wonder we fought."

He and I had said some awful things in the heat of the moment, blaming each other for events out of our control. The stress of being a foundation for our friend through her storm, the helplessness we'd both felt, the inability to do more...we'd bottled it up for so long that it all came to a head. And we exploded.

"I gave him space afterward, but I didn't think we were actually done. Silas must have, though." I keep talking as I put away the rest of my pants, unable to meet Leah's steady gaze. "I went to surprise him at a party at our mutual friends' house four days after the fight, hoping to make up and move forward."

My throat is thick with the painful memories, and it takes me a moment to continue. "Instead, I found him making out in a dark corner with a curvy dark-haired woman."

Leah gasps, and I glance up to find her eyes wide, full of shock.

I hurry to reassure her. "We hadn't made any commitments or promises, so it wasn't like he'd cheated." But I'd also vowed never to let him get close to me again.

She nods, still frowning, and I know she's processing.

I walk over to sit on the bed next to her then grab her hand. "I'm so sorry I kept this from you. We both wanted to tell you, but it never seemed like a good time. You had enough going on without worrying about us."

She squeezes my fingers. "I understand. I mean, I wish you'd told me, but I get why you didn't. We all had a lot going on." Lee pulls me in for a hug. "And I'm sorry, too. I hate that you were hurting and I didn't even know."

I hug her back, feeling a big weight lifted off me. Keeping secrets sucks, but keeping them from your best friend? Zero out of ten, do not recommend.

She pulls back with a frown. "I can't believe Silas kissed someone else, though. That doesn't seem like him. I always thought he liked you, too."

A pang stabs at me, followed by a prick of bitterness. "Yeah, so did I." And look where that got me.

"Did you ever...talk to him about it?"

I raise my eyebrows before I finish taking care of my laundry. "Nah. I know what I saw. If I'm that easily replaced, then we're not meant to be."

She tilts her head, and I recognize the pensive expression. She's analyzing the whole situation, running it through her mind with the new information. Just like Sebastian does, another reason they're such good friends.

"Let it go, Lee."

"Nope," she says, and I sigh. "You two still pick at each other, so obviously not all the feelings are gone."

I let out a *hmph* as I yank open my underwear drawer in my dresser.

"Hah, see?"

Evidently my grunt didn't count as outright denial. I fight the urge to roll my eyes.

"Every girl he's dated since then has looked similar to you. Don't you think that says something?"

I set my jaw, then suck in a calming breath before I turn to face her. "Yeah, Lee. It says he wants someone that looks like me. Just not *me*."

I've thought this through from every angle and it's the only conclusion I've been able to reach. Saying it out loud hurts more than I thought, but the truth settles into my chest, adding another barrier to the layers of protection over my still-bruised heart.

Chapter Three

Silas

I lie on my back in my bed, tossing my soccer ball toward the ceiling then catching it and tossing it again. Over and over. I threw in my load of laundry when I got home from work, so now I've got nothing but time.

And all I can do is think about this morning.

The secret is out. I should be relieved that everyone knows, that I don't have to keep what happened with Meg from those closest to me. But that means I also have to face the complicated feelings that got me into this mess in the first place.

I forget what I'm doing and almost let the ball drop on my face. With an annoyed sigh, I toss the ball to the ground, then a knock sounds at my door, and I call, "Come in."

Steven peeks in, raising his eyebrows. He hadn't been downstairs when Sebastian outed us, but news spreads fast in this house. I sit up, then shove some clothes off the end of my bed to make room for him.

He gets comfortable and says, "Spill."

Steven and I are close, despite the five years between us. I've always looked up to him, tagged after him, and he's never made me feel like the annoying pest the others had. Shawn and Sebastian are pretty tight, so it actually works well.

I start talking, telling him everything that happened. Moments bob through my mind—her soft, full lips touching mine. The heat of her palm burning through my thin T-shirt. The sweet scent of her shampoo as her silky hair brushes my cheek. The memories of us in that tree house are some of my favorites, and I've been chasing that level of connection ever since.

But the days and weeks that followed are still hard to talk about.

"I'm sorry I wasn't there to run Vance down. I'd really like to get my hands on that fucker." His name leaves a bitter taste in my mouth as I think of all the damage he's done.

"It wouldn't have changed anything."

Steven's matter-of-fact words jolt me back to the present. "What?"

"You coming with us to teach Vance a lesson." He studies me. "In fact, it was probably good you weren't there. We barely held it together between the two of us. I don't know if even Judge Paulson would've been able to get us off if we'd beat him up any worse."

Some of my guilt eases, and I manage a wry smile. "That's true. I doubt he'd have been able to walk."

We both share a chuckle, then he says, "So how'd things get so fucked up with you and Meg?"

I swipe a hand over my face. I don't like thinking about that, let alone admitting what happened. Especially to my older brother.

Steven and I are opposites in a lot of ways, but where Sebastian and I butt heads, Steven balances me. He's neat and tidy to my mess. We both have brown hair, but his is darker and always perfectly styled while my curls have a mind of their own. He's quieter than Shawn and I, and he chooses his words carefully. When he speaks, he puts thought into what he wants to say and how it will affect everyone.

Unlike me.

"We fought." I rub the back of my neck, not meeting his knowing gaze. "Emotions were high with everything going on... I guess I blamed her. I made her out to be the reason I wasn't there to help you guys, and I think she resented me for not being there for Lee."

Steven hums, letting me know he understands.

"Add in the pressure of keeping things a secret, and well..." I spread my fingers, simulating an explosion. "Kaboom, that was it."

When I finally glance up, Steven shakes his head. "You're an idiot."

I roll my eyes. "We all know that."

"You never apologized?"

"We both said shit we didn't mean, and it was easier to let things be, you know?" She'd shut me out after that fight. Her cold shut-out had hurt even more than her harsh words, and that sting still lingers.

He shoves my shoulder. "No, I don't know. I can't believe you'd let her walk away without a word." His scrutinizing gaze pierces me then he adds, "Unless there's more."

I never could hide anything from him. Even this whole secret with Meg, I'm sure he knew something had changed between me and her. He'd just let me keep it quiet until I was ready. I play with a loose string on my shorts as I struggle to find the courage to say the words out loud. "I, um, kissed another girl at a party after our fight. I was drunk and thought it would be a good distraction. It didn't last long, but I think Meg found out somehow."

"Seriously? And you *still* didn't apologize?"

"I tried!" I protest. "She wouldn't even look at me, let alone talk to me after that. I texted her too, but she never responded."

He shoots me a dry stare. "You're an adult, Silas. You both are, and you should act like it." When I stay quiet, he sighs. "You and Meg, man, that was a long time coming."

I fold my arms, hating how right he is. As the youngest in our group, she and I were paired together often. Then in high school, I realized she had a crush on me and it made me feel...special. Out of all my brothers, out of all my friends, she had a crush on *me*. Once I started seeing her as a woman, it wasn't hard to fall for her too.

But there were complications.

Lee is like my sister and Meg's her best friend. If something went wrong between us, it could be detrimental. We didn't like the idea of rocking our perfect little boat, so we took our time, dancing around those feelings for years until we were sure. And it still turned out shitty.

"Maybe it's for the best." I shrug. "We tried, we failed, we can move on."

"But you haven't," he points out gently. "Every girl you date looks like Meg."

"What?"

That dry stare is back. "Think about it, Silas. You always said that Meg is your type, but maybe it's more than that."

The litany of women I've dated runs through my head, and I picture their similarities. Long, dark hair. Luscious curves. Several inches shorter than me but not too tiny. I frown at the one thing they all have in common — they all look a hell of a lot like Meg.

"There's still something between you, and you need to figure it out before you let her get away."

I jerk my head at his words. "What do you mean?"

"Think about it. Why are you trying so hard to find someone like her? Why are you still so pissed?"

The words dance around my mind, and one realization floats to the surface. *She's perfect for me.* The phrase pokes and prods at some sore spots, as the truth often does, and I try not to wince.

"Listen, I know what happens when the girl of your dreams gets away and it's not pretty."

The pain in his voice has me reaching over to touch his shoulder. His high-school sweetheart Bianca left town the night of their high-school graduation and never looked back. I'm not sure he'll ever get over her. But I can learn from his mistakes, and not repeat them.

"You need to fix this. If I'm wrong and nothing is there, then you two can at least be friends again." He grins. "I think we'd all love a break from your bickering."

I chuckle. "Fine. I'll think about it."

"That's all I ask." He stands then picks up the soccer ball, raising his eyebrows in a silent offer to go kick it around.

"Hell yeah." Burning off some energy is exactly what I need after the day I've had.

First, though, I stop and put my clothes into the dryer. Shawn comes outside after we've been out there for a few and takes turns being goalie in the net I have tucked in the back corner of the yard, opposite Leah's tree house.

As we're finishing up, I glance between my brothers, knowing there's one more piece of news I should share. "So, I got this email this morning." I run through my ADHD diagnosis and how Sebastian pointed me in the right direction.

Shawn grins. "Well, that explains a lot."

We all laugh, lightly at first, but as I look at my brothers, I can see that unhindered acceptance and it makes me laugh even harder. Because it's true, because there's no judgment, and I feel free.

As we reach the house, I call dibs on the shower, thrilled I can grab my clean clothes so I've got something to wear. After I'm washed and dressed, I trot downstairs to grab a snack.

Leah's at the table, reading. I put a small bag of chips and a cheese stick on the table, then go give her a quick hug from behind.

"Sorry we didn't tell you, Lee-bug."

She pats my arm, turning so I can see her smile. "It's okay. Meg explained and I get it. I wish I'd been there for you guys while you were going through that."

That's Lee, always wanting to take care of everyone. I plop into my seat and pick up my cheese. "You were going through plenty."

She slips a bookmark between the pages before setting her book down. "Now that I know what happened, maybe I can help fix it."

I don't like the gleam in her eye or the pensive expression on her face. Lee is tenacious when it comes to looking out for us, and I know this thing between me and Meg has bothered her for a while. But Meg is stubborn and loves to hold a grudge. Even if I apologize, I doubt things will go back to the way they were before.

The last thing I need is Lee roping me into some scheme and making things worse. I take my phone out of my pocket, pretending I felt it buzz. "Oh, Steven needs me. Guess I'll take this upstairs."

I wave a quick goodbye, then I do just that, ignoring the weight of her assessing gaze on my back.

* * * *

Meg

My mind won't let me concentrate on my Trauma Basics homework the next day. I've been staring at the same sentence for ten minutes, but I still don't know what it says. I need a change of scenery. I focus better with ambient noise and could definitely use some coffee. My stomach growls, reminding me it's past lunch time.

After I pack my things, I sling my backpack over one shoulder and tuck my phone into my shorts pocket. Callie and Sebastian are snuggled on the couch as I walk out, and they both look up from their books.

Sebastian sets his down and pops to his feet, then shoves his hands in his pockets. "I'm sorry, Meg. I didn't mean—"

I raise my hand and give him a heartfelt smile. "It's all right, Sebastian. It was bound to come out sometime. I can't believe it took this long, actually."

"You and Leah are okay?" he asks, pushing his glasses up on his nose.

I nod. "Yep. We talked, and we're fine."

"Good." His smile is relieved, and I grin back before waving at both of them.

Outside, the sky is gray, but it's not raining and I decide to walk to the coffee shop. Not Your Average Joe is only a few blocks away. Besides, the end-of-June heat is in full swing so even if it does rain, it'll be warm.

My talk with Sebastian has me thinking how lucky I am to be friends with the Wrightings. I may not be in their little group like Leah is, but I'm on the edge. They watch out for me by proximity. They care about me because she loves me.

And it's nice to be cared for, even if only by association.

Silas' face pops into my head, understandable with so much of the past being resurrected. An ache fills me as I walk—not quite for Silas but for how he made me feel.

While Lee would flit from one brother to another, finding common ground with each of them, catching up with their lives, playing games tailored to their likes, I would hang back. She didn't mean to leave me out. She just thought I'd do whatever I wanted to, that I could fend for myself.

Steven, Shawn, and sometimes Sebastian would stop and talk to me. Often they'd invite me to play, but I usually said no. I didn't always feel like playing at that time.

Silas never gave me a choice. He'd come up with idea after idea until I finally said yes. Or he'd construct a game that involved all of us then beg me to play so we had even numbers. Every time, he made me belong.

That feeling transferred over to school. I always thought of him as the popular guy—because it was true. He seemed on a plane high above me.

Everyone liked him, so many of our classmates fawned over him, but he always took the time to wave or say hi when he saw me. Like a flower opening in the steady rays of the sun, I blossomed under Silas' attention. I rarely felt wanted or needed in those days, but he made me feel seen.

A heady feeling indeed.

It's no wonder I fell so hard. When he actually kissed me back that day in the tree house, I had no hope of rescuing myself from the sea of love. I clung to him, trusted him, and he left me in the waves without a life raft.

The image of him kissing that other woman fills my mind. Even after I push the memory aside, the bitterness remains. I hate that he'd been my end goal while I'd just been another notch on his bedpost. I'd vowed never to open my heart to him again.

Pain that deep can't be survived twice.

My spirits match the heavy clouds filling the sky as I continue my walk to the coffee shop. Hopefully a mochaccino and a sandwich will brighten my mood.

Several minutes later, the bells jangle as I push the door open but I deflate at the sight of Silas behind the counter, glancing at me. It'll take a while to get used to him working weekends. The interaction here yesterday plays before me, and his gaze flits from me to the tip jar and back.

Just because I did him a favor doesn't mean I forgive him. The past is too close, my scars too raw after revisiting it with Leah. I'm not at all in the right headspace for dealing with him, but it's too late to turn tail now. Plus, I want my coffee.

"Hey," he says, giving me a grin.

"Hey." My answering smile is tight, and I hope he'll get the hint that I'm not in the mood to argue or banter, or whatever he calls it.

I say no more as I focus on the food menu. For once, I wish there was a line so I didn't have his undivided attention. Each moment drags on, like a kid in over-sized galoshes and shin-high mud.

"Is that your boyfriend?" he asks, breaking the tension before he nods at the door.

I turn and, sure enough, Chad's on the other side of the glass, pacing as he talks on the phone. I groan, wishing I could disappear.

"Uh-oh, trouble in paradise?" Silas teases.

I glare. "He broke up with me, you jerk."

Chagrin crosses his face, but he doesn't get to respond before Chad walks in. My ex stops at the sight of me, then sighs, as if I'm one more thing he has to deal with. My spirits dip even lower.

"So, Meg," Silas says in a deliciously husky tone that has me jerking my gaze back to him.

The dazzling smile on his face is one reserved for flirting, and it startles me, butterflies dancing in my midsection. Confusion washes over me, amplifying when he reaches across the counter to trail his finger along the inner edge of my wrist. My heart flutters as my stomach dips. I forgot how intoxicating his attention is, forgot how good his touch feels.

"What are you having? Sticking with your usual order, or maybe you want to try something..." He pauses to trace the same path then meets my eyes with his twinkling amber ones. "New?"

Oh, he's giving me an out. Helping me through this awkward moment. My carefully erected barriers crumble in the face of this realization, and I'm left staring into the deep, pure well of longing that has always resided within me. I try to pretend it's not there, pretend I'm over this man.

Then a moment like this comes along and I'm blindsided again. I swallow at my now dry mouth as I try to catch myself before I fall completely. It's all an act, a game.

One I can play too.

I toss my hair over my shoulder, returning the flirtatious smile. "Surprise me. Just make it hot, okay?" I add a wink for good measure.

He doesn't move for a second, then jerks as if remembering himself. "You got it." He gives me a wink of his own before going to make my drink.

I risk a glance at Chad, who studies the menu with all the focus of an archaeologist uncovering a new skeleton. His blatant avoidance tells me he heard every word and satisfaction ripples through me.

"Here you go," Silas says.

"Thanks." As I lean in to take the coffee from him, our fingers brush. A jolt darts up my arm and zings straight to my core, but I keep my smile in place. "What do I owe you?"

"Nothing, Meg. It's on the house."

His smoldering grin and husky voice have my cheeks warming. I stutter out another thanks before I wander to a booth, trying to rein in my over-the-top reaction. He was only playing a part, just helping me out.

"You're one of the Wrightings, aren't you?" Chad says when he steps closer to the counter.

At Silas' nod, Chad looks my way and, before I can avert my gaze, he shakes his head disapprovingly. As if I'm doing something wrong. As if he *suspected* this. I glare back before I settle into my booth and take out my homework.

To my relief, he's gone in minutes, and I grab my wallet then hurry to the counter again. "Seriously, let me pay for the coffee." Silas already gave me a free one yesterday. Two days in a row is too much.

He stares at me like I've grown a second head. "No. You've had a rough couple of days and you saved me yesterday. It's the least I can do."

"Oh, well, thanks." My stomach growls impatiently, and my cheeks heat. Again. "Um, with everything going on, I forgot to order a sandwich like I'd planned." I put in my order and pay, thankful for the card reader so I don't have to risk brushing hands with him again.

"I'll bring it out in a few."

I nod, then hurry back to my booth, overwhelmed. I contemplate getting the sandwich to go, but when I glance outside, the rain that has threatened all morning pelts the window. There's nowhere else I'll be able to concentrate anyway. The library is too quiet, and I don't want to go back home.

There aren't many people here, but the casual chatter is just right, allowing me to tune out and focus on my studying. I open my book and am engrossed in reading about splinting injuries in no time.

"Here ya go."

Silas scares the life out of me, making me squeak and flail my hands in the air.

He stares at me with wide eyes and a bemused grin. "You good?" He chuckles before he sets the plate on the table.

I rest my hand on my chest as I suck in a deep breath. "Sorry, guess I was concentrating harder than I realized."

"You hanging out a while?" At my nod, he grins wider. "I'll try not to scare you anymore."

Then he leaves. I stare after him for a second, wondering when the nice guy act will drop and the Silas who's annoyed with me breathing in his space will reappear. The butterflies shimmy at the memory of his earlier flirting, but I tell them to calm down. Any second now, he'll be pushing my buttons again.

He doesn't want me. I take a deep breath, then I pull my walls up so they're firmly in place. And I get back to studying.

An hour later, I stretch, my neck and back popping from being hunched too long over my textbook. The rain pours down steadily now, and two women race inside with their hoods up. The taller one pushes her hood off, her beautiful strawberry-blonde hair cascading down her shoulders as she removes her rain jacket to hang on one of the pegs inside the door.

She looks the place over with a wide, nostalgic smile. The shorter one seems annoyed, huffing as she hangs her sopping jacket on a peg. She shakes off her hands, grumbling under her breath before she runs her fingers through her short dark hair.

Silas emerges from the back and a huge grin spreads over his face. "Avery Milbourne, is that you?"

She spins on her heel, her smile even wider as she calls, "Silas!"

He rushes from behind the counter to give her a big hug, and I shake my head. He's got too many women for me to keep track of. Good thing I didn't get my hopes up.

Chapter Four

Silas

I can't believe Avery is here. It's been a couple years since I've seen her, but we worked together for quite a while. She showed me the ropes of this place, taught me some of her best shortcuts, and we always had a blast when we worked the same shift.

"It's Avery Elgin now." She holds up her hand with a massive ring on it, and I gape.

"As in *the* Elgins? The one the study hall is named after?" I walk by it every day I'm at SMU.

Her best friend Gina appears at her side and chimes in, "That's right. She's one of them now."

"Hey, Gina, how are you?" My gaze dips to her finger, which is bare.

"Oh, I'm not married."

"But you should be." Avery glares at her friend. "You and Liam need to tie the knot someday."

"We're happy just being together." She rolls her eyes, making me laugh.

"I see nothing has changed," I say, loving how they pick on each other in exactly the same way.

Avery nudges Gina, then they both turn expectant eyes on me as Avery says, "And you? Got someone special in your life?"

I can't help glancing in Meg's direction, a sour taste flooding my mouth at the reminder of my failure. I shake my head and force a smile. "Nope."

"I can't believe no one's tamed you yet." Avery sighs.

"Yeah, well, I'll settle down. Someday." *I hope*. I head back behind the counter as they shift to study the menu.

They put in their orders, and I bring them right out. We're slow, so I grab a coffee for myself, sipping on it as we stand at the counter, catching up. Avery and Gina take turns filling me in, and I love how amazing their lives have turned out.

We exchange numbers then they take their coffees to go, both giving me hugs goodbye before heading out into the rain once more. Meg comes up a while later to get a second coffee and a water, keeping her words to a minimum. She goes right back to her book, her laser focus perplexing me.

I don't know how she can study in a place like this. I get so distracted every time someone walks in and makes the bells jangle. Sometimes I have to ask customers to repeat their order — annoying, but I don't know how to prevent it.

The email with my diagnosis pops into my head, and I mull over the connection. Maybe that's something I can talk to the therapist about when I see them. The thought energizes me, that maybe I can fix some of these things I find so frustrating. Maybe someone can give me a road map to help me learn how to navigate my own brain.

Another hour passes, and my manager Pattie comes up. "Hey, it's pretty slow. Would you be interested in leaving early?"

I lift a shoulder. "Sure."

She glances at the clock. "Say, six?"

I nod, and she heads to the back once more. Forty-five minutes to go.

My friend Lyssa comes in with several women I don't know. One of my favorite parts of this job is seeing my friends and meeting new people. Lyssa and I connected in my English class last semester, but she's also close to Callie. We've all hung out a few times outside of class and it's been fun.

We chat for several minutes while the other women decide what they want, and she introduces me. The last woman slips me her number on the receipt, giving me a flirtatious wave before tossing her short, blonde hair. She giggles with her friends as they walk out of the door.

I smirk at the number, even though she's not my type. The thought gives me pause as I throw the paper away, Steven's earlier comments echoing in my head. I automatically glance at Meg, only to find her packing up. A quick look outside shows that the rain has turned into a downpour.

"Did you walk?" I call from behind the counter.

She grimaces. "Yeah."

"If you wait half an hour, I can take you. I'm leaving early."

To my surprise, she shakes her head. "Nah, I'm gonna head out."

My reaction to her words surprises me even further. I'm not only hurt, I'm pissed, and I don't know why. It's her hide that's going to get soaked. "It's just a ride," I mutter, loud enough for her to hear.

"And it's just a little rain," she retorts, pulling on her backpack.

"You just can't stand being stuck in the car with me, even for a few blocks. Grow up, Meg."

A stony expression crosses her face as she straightens to her full height and her brown eyes flash with undiluted anger. "I'm an adult, Silas. I won't melt, and I can make my own decisions. Besides, I wouldn't want you to miss an opportunity to flirt, since you so obviously need it."

"What?"

She gestures to the door. "After spending your entire break with those two women, you got a number from at least one in that last group. Always gotta have someone standing by, don't you?"

I feel like I'm only in on half of this conversation. The bitterness seeping into her tone tells me something more is going on, like she's bringing up a piece of our past, but I have no clue what she's even referencing. "Meg, what are you talking about?"

A raw vulnerability appears as her walls crumble for a split second, and my heart wrenches at the sight. Then her face pinches with fury before she flips her long, dark hair over her shoulder.

"Thanks for the coffee." She strides out into the rain without answering my question.

But I refuse to let her go like this, especially after the advice Steven gave me. That conversation slams me in the face and I remember my other admission—how I'd kissed that girl at the party and Meg found out. Maybe that's what she meant?

Frustration surges within me and I rush to find my manager. "Pattie, any way I can leave now?"

She shoots me a knowing smile. "Something to do with that girl?" At my frantic nod, she sighs. "Go on with ya."

I punch the air then give her arm a quick squeeze. "You're the best."

I rush to take off my apron and grab my bag, then I zip out of the back door, only to skid to a stop. I forgot to punch out.

Pattie laughs through the slowly closing door. "I got you," she calls.

"Thanks!"

I race to my car, tossing my bag into the backseat and pulling out of the parking lot while buckling. I have to crank the windshield wipers to even be able to see, and I turn right, peering through the sheets of rain, hoping for a glimpse of Meg. One block up, I see her, hunching against the weather.

I unlock the doors and roll down the window. "Meg!" I have to yell a few times to finally get her attention, then she frowns.

"Silas? What are you doing here?" She doesn't even bother coming closer.

"Get in."

She trots over to lean in the window. "You still had a half-hour of your shift."

"I left early. We were slow." I jerk my chin. "Come on."

"Go back to work, Silas." And she starts to turn away.

"Dammit, Meg! Get your stubborn ass in here." She pauses, and I add, "Or else I'll come out there and walk with you." It's the only threat I can think of, because she hates inconveniencing people.

I watch her shoulders slump and I know I have her. She turns around, opens the door, and flops in with a huff as I roll up the window. She struggles with her backpack, finally yanking it off to throw on the floor.

"Here." I hold out the beach towel I always keep in the backseat.

She stares at the offering as if it had been dragged through a pile of manure.

"It's clean," I insist. "I always keep one in here. Never know when an impromptu beach trip will come up."

"Thanks," she mutters, snatching the towel from my hands.

Once she's buckled, it's a quick drive home. Right before we pull into the driveway, I break the tense silence to ask, "What'd you mean back there? About me having someone standing by?"

Does she really think that's why I kissed the girl at that party? That I moved on that quickly? Is that why she shut me out? I hold my breath, needing her to answer. Needing her to open up.

But she just presses her lips together. "Forget about it."

"I don't want to."

She turns her glare on me. "Well, I do."

I huff, reaching into the back to grab my bag, then I stomp outside, around the car, to open her door. "I wasn't trying to parade anyone in front of you," I growl as she steps out.

A gust of wind has her squinting at me in the sideways rain.

I feel like I still owe her an explanation, even though I don't know why. "Those are my friends. Well, most of them. Even if they weren't, I'm allowed to search. I want my happily-ever-after too." It's not like she's ever given me any reason *not* to keep searching.

When I look at her, resignation fills her gaze, and I feel like I said absolutely the wrong thing. I wish I could take the words back. That we could start over and say what we both mean.

But it's too late. I want to crumple at her cold expression, her gaze firm and unwavering.

"Of course, Silas. You just keep searching."

She leans in to grab her backpack before stepping out of the way for me to shut the car door. Then there's nothing between us as she stares up at me with those big brown eyes, holding a turbulent mixture of pain and hope and confusion. Her dark hair is soaking wet with several strands plastered to her face. She's drenched to the bone.

And she's never looked more beautiful than at this moment. My gaze drops to her full lips, beaded with raindrops. I want nothing more than to pull her to me and kiss her soundly. Despite the storm.

"Silas, I don't know what's going on in that head of yours, but you are all over the place. I swear if you try to kiss me, I'll punch you in the nose."

Her half-hearted threat breaks me out of my daze, and I step back with a teasing grin. "What? Me buying you coffee and being nice threw you off?"

"Yes!" She tosses her hands then stomps past me.

"Who gets angry because someone's being nice?" I call after her.

She storms into the house, but I stand there for a few more minutes as Steven's earlier words echo back to me. That Meg is the one I've been searching for all along and I'm this close to letting her get away.

When I shut my eyes, all I can see is her upturned face and those parted lips, and every minute of the last two years finally makes sense.

I'm not an angry person—I don't hold grudges. But I did with Meg, and it's all because I fell for her a lot harder than I was ever willing to admit.

I'm so screwed.

* * * *

Meg

I've just put on dry clothes when someone raps on my door. I open it to find Leah with her hands on her hips.

"Hey," I say, brushing by her to duck into the bathroom and get a towel for my still-dripping hair. "What's up?"

"Why did you and Silas come in looking like drowned rats? I tried to ask him about it and he said he felt off. That he was going to lie down upstairs."

I frown. Maybe that's why he left early—because he wasn't feeling well. Guilt snags at me for laying into him like I did. The frustrated words had just tumbled out. That heated moment after replays in my mind— when he shut the door and we faced each other. How his gaze dipped to my lips and my stomach flipped as anticipation shot through me.

A flutter of longing dances in my midsection at the memory, followed quickly by annoyance at my reaction. It was a hell of a lot easier to keep my barriers up when he was mad at me. This new back and forth has me all over the place.

I realize Leah's still waiting for an explanation. "I did my homework at the coffee shop this afternoon and Silas gave me a ride home. Then we talked for a few minutes."

"In the rain?" Her hands are on her hips again, her gaze boring into mine.

Exasperation fills me. "Lee, don't make more out of this than there is. Silas and I tried, okay? We didn't work. End of story."

A sharp stab hits my heart at my own words, even as I roll my eyes at my pathetic self. The definition of insanity is repeating the same action over and over, while expecting different results. Silas and I have been there, done that. He left me, like every other man in my life.

I'd be a fool to think a second round would fix anything.

"Meg..." Her hands drop and her breath whooshes out of her. "All this history with you two has my mind going places and I keep picturing you together, how great you'd be as a couple. I'm sorry. I just want to see both of you happy."

"I know, Lee. I'm working on it, but Chad and I did just break up, so maybe I could have a little space?"

She wraps her arms around me, despite my damp hair and the towel in my hands. "Of course. Love ya!" With another quick squeeze, she steps back and starts to walk away.

"You too," I call, then go back to drying off.

* * * *

Monday after my morning classes, I walk home, still not sure what to think about Silas. Luckily I haven't had to face him today, since he was gone for his internship before I emerged from my room. That doesn't mean he hasn't been haunting my thoughts.

That moment in the rain won't leave me alone. It teases me, waking or sleeping, as does the longing that followed. I briefly imagine starting another chapter between me and Silas, then I remember how crushed I was after our fight. How much it hurt seeing him with that other woman.

My resolve solidifies once more, and I'm determined not to let hope seep in because I won't go through that again. I'll stick to my fringe friendship with the Wrightings. I can survive on that.

Maybe if I tell myself that enough times, I'll actually believe it.

I walk up the steps right as Callie gets dropped off by one of her friends, and I greet her with a grin. "Hey, what're you up to?"

"I don't know!" She tosses her hands in exasperation. "Sebastian got into a fight with my dad in the dean's office this morning."

Taken aback by her vehemence as well as her statement, I blink and try to process. I can't imagine Sebastian fighting with anyone. "I'm sorry...he did what?"

She nods. "Now he's on forced leave for the rest of the week and he has some plan but won't tell me what it is."

I've never been one for surprises either, so I give her an empathetic smile. "Well, good luck."

"Thanks, I need it," she says as we go inside and head our different ways.

I spend the afternoon doing homework at the kitchen table. I'm still there when Leah and Shawn walk in, hand in hand, and a familiar lovey-dovey gleam in their eyes. Shawn kisses her temple then trots toward our suite, but Lee hangs back.

"Um, Meg?"

I sigh, knowing what she wants. "You want me to make myself scarce for a while?"

Her cheeks turn pink as she nods. "I don't want to kick you out, but..."

I'd been spending several nights a week at Chad's before our breakup, and I'm sure she and Shawn are missing that privacy. She's never been comfortable going upstairs either, plus Shawn's room is a mess and there would be even more people within earshot. Giving up our mini-suite may inconvenience me, but I don't mind. Not for Lee.

"No problem. Just let me grab a few things." I hurry into my room, ignoring the mostly closed door of Leah's room and trying not to think about Shawn waiting for her. I pick up a book plus my charger, then head back out. "All yours."

"Thanks." She disappears into our suite and closes the door.

I plop on the couch, turning on the TV for good measure. Some basketball game that I couldn't care less about fills the screen, but it's background noise, so I leave it on as I open my book. The dark romance I'm reading has all the right elements — a stalker, so much tension, and an even worse bad guy. I love reading about morally gray anti-heroes.

Though I don't think I'd want one in real life.

The front door opens several minutes later and in walks Silas. My heart stops as I take in the whole picture—him in a suit and tie, carrying a sleek briefcase. No one has any right to be that fucking handsome. When he sees me, a big smile crosses his face.

Someone needs to call nine-one-one before I have a heart attack.

"Hey, Nutmeg."

I gape, the old nickname sending me reeling. I'd always loved the endearment that came from him alone. I haven't heard it in years, and so many memories pop into my head. Endless moments I used to replay when I thought I had a chance with him.

"What are you doing watching basketball?"

The question yanks me back to the present and I scramble to form a coherent thought. "It's on for the background noise." I hold up my book. "Not actually watching it. What are you doing in a suit?"

He glances down and chuckles as he adjusts his tie. "Wanted to look good for my first day."

A beat passes, and I realize I don't want this to end. I hurry to add, "How'd it go?"

He stares for a second, as if he's surprised I asked. "Actually, pretty well. I'm working every day for this week, but after that I'll only be going in Tuesday through Thursday. I think I've finally found what I've been looking for."

A weight underlines his words that I don't understand, and his gaze rests heavily on me. But I take his declaration at face value. "I'm so happy for you."

I've always known what I wanted to be—a nurse—and I jumped on that career path right out of college. It's slow going, with how expensive it is, so I started with my medical assistant certification, knowing I could get on-the-job experience and earn money while taking the next classes.

Silas, on the other hand, has switched his major multiple times, but he recently helped Callie sort out a trust left to her by her deceased mother. It made him decide that he wants to be a lawyer, so something good came out of an otherwise crummy situation.

He shifts his weight. "Where is everyone?"

I glance at our suite. "Shawn and Leah asked not to be disturbed."

"TMI, Meg." He grimaces.

"You asked." I shrug and continue. "Callie and Sebastian left a few hours ago, but he wouldn't say where they were going."

He shoots me a knowing grin.

I frown. "Wait, you know?"

Holding up his hands, he shakes his head when I press him. "Nope, I'm sworn to secrecy."

An exasperated sigh whooshes from me as I slump against the couch.

A bemused chuckle rumbles out of him, and he arches an eyebrow. "Have you eaten yet?"

"No," I grunt.

"Me neither. Maybe we could grab a bite, see if Steven wants to come?"

I glance over, surprised and confused. Our last interaction wasn't exactly pleasant, and now he's inviting me to dinner?

"We could even play a game afterward. Just let me know." He drops the casual invitation then heads upstairs without glancing back.

I stare after him, my mind working overtime as I try to figure him out. But I feel like a car stuck in the mud — my wheels spin, never gaining ground.

Steven walks in from work a few minutes later, giving me a nod and a wave before trotting upstairs. I pick up my book but don't read as I mull over what I want to do. A game should be safe, right? And if Steven is there too…

They both come downstairs, Silas' booming laughter making me smile before I realize what I'm doing. I don't understand why he still affects me so, especially since I know I'm just going to get hurt if I let him in. *Stupid heart not knowing what's good for it.*

"So, Meg," he says, coming to lean over the back of the couch and into my space.

His fingers brush my shoulder, and my stomach flips even as the red alert siren goes off in my mind. Silas is a toucher, that's his love language. When he's comfortable with you, you know it. He pats and hugs, nudges and bumps.

Over the past two years, he has rarely touched me, has held himself so stiffly that there's been no accidental grazing over here. We shared a couple of rigid hugs at Christmas and birthdays, but otherwise? Nothing.

This is the second time since our secret came out that he's broken that barrier. Something has definitely shifted between us, at least for him. That knowledge puts my guard up even more.

I shake my head, leaning away to grab my book. "I think I'll read."

Steven pipes in. "C'mon, Grimm Masquerade is more fun with three."

That's just playing dirty. Everyone knows it's my favorite game, and I shoot Silas a glare while he stares back wearing an innocent grin.

"We can throw in a couple of pizzas," Silas says, sweetening the offer.

"Fine." I push to my feet. "You guys put in the pizza, I'll get the game."

Several minutes later, the three of us are seated around the table and drawing character cards. There are three rounds and each round we randomly select a fairy-tale character. The goal is to collect three objects that match your card while not tipping your hand to let others discover who you are.

I enjoy the game because it takes some skill and strategy. It's not all random luck, though that does help. We make it through all three rounds before the pizza timer dings. I won the first two rounds, but Steven won the last, which is worth the most points.

Silas lost by a lot, but he swears he had fun. His grin never dims. His unflappable cheeriness grates on me sometimes, but I will say this. He's never been a sore loser.

Chapter Five

Meg

After we've packed up the game, we each grab a
couple slices as Shawn and Leah walk into the kitchen.

Shawn sniffs the air. "Pizza?"

Steven rolls his eyes. "You and your timing."

"You guys played Grimm Masquerade without us?"
Leah cries, spying the box on the counter.

We don't get to play this game often on our game
nights. It has a max of five players, and we usually have
more people than that. Silas and Steven turn to me, the
same silent question in their eyes.

"Let me finish eating," I say with a huff. "Then we
can play again."

Leah whoops joyfully before she grabs a plate.

Shawn starts doling out beer. "Want one, Meg?"

I wrinkle my nose. "Not unless we have any more of
those fruity ones." Beer is so not my thing, but with
fruit, I tolerate it.

He crouches to paw through the bottom drawer, emerging triumphantly with a blueberry ale. "Your wish is my command."

Leah glares. "Hey, you're only supposed to say that to me."

He hands me my beer, then kisses her cheek, murmuring in her ear. Her cheeks get bright red, and he smirks before grabbing his pizza.

Lee quickly changes the subject by asking Silas about his first day at the internship. I sit back, content to listen as I bask in the feeling of being with these amazing people. Even with everything between me and Silas, I could never stop caring about him. They all mean a lot to me, even if I don't mean as much to them.

My phone chimes at the same time Leah's does, and I pull it out of my pocket to find a group text from Callie saying they're at Mackinac Island.

"He took her back to Mackinac?" Lee asks, grinning wide. "That man is head over heels."

Silas grins before he drops his gaze down to the table.

"Seriously," I demand, staring at him. "What do you know?"

He shakes his head.

Lee and I exchange a look then she takes over. "Silas, tell us."

"Sebastian made me swear."

I realize Shawn isn't protesting either, just calmly eating his pizza, and I glare. "You know too!"

He smirks.

Lee and I turn to Steven, who zips his lips, then he gives us an empathetic smile. "If it helps, Callie doesn't know either. But they'll catch everyone up when they get back on Wednesday."

With a sigh, Lee juts her lower lip. "I hate being in the dark."

I study the guys once more, realizing none are going to crack. "Well, we've still got Grimm Masquerade."

Lee brightens at that. We finish eating and clear the table once more, then play a lively game that stretches on much longer than the first. Shawn wins with me in close second and Silas bringing up the rear. Again. His loss doesn't dim that constant smile or teasing disposition, and I can't help wishing I could let things wash off me like that.

We relocate to the living room where I sit on my spot on the couch and Lee settles next to me, both of us content to read while the guys watch some big soccer match Silas is geeked about. He plays on an intramural team. That's one thing he's always been constant about — his love of soccer.

The next two days fly by while I work my usual shifts at a family doctor's office. Tuesdays are their late night, scheduling patients until seven p.m., so sometimes I'm not home until eight, depending on how late things run. Wednesday we get out around five-thirty, and I hole up in my room to finish an essay.

I usually work Thursdays, but this week I don't because it's the Fourth of July. I'm looking forward to our usual tradition of hanging out at the Wrightings' parents' house. Trey always has something on the grill while Judy cooks some delicious sides. We're expected to bring snacks or drinks, and we make a whole day out of it.

Leah's parents often come too, so I get to see my favorite aunt and uncle. But the best part is that Trey and Judy live close enough to the park that we can watch an amazing firework show right from their backyard.

I ride over with Leah and Shawn, asking if she's heard anything from Callie on the way.

Leah shakes her head, glancing at Shawn. "You?"

He shakes his head too. "Nope, nothing from Seb. They're planning on meeting us here this afternoon, so I'm sure we'll hear all about it then."

Lee needles Shawn the rest of the drive, trying to get him to spill his secrets, but he doesn't budge. I tune them out, content to wait, and stare out of the window.

When we finally arrive, Lee gives Shawn an apologetic hug and I exit the car before they kiss and make up. My bag over one shoulder and my contribution of mixed fresh fruit in my other hand, I hurry inside.

"Meg," Aunt Mary exclaims, rushing over from her perch near the counter.

I greet her and give her a quick one-armed hug. Judy takes my fruit and I get a hug from her too, then I step out of the way for Shawn with his cooler. I stay off to the side watching him greet his mom before both women greet Leah.

My heart twists painfully as longing stabs my gut. I wish my mom and I had the easy closeness I see between my friends and their parents. Standing off to one side, I feel invisible as the four of them chatter away, catching up despite the fact that they talk often.

I just wish I had a place that I knew I fit.

Lee glances my way and I force a smile as I put my mask back into place. No need to ruin anyone else's fun with my crappy situation.

We're all making our way outside when Steven and Silas arrive. I hurry out to the patio, where Uncle Bob is helping Trey man the grill. I give them both quick hugs, then I crack open a seltzer, more than ready to lounge by the pool and soak up the sun. Maybe that'll help get me back in a holiday mood.

I start to leave, but Silas pokes his head out of the door and says, "Hey, guys, I want to tell you all something."

Everyone comes outside onto the patio, staring at Silas expectantly.

To my surprise, he seems nervous. His usual grin is missing and he shifts his weight to his other foot, not meeting anyone's eyes. "So, I have ADHD."

Nobody moves other than a few eyebrow raises, and we all listen as he explains how Sebastian started him on the path to a diagnosis. How he's got an appointment for therapy next week. How he's not planning on going on meds at this time.

Trey is the first to speak after Silas is finished. He rests his hand on Silas' shoulder and looks him right in the eye. "We love you, son. Let us know if you need anything."

Silas' gaze glimmers more than usual as he nods then Judy pulls him in for a big hug. He meets my eyes over her shoulder and I give him a real smile, which he returns. Then I make my way to the pool, wanting to give the family a moment to themselves.

I settle in one of the lounge chairs, sipping my seltzer as I think about Silas and his diagnosis. It explains a lot, and I can't believe I never suspected it before. We've touched on some different neurological conditions in my classes, and he fits the bill for ADHD.

I guess with his sunny attitude and the way things roll off him, I never thought further than that. Why would someone need a diagnosis if things were going well? I know better than that now, of course. Just because someone isn't negatively affected by a condition doesn't mean there aren't benefits to knowing they have it.

A diagnosis and understanding how one's brain works can help a person navigate their world better. Knowledge is key to learning how or why one might react in certain situations, and it can make someone feel not so alone. Or out of place.

I glance at the patio where the family still surrounds Silas. I wonder if he ever feels out of place... He's always been Mr. Popular, fitting in wherever he goes, and I can't imagine him feeling alone and unsure. Not when he's the poster boy for confidence.

Trey calls out that the burgers are done, so I head back to the patio to crowd around the outside table with everyone else. We take turns catching up on our lives then Trey teases us with the prospect of ribs for dinner, which is when the real spread happens. Judy promises her famous mac-and-cheese bake that everyone fights over, and I can't wait.

After we're done eating, Shawn and Leah want to play volleyball. Steven volunteers to help clean up, so it'll be me and Silas versus them. Silas raises his eyebrows, asking if I'm up for it.

I love volleyball, so I nod, then we begin discussing teams. Lee hovers next to Shawn, a sure sign she wants to be paired with him, and while I'm not thrilled with being Silas' partner, I'm sure as hell not letting him and Lee play together. Those two on the court are unstoppable. And guys against girls gives the brothers an unfair advantage since they're both that much taller than us.

The mood is happy and light as we make our way to the makeshift court on the side of the perfectly manicured lawn, Lee holding Shawn's hand, thrilled to be on his team.

After the game starts, it quickly becomes clear that Silas is in rare form today. He's always sunny, but he must be riding the high of the family's acceptance because he's teasing, joking and laughing as if he had an extra dose of sunshine with his morning coffee.

When it's our turn to serve, we take our places, and he tugs my ponytail with a wide grin. "We've got this, Meg."

The overly familiar gesture grates on me. I don't mind his good mood, but I'm not ready to be the recipient of all the many touches he usually gives his teammate. With the distance that's been between us for so long, the casual affection feels weird. And I can't help bristling more with each one.

We volley back and forth, and I get lost in the game, forgetting about my annoyance. Silas and I tune in to each other, reading one another perfectly as we help cover the court. When I'm close to the net, he hangs back and vice versa.

Shawn slams the ball past Silas' waiting fingers, but I dive, managing to pop it up to Silas. I scramble to my feet as he sets it back to me, nice and high. I pull back like I'm going to spike it, but at the last second, I tip it over Leah's outstretched hands to a spot too close to the net for Shawn to save.

"Yes!" cries Silas as the ball hits the ground. He races over and wraps an arm around my shoulders for a quick squeeze. "Way to go, Nutmeg!"

I manage a smile but hurry to extricate myself from his grasp. I don't like him being this nice to me. It's like he's trying to step back in time to where we were before we got together, before our fight, before he kissed another woman. I can't just erase that.

And I don't like that he seems to be trying to.

The black tendrils of my earlier mood begin to resurface, ebbing out the joy from a good play. Annoyance bubbles within me each time he holds out his hand for a high-five or fist-bump. He pats my shoulder or back when I do well, not seeming to notice how I grow more rigid with every touch.

Leah shoots me a concerned glance but I wave her off. I'll be fine.

We volley back and I lose myself in the action, exhilarated at the thought of winning the game with this next point. I get a spectacular dig off Shawn's spike, popping the ball right to Silas who smashes it over the net. And Lee misses.

I raise my fists triumphantly in the air, so caught in the moment that I don't register Silas barreling toward me until he grabs me and picks me up to spin me around. I yelp and push at his shoulders. "Put me down!"

Hurt flashes across his face, but he obeys and steps back. My heart pounds as we stare at each other, anger simmering in me. Anger at him for being so cavalier right now. For thinking everything can be fine between us when he hurt me so badly.

"Meg? You okay?" he asks, his brow furrowed.

I shake my head. "No, Silas. I'm not okay. *We're* not okay, so stop acting like we are." He rears back, but I ignore him and turn to Leah and Shawn. "Good game, guys, but I'm gonna sit the next one out. I'll see if Steven wants to play." And I rush off before anyone can stop me.

I nearly run into Steven as I hurry into the house.

"You okay?" he asks, worry crinkling his forehead.

"They need a fourth, maybe you should go fill in for me." It's not an answer but it's all I can give him.

I grab my bag and head for one of the bathrooms with my swimsuit. After I close the door, I rest my hands on the cool, smooth surface of the sink and stare at my reflection. That anger still boils within me, and I don't understand why it's coming to such a head now.

I thought I'd dealt with all of this. I thought I was over Silas and what he did to me, that I'd moved on, but my reactions lately keep proving that I'm not. My conversation with Leah replays in my mind, her asking if we'd ever talked.

The answer weighs on me.

No, we never spoke about our fight and I never confronted him about that kiss. He tried to talk to me a few times, both in person and in text, but I was so hurt, so furious over what he did to me…I couldn't respond.

All this time, I thought I'd moved on when really I've been in stasis. Just existing in that plane of 'after Silas'.

I need closure. If I'm ever going to truly move forward with my life, Silas and I need to talk. Like, really talk. The thought makes my stomach churn, but I remind myself that there's not much more that he can do to me now. Sometimes you have to reopen a wound to let the infection out. It's the only way it'll heal properly.

Even if it hurts.

Resigned, I change into my swimsuit. I'm not going to do anything more today. I've already caused a scene and I don't want any more drama when we're supposed to be celebrating. Right now, I'm going to go relax by the pool and try to enjoy what's left of my holiday.

When I emerge, Sebastian and Callie are walking through the house. Callie's smile is huge and Sebastian wears a matching one. I immediately notice the ring on her finger and gasp, raising my eyebrows as I wait for her to spill.

She just grins bigger and says, "Come on. We want to tell everyone together."

We hurry outside. A mixed storm of emotions loops through me, and it takes a few minutes for the family to gather on the patio, giving me time to work up my happy face. I mean, I am happy for them...I just wish I had something going for me in my love life.

Sebastian loops his arm around Callie's waist, pulling her to his side. "Calliope and I are getting married."

Stunned silence reigns for a brief moment before whoops and congratulations sound as everyone rushes in to hug the smiling couple. I stand off to the side, feeling alone in the chaos as I stare at my empty life. I'm two years older than Callie and Sebastian is one of the least romantic people I know.

But here they are, perfect for each other and glowing with that loving bliss I wish I could have for once in my life.

My turn comes to hug them and I go to Callie first. I mean it when I say, "Congratulations!"

She grins back, then I pause in front of Sebastian, making sure it's okay to hug him. He nods. I step in awkwardly to embrace him, and he pats my back. When I move away, Silas catches my attention and our gazes meet for the briefest of seconds. I feel his concern, and I know he's wondering if I'm okay.

Again.

But the truth is… I don't know. This last week has been like opening the Pandora's box of my past, complete with all the pain and feelings and scars. I've already lived through it once. I'm not sure how I can survive confronting it again.

Leah bombards Callie with all sorts of questions as the guys drift to one side. I stick with the girls, happy to keep my distance from Silas. I try to hold the negative feelings at bay, giving Callie my full attention as she gives us the details. It all sounds so romantic — how Sebastian proposed at the butterfly house on Mackinac Island, how he rented the whole place for them after hours, and how they'd talked about the wedding the whole way home.

Then Callie turns to Leah and asks, "Leah, will you be my maid of honor?"

Leah's eyes shine as she grabs Callie's hand and nods. I hold my breath when Callie shifts her attention to me, not sure if I want her to ask or not.

"Meg, I want you to be a bridesmaid too, along with my friend Jess."

"Of course," I manage. I'm honored to be her bridesmaid. We haven't known each other very long and it's a sweet gesture. But now, I'll have to live and breathe this wedding and I swallow down my doubt at the thought. Clearing my throat, I ask, "How soon are we talking?"

"Well, I've got to ask Trey and Judy, but we're hoping to get this done in a couple of weeks. I called Jess on the way home and Lyssa's apartment is up for grabs, so Sebastian and I are going to check it out tomorrow."

My mind spins with all that has to be done in that short amount of time, and Leah stares at her wide-eyed.

Judy steps closer. "Did you say a couple of *weeks*?"

Callie nods. "I know it's a lot, but we want a simple wedding. Here, if possible. We want it done before the next semester starts, and the sooner the better so I can get my trust transferred over."

Judy's expression falls slightly. "If this is only about the trust—"

Callie shakes her head, her giddy expression never dimming. "I know I'm young and I know this is fast, but I can't imagine spending my life with anyone else. I know exactly what I want." She glances at Sebastian. "He's my forever."

Sebastian gives her a soft smile that melts my heart even as jealousy pricks me.

I want my forever. I want my happily-ever-after. My gaze inadvertently finds Silas, who stares back at me with a longing expression that disappears when he registers I'm watching. It unsettles me, how closely it matched my own thoughts.

"You're walking with Silas," Callie says, nudging me. "So you two better figure things out."

The words hit me like a sledgehammer, and I steel myself even as I nod. "Okay."

My previous resolve rises within me, and I know we need to talk. When my gaze finds his again, I straighten my chin as determination surges through my torso.

There's no time like the present.

Chapter Six

Silas

I knew why Sebastian had whisked Callie away. Knew that he wanted to propose.

But I'm still shocked that she said yes.

I see how they are together, a perfect fit. She gets him in every way, reads his movements, knows what he needs, and he does the same for her. They orbit one another, and I'm beyond jealous. I can't help thinking back to the night we had pizza — how Meg knew I was hiding something.

She's always seen me — the good, the bad, the in between. Like the other day when she brought my wet laundry to my room. She knew I'd forget again unless it was right in front of my face and she took the time to do that.

For me.

So I've never understood why she wouldn't let me talk to her after our fight. She had to know I didn't mean what I said. Even if she does know I kissed someone else, the least she could do was let me explain. To apologize, to tell her I was drunk and I stopped as soon as I realized the mistake I'd made.

I expected some distance, both of us giving the other space before we could work things out. But that reconciliation never came.

I realize I'm staring at her when she turns to me. A hint of embarrassment creeps over me but it turns to curiosity when Callie says something and Meg nods, determination written on her face. I barely have time to wonder about it when Meg strides over in her sleek two piece that hugs her curves perfectly, grabs my wrist, and drags me into the house.

It's the first time she's voluntarily touched me in two years and I can't stop staring at the spot where her hand encircles my wrist. Electricity shoots up my arm. *Fuck me.*

"What's going on?" I manage to ask, glancing over my shoulder and finding my family grinning back with bemused expressions.

"You and I are walking together for the wedding. We've got to figure this out, and to do that, we need to talk."

She'll get no argument from me. I stumble as she pulls me through the kitchen and down the hall, righting myself before I faceplant. Talking sounds great. Maybe I can finally apologize for the fight. Maybe I can figure out why she got so pissed earlier when we were playing volleyball.

Maybe I can confess that I've never stopped wanting her.

One peek at her stormy face as we head into my old bedroom tells me she's not looking for a warm fuzzy talk here. She means business as she folds her arms and raises her chin, then nods to the door. I shut it behind me, trying to distract myself from the fact that she's wearing next to nothing. In my old bedroom. Next to my bed.

Now is not the time for a hard-on.

"So…" I start, easing onto the bed and leaning my elbows on my knees.

"I realized earlier today that we haven't really talked since…well, you know."

This isn't going to go well if she can't even say that we were together. "Since we had sex?" I say, wanting to get that out of the way.

Her cheeks flush, and she glares. "Yeah, Silas, since we had sex. Although it was a bit more complex than that for me."

I backpedal, holding up my hands. "It was more than that for me too. I just—"

"Yeah, sure." She rolls her eyes. "That's why you moved on so quickly."

Popping to my feet, I frown. "I didn't move on, Meg. I—"

"I saw you."

Her eyes well with unshed tears as she stares at me and I'm taken aback by the depth of the pain in her gaze. I'd ask who hurt her, but I'm afraid I know the answer.

Me.

"I gave you space after our fight," she says, crossing her arms over her bare abdomen and wrapping her hands around her opposite biceps. "A couple of days later, I knew you were at a party, at Ben's house. I wanted to fix things. I know we were both under a lot of pressure with everything and we both had some horrible guilt."

I know what she's going to say and steel myself against it, not wanting to hear this from her perspective. But at the same time, I need to know her side. Need her to let it out. Then I need her to let me explain.

"It took a while to find you, and when I did, you weren't alone. A dark-haired woman was with you, in the corner. You…" She trails off and sucks in a breath. "You were kissing."

I nod, not dodging the statement. "Yeah, Meg. I messed up. I kissed her."

Meg's lips press tight together in a stony expression.

I take a deep breath then speak the words I've waited years to say. "I got really drunk that night. I missed you. I wanted *you*, Meg." I don't look away from her turbulent gaze. "She kissed me, but I didn't stop it. I thought maybe I could distract myself from everything going on with you and me."

Hurt pools in her dark eyes and her shoulders slump.

"It didn't help, though," I say gently, relieved when a glimmer of hope appears on her face. "I couldn't stop thinking of you, and I knew right away I'd made a mistake. I broke off the kiss and went to bed. Alone. I promised myself that you and I would work things out the next day."

Her hands drop to her side as she stares at the floor. "Then I wouldn't even talk to you."

"Yeah…evidently you and I both have crappy timing."

She raises her head once more, and some of the tension eases between us as her mouth tips up. But there's still so much I want to say. I don't know when

I'll get another chance, so I take a deep breath and go for broke.

"Meg, I'm so sorry. I'm sorry for taking my anger out on you. I'm sorry for what I said in our fight." I step closer, hoping to close the distance between us — physically and emotionally. "I didn't want anyone else, wasn't intentionally looking for someone else. I didn't go on a real date for months after you."

She stares back at me, searching my face as if she might find the evidence she needs there.

"Please, Meg. I never meant to hurt you." My voice cracks with the weight of my emotion. I want her to believe me with every fiber of my being because it means she didn't actually reject me. And I need that. Desperately.

"I'm sorry I didn't let you explain," she says, her words hoarse with unshed tears. "This is my fault."

"No," I say firmly, reaching out to touch her arm. "No. I could've tried harder and I shouldn't have gotten that drunk. As for the fight, we both said things. We both let that resentment grow. And it'll take both of us to fix it."

I need her to see that I'm still in this, that I'm willing to do what it takes to make this work. But I can't do it alone. She doesn't pull away, which I take as a good sign. I step closer, noting how her chests rises, her breath hitching at my proximity. She blinks rapidly, as if still fighting tears.

Then she steps backward, again.

I remember her anger before on the volleyball court when I picked her up. How rigid she felt in my arms. "Meg? You don't want me to touch you?"

One tear spills down her cheek and she swipes at it, then sniffs. "I can't handle it, Silas. You keep acting like nothing has changed between us, as if we're great friends like we used to be. But we're not."

The words sting. I had wanted to show her that we're okay, show her that I'm interested, and here I've been pissing her off and making her uncomfortable. "I'm sorry, Meg. I didn't realize…"

I thought maybe I'd get to spill my heart to her today, tell her everything I've figured out this week. But I see the edge in her posture. I wanted to ask her for a second chance, wanted to beg her to let us try again.

Only to find out she doesn't even think we're friends.

Meg stares at me, waiting, as silence hangs between us. She's always been wary. Even as a kid, she had walls up and kept herself apart from everyone else. I tried my best to show her she was welcome with us, and I worked hard to earn her trust.

Then I went and threw it all away.

But things that are broken can be mended, and I can rebuild that trust, if I'm willing to put in the work. "We still have the wedding to get through," I say slowly as my resolve strengthens.

I know what I want, and it's Meg. I'm done looking anywhere else, and I'm not giving her up this time without a proper try. She doesn't have to know that, but I'm not leaving it like this. So I pull out my ace. "And we're walking together, right?"

A frown crosses her face, but she nods.

"So we have to make this work. Maybe…can we go back to being friends?" Her searching gaze lingers on my face, and I try to remain open and hopeful.

"*Just* friends?"

"Yes," I answer without hesitation. Whatever it takes to get a foot in the door. I can be whatever she needs, even if that ends up being just friends. I'll be the best friend she could ever have.

Some of the tension leaves her body, and she nods. "Okay. I'm willing to try."

I beam. "Good." Then I step forward with open arms. "Can I hug you now?"

She purses her lips for a moment before she sighs. "Fine."

With a huge grin, I give her my most playful hug, picking her right up off her feet. "I missed you, Nutmeg."

It takes a beat, but she reluctantly whispers, "I missed you too." And she hugs me back.

It's a win I will take.

* * * *

Between swimming and dinner, I coax Lee into taking a walk with me. I need her advice. I explain what went down when I talked to Meg earlier. "I still can't believe I kissed that girl. That I thought it would help."

Lee gives me a soft smile then squeezes my arm as we walk through the trail in the woods. "Everyone makes mistakes, Silas. You were going through some tough stuff."

"I wish she'd let me talk to her afterward." I could've pushed harder but I've never been great with rejection. When she'd shut me out without explanation, I didn't know how to handle it. I'd just let the anger and resentment build.

What a fool I've been.

"You have to remember that Meg has never had a constant in her life besides us."

Meg doesn't speak much about her home life, and I frown, trying to piece together what I know. "Her dad left…"

"And her mom jumped right into finding a new guy. Every time she came to hang out with me, that's what her mom was doing. Her mom thought a new husband was her meal ticket or something. Then, when she found George, her mom threw herself into that life. I don't think she left any room for Meg."

The realization sinks in, weighing me down further.

"You were it for her. She's had a crush on you for as long as I can remember." Lee gives me a wistful smile. "I used to be jealous—not because I was into you or anything. But because she knew who she wanted to end up with."

Another stab of guilt pricks me.

"She's never been great with speaking her feelings. I tell her I love her all the time, and she still has trouble saying it back."

I'm feeling worse by the minute.

"She's only seriously dated one other guy in her whole life, right after high school. They had a summer fling, then he left her to go to Arizona, but that's it." She stops, placing a hand on my shoulder until I turn and meet her steady gaze. "Every guy in her life left. Not a single one has stayed. Yeah, there's your brothers, but that's not the same."

And I left her too. I hate that I hurt her, hate that my careless actions made her think less of me. My shoulders slump. "I really fucked this up."

She rubs my back. "You both did. You stopped trying, and she stopped hoping. You've got some scar tissue to get through, but I really think you can salvage this if you're sure that's what you want. Although, it won't be easy."

I've never been more sure of anything. "The best things in life are worth fighting for, and Meg is definitely worth it." Lee's optimism gives me hope, and I manage a smile. If Leah thinks we can do it, we definitely stand a chance.

The call for dinner echoes to us, summoning us to the house.

I loop an arm over her shoulders as we walk back, knowing exactly what I need to do. "I'm gonna need to raid your romance collection, Lee-bug." *I gotta consult the manuals.* "I need all the second chance romances you've got."

* * * *

Meg

I avoid Silas on Friday, first by going to work, then I finish a paper I've been writing. Our conversation replays in my head, and I know can't avoid him forever. Know I said we'd be friends.

I'm just not ready to start that next step of our journey. *Yet.*

Saturday, Leah barges into my room with a steaming cup, waking me from a pleasant dream. She plops on the edge of my bed, using her free hand to waft the smell of coffee toward me. I reluctantly sit up and take it, bracing myself for whatever's causing the excitement to pulse from her in waves.

"We're going to the ropes course. All of us. Forced family time."

I don't even hide my groan.

She keeps going like she didn't hear me. "Us girls will ride together, do some more wedding planning on the way." She stands with a grin. "Leaving in an hour, and you're coming—no matter what state you're in."

Fifty-five minutes later, I've showered, my hair is in two braids, and I have on a cute but sensible outfit of a fitted tee, jean shorts, and tennis shoes. I walk into the living room where everyone is waiting for me, all smiles.

It's the first time I've seen Silas since the Fourth, and I can't help being wary. But his expression is easy and he gives me an acknowledging nod, like we truly are friends again. I relax, happy to be on the same page for once.

"I'm ready, let's go." I offer to drive, so Leah hops in the front seat and Callie takes the back, leaning in toward the console.

"How was the apartment?" I ask Callie.

She gushes over it. There are two bedrooms and it's small, but great for their first place. Lyssa's roommate will be out sometime next week, so Callie and Sebastian can take it over any time after that. They've already signed the paperwork.

I'm so happy for them. Even if they are moving at breakneck speed, it seems to be what they both want. I mean, they decided to have the wedding the Tuesday after next. Talk about a whirlwind.

Leah starts going through her list on her phone of all the prep that still needs to be done. "I'm handling decorations. Do you know who you want to cater?"

We'd offered to all bring something foodwise, but Callie didn't want to add to our stress. She sighed. "Not yet."

"How about a dress?"

She shrugs. "Well, I want my bridesmaids in red."

I grin at the mention of my favorite color.

"Jess is planning to wear a suit, but her shirt will be red. I have some ideas for my dress, but I don't know where to go. I haven't had many occasions to get dressed up."

Leah and I exchange a look. I always forget how sheltered Callie's life has been. Her mom had some lung condition, keeping her from having many friends over or going anywhere. After her mom passed, Callie's dad kept her on a tight leash, so this is all new to her.

Leah gives her a reassuring smile. "Don't worry. We'll figure it out."

I meet Callie's eyes in the rearview mirror and nod encouragingly. It must work, because she switches subjects to one of the botanists on campus doing the flowers, and Leah checks one more item off the list.

The ten-minute drive goes quickly, and we pull into Branching Out. We climb from the car as the guys park behind us. Shawn and Sebastian hop out, immediately finding their respective ladies. I hang back for Silas and Steven, letting the couples go ahead.

"So have you guys done this before?" I ask.

Steven nods. "Yeah, it was a family thing we did a few times each year for a while." A nostalgic smile tips his lips.

Silas almost bounces beside me. "I cannot wait! It's been forever, but there's nothing like it." He pauses to glance down at me. "You're good with heights, right?"

"Yeah." I wave him off, but he keeps staring, waiting for me to elaborate. "I've never had a problem climbing trees or going on Ferris Wheels."

"Have you ever been mountain climbing, or hiking up steep surfaces?" Steven asks, a hint of concern in his voice.

I shake my head, not worried in the least. How different can this be from being in a tree? Leah calls for us to hurry up, cutting off any further discussion on the matter. We join the group, all pitching in to pay for entry, then we get our yellow beginner wristbands and move on to the harness shack.

Several employees dole out harnesses, helping each of us into them. The staff is perfectly professional, but it's still odd having a stranger that close to me. They hand me a heavy cable to drape over my shoulder as they check me over one last time. Then I stand off to the side to wait.

I take a moment to look up, finding one of the black advanced courses to my right, and a zing of excitement zips through me.

"You good?" Silas asks, appearing at my side.

"Oh, yeah."

I follow the others to the beginner's course Leah picks. At the base of the stairs, an attendant helps us hook our line into the metal track that runs above the entire course, then they have us each hang from the cable to double check it holds our weight. Leah and Shawn go first.

The course is a series of obstacles about thirty feet in the air, most metal, some wood, and they're strung between several massive trees, with wider platforms here and there for more than one person to gather on. Only one person is allowed on an obstacle at a time, and there are two attendants per course if anyone needs help. I like the idea of someone being nearby if anything goes wrong.

Steven goes next, followed by Sebastian and Callie. I watch from the stairs as I wait my turn, smiling at Leah and Shawn racing each other on parallel obstacles. Silas stays behind me while I climb the stairs, push my cable along and nod to the attendant. I scan the obstacles as I cross the platform, then I move toward a balance beam, getting right to the edge.

Where I make the mistake of peering down.

The ground seems impossibly far away, and my vision swims at the thought of having nothing between me and the empty space. I clutch my cable with a frightened squeak, frozen in place and beyond shocked at my terrified reaction.

"Meg?" Silas says behind me. When I don't answer, he comes up next to me, resting a hand on my back. "Hey, it's okay."

The warmth of his touch comforts me. But my heart is still pounding, my palms are sweating, and I can't look away from the ground. This is night and day compared to climbing a tree or a ladder. No branches to hold, no rungs to cling to.

"Steven freaked out his first time too. It's a whole different experience than any of us are used to, isn't it?"

I manage a nod, concentrating on his easy, calming cadence.

"It's all about trust." He tugs on his cable, making it clang against the track. "You have to trust that the cable will hold you. You have to trust the harness." He grins. "Trust me."

A weight underlines his words, an imploring that strikes a chord within me even as his relaxed smile stays in place. My head gets what he's saying, but my heart... Why are the two never in agreement?

He rubs my back, nodding in encouragement. "You've got this."

I take a deep breath, determined to try. I cling to my cable, then put one foot onto the balance beam. My leg feels weak and wobbly, which isn't like me at all. I get two more steps out, then I'm completely in the open. I pinch my eyes shut as my vision swims again.

"Meg, I'm right here," Silas says from behind me.

I grip my rope, focusing on his words.

"You've got to fall."

What? He must be crazy if he thinks —

"Trust me," he says again. "It'll show you that you're safe."

I swallow at the lump in my throat. It makes sense, but I've never wanted to do anything less. I suck in another ragged breath as everything in me screams that I'm going to regret this. Then I let go of my rope as I lean over the edge and fall.

The rope jerks me to a stop as I bite back my panicked shriek. I swing next to the beam, my feet dangling in mid-air as my body realizes it's not plummeting to the ground. I am also still three-dimensional, rather than a flattened pancake like my fear told me I'd be.

"Yes, Nutmeg! You did it!"

My rope slowly spins until I face him, and I soak in the proud grin on his handsome face. I manage a tremulous thumbs up, then set about climbing back onto the beam. It doesn't take much before I'm upright again, and while I still have a flutter of nerves in my midsection, it's nothing like before.

"You good?" he calls.

I manage to swivel partway around as I give him a real smile. "Yeah, I'm good, Si."

He sucks in a breath at the nickname. I'm the only one who's ever called him that, and it hasn't passed my lips in two years. The fact that it slipped out now has me stunned, but I try to hide it, not wanting him to realize how affected I am.

"Good." His smile seems a bit forced. "Okay then, I'm gonna..." He jerks his thumb toward a different obstacle.

I quickly nod.

He waits another beat, studying me, then his shoulders drop and he gives me his usual grin. "You got this, Nutmeg."

I stare after him as he races off, trying to convince myself the butterflies in my stomach are from facing the course.

And not from him.

Chapter Seven

Meg

I have no other problems as I navigate the course. My pulse is elevated the whole time and I never feel completely comfortable, but I refuse to let my fear get the better of me. I take an intentional breath before each obstacle, then I conquer it.

I win over the wobbly bridges, the rolling log, the uneven pedestals. I feel a thrill of fun as I race along the alternating steps then follow a zigzag metal path.

Each time I reach a platform, my eyes automatically find Silas. The way he'd coaxed me through my fear replays in my mind, and I've had other memories pop in too. In all of them, Silas calms me down or bolsters me. I forgot how supportive he can be, how much I leaned on him. And my chest aches as I allow myself to miss it.

To miss him.

As I approach the only obstacle I have yet to conquer, I exhale with a whoosh and bring my focus back to the task at hand. My legs feel strained from the extra force of keeping me balanced. My hands ache from continuously gripping the rope. And my mind itself is tired after holding off the fear that lurks around each corner, but I press on.

I read the plaque, seeing it's called the flea jump. I skirt the platform and step up to it, finding an extended two-foot by two-foot platform jutting into mid-air followed by a space between it and the matching extended platform across from it. The gap is only two to three feet across, a distance I could easily cross if I were on the ground.

Taking my usual bolstering breath, I move to the edge and prepare myself to jump. Instead, all the panic I've been holding at bay comes crashing in as my system overloads. I freeze, every muscle locked tight as I stare at that empty space.

"Meg?" Leah asks from a few obstacles away. "You okay?"

I can't move, not even to shake my head, but one face swims in my mind. "S-Silas," I manage to say. A smidgen of relief trickles through me at his name. I can't even bring myself to worry about my reaction – I just know I need him. "Get S-Silas."

The next few minutes slog by at an interminable pace. It feels like I have been stuck here for hours, struggling for each inhale. Then movement catches my eye on the larger platform beyond the flea jump.

"Hey, Meg, I'm here."

His welcoming voice has the air whooshing out of my lungs as I lock eyes with him. "I c-can't..." is all I'm able to say.

He nods, keeping my gaze. "You've done great so far. I've been watching you, and I'm so proud."

My lips twitch, a smidgen of warmth blossoming in my chest amidst the icy grip of fear. This is why I need him.

"Is this your last one?"

I nod.

"You're not gonna let one tiny little jump beat you, are you?"

The teasing edge to his words buoys me, and I know he's trying to help me regain perspective. I close my eyes as I think of all I've accomplished, then open them as I replay his words. That's all this is, a tiny little gap. A mere step if I was on land. If my feet were on the ground —

They're not, my brain reminds me helpfully and I tell it to shut up.

"Meg, look at me."

I do, my gaze colliding with his warm amber eyes that hold such tenderness, my insides begin to liquefy.

"I'm right here. Jump to me. Make this obstacle your bitch."

My vision narrows to the small platform on the other side of the gap. One tiny jump, that's all I need. I steel myself, ignoring my racing heart and trembling legs, then I bend and launch myself into the air.

Silas

I watch Meg fly through the air and brace myself to catch her when I see she's overshot the distance. My mind can't wrap itself around the fact that she listened. She jumped to me. Her feet hit the platform with enough force that she stumbles. But I'm right here and I pull her into my arms as she sags against me.

"You did it, Nutmeg," I say, loving how she clings to me even as she starts to tremble. I stroke her hair, catching a hint of her fruity shampoo and wanting to bury my face in the silky strands. "You did it."

When Lee had the idea to go to a ropes course, I never dreamed it would bring me and Meg closer. I remember how Steven reacted that first time. His fear is ingrained in my memory like a burn mark on a log, and my gut told me to keep an eye on Meg.

I'm so glad I did. And I'm so very proud of her for not giving up.

I hold her until she shifts backward, then I drop one arm, giving her space. But she doesn't move away, doesn't push my other arm off. My heart beats faster knowing she wants me to keep touching her.

She stares at me with a pleading gaze. "I just want to get back on solid ground again."

The words resonate within me, and I know she means them in a literal sense, but they match my hopes for where I want things to be between us as well. I follow on her heels, nudging her to the easiest path to the exit.

As soon as her feet hit the ground, she rushes to the harness shack to rip the thing off.

She waits while I shed my own, then I ask, "You want to wait for the others? Or I can take you home now?"

"Home," she says without a speck of hesitation.

I text the group, letting them know I'm taking her back to the house. She walks close to me as we head toward the exit, our hands brushing more than once. I gingerly lift my arm in a silent offering, and she leans into my side. I wrap my hand around her shoulders, happy to provide her comfort, thrilled that she's accepting it from me.

I pause at the car before I open her door. "You good?"

She seems exhausted, but she gives me a big smile. "Yeah. I really am."

Meg falls asleep before we're out of the parking lot, and I don't have the heart to wake her, so I meander my way home. I wonder if she's ever trusted someone like that before. I've had my family to lean on my whole life. If I fell, someone was always there to pick me up and dust me off. I could count on it.

Has she ever had that?

It's a huge step, letting go and trusting something else with your life. Even Steven had trouble. He's one of the most in control people I know, examining every angle before taking a step. Meanwhile I'm over here jumping off roofs and hoping I will fly.

But I've never been burned by gravity, have always been caught by the safety net of friends and family.

Today gave me a glimpse into Meg that I never would have had otherwise. True fear is unmistakable, yet she didn't let it stop her. I knew she was stubborn, but this outing proved her grit on a whole new level. I've never found her more attractive than I do at this very moment, and I can't help stealing glances at her sleeping form.

At a stop sign, I brush a piece of hair away from her face. Then I take an extra moment to bask in the fact that she's here.

And she jumped to me.

* * * *

We finally make it home, and Meg begins to stir when I shut off the engine.

"Hey, sleepyhead."

She yawns and stretches, frowning when she sees the dash clock.

I grin sheepishly. "I took the long way home. Thought you could use the rest."

"Thanks." Her smile is sheepish too. "I guess I did."

I'm not ready for my time with her to be over yet, and my mind races with ways to keep her near me. "So I was thinking about dinner…"

She giggles and shakes her head. "Of course you were."

I grin wider at her teasing. It's a well-known fact that food is rarely far from my thoughts. "Maybe we should get Chinese for everyone? Have a game night?"

Her beautiful eyes light up. "That sounds great."

"I thought so too, but wanted to make sure you're up for it. I'll text Lee, see if it works with everyone else." After confirming they're all in and getting a text with what everyone wants, I put in our order. We'll have half an hour before it's ready, and I know how I want to spend the time. "Want to walk there?"

She hesitates for a moment, then smiles. "Yeah, it's so nice out. A walk sounds great."

We both exit the car, then fall into step with one another. It'll only take fifteen minutes to get to the restaurant, but we can take our time.

A robin flits in front of us and a memory pops into my head. "You remember when Shawn dared me to climb the tree and I didn't realize there was a nest on one of the main climbing branches?"

Meg starts laughing. "That mama bird was so mad!"

The bird had dived at me over and over for getting too close to her nest.

"The way you flailed..." She trails off in another peal of laughter that has me grinning. "Then you fell right out of the tree!" She doubles over.

I chuckle too, though it had been terrifying when it happened. I was twelve and my ego had been pretty bruised then, but now, it's fun to laugh about. We keep reminiscing as we walk and it feels like old times. Although I never had feelings for her when we were growing up.

Whenever she turns her smiling face toward me, my heart stutters. The distance that had spanned between us is gone, all because of Leah's bright idea to make us all go to a ropes course. Meg's hand brushes mine as she sidesteps a missing brick, and she doesn't jerk away. My stomach flips at the contact.

I wish I could hold her hand. Just reach out and twine my fingers through hers as we walk along. I want the privilege to have that casual contact, to have her permission to connect us physically, but I know I need to be patient.

A familiar laugh sounds and I peer up the street, grinning wider when a strawberry-blonde woman steps out of a shop. "Avery!" I call. Then I reach for Meg's hand and tug her forward. "Come on, there's someone I want you to meet."

Her forehead furrows as if she's confused but she doesn't pull away as I rush to meet Avery. Gina steps out after her, both of them exclaiming at seeing me again so soon. Avery gives me a quick hug, noticing Meg afterward. "Who's this?"

"Avery Elgin, this is Meg Parker. Meg is Leah's cousin and she lives with us." I give Avery a stern look when her eyes widen in excitement, letting me know she remembers me talking about Meg from our days working at the coffee shop. I turn to Meg. "Avery and I used to work together."

Her lips part as she glances from me to Avery then back, understanding dawning in her eyes. "You worked together?"

I nod.

Avery holds out her hand, and Meg tentatively takes it. They exchange 'nice to meet yous' before I introduce Gina.

"What are you two doing on this gorgeous day?" I ask.

Avery holds up a shopping bag. "Just having some fun, checking out all the cute little boutiques over here."

Meg asks which stores they've been to as my phone buzzes in my pocket and I take it out. "It's Leah. I'll be right back."

When I answer, Lee asks, "Is Meg all right?"

I grin, turning back to see her chatting with Avery. "Yeah, Lee. She is."

Meg

I feel like an idiot for judging Silas the other day over taking his break with these two women. Avery has a wedding ring on her finger and she's mentioned Liam in conjunction with Gina several times. I guess I overreacted.

I recognize Avery's last name too, as one of the names displayed on the buildings on campus. Her clothes are obviously expensive, and she has a gorgeous style that I envy. My thoughts turn to my discussion with Callie and Lee on the way to the ropes course, about the wedding.

"This is kind of an out-of-the-blue question, but would you happen to have any good recommendations on where to get a wedding dress on short notice?"

Her eyes grow wide, and she looks at Silas then back to me before her gaze dips to my finger.

I burst out laughing. "Not for me! Silas' brother Sebastian just asked his girlfriend to marry him. They don't want a big to-do, so they're having a fairly quiet affair, but it's a little over a week away. We're at a loss for where to get a dress. And a caterer, for that matter."

Understanding dawns, and she nods. "Actually, I might be able to help." Holding up a finger, she quickly places a call. After a few minutes of murmuring, she turns back to me. "Are you guys free Wednesday afternoon? And how many are in the bridal party?"

I'll have to leave work early, but I nod, hope bursting within me. She confirms the appointment, then hangs up with a big smile.

"The place is called Lit, and trust me—Serena is a bit, um, unique, but she knows what she's doing. She is the *only* one I let dress me for big events." Avery and I exchange numbers, then she texts me the address, as well as the confirmation of appointment.

"Thank you," I gush. Callie is going to be thrilled. "Now all we need is a caterer."

Gina arches an eyebrow at Avery. "I'm waiting for you to leap all over that."

"You know a caterer?" I ask, hoping beyond hope.

Avery's cheeks are pink. "Actually, I am one."

"And a damn good one, at that," Gina adds.

"I'm just getting started with my business so I'm not quite—"

Gina clears her throat and gives her an admonishing look.

Avery takes a deep breath and straightens, turning on a professional charm that transforms her from friend to businesswoman. She pulls a card from her clutch and hands it to me. "This is my card. Have your friend call me, and we'll discuss numbers and menu options. I'd be able to arrange a taste test right away to see if we're a good match."

I take the card, loving the adorable cupcake on the front. *The Cupcake Standard, for all your catering needs.* "I'll pass this on. Thank you so much."

Silas comes back and we all chat for a while longer, then his phone buzzes again, letting him know our food is ready. I thank Avery and Gina once more before we say goodbye and go our separate ways.

As he pays in the restaurant, I grin, remembering how he checked with me before even asking Leah about having a game night. I appreciate him watching out for me — as a friend. He's been so gentle and supportive all day.

I can't believe I survived two years with us at odds. I forgot how fun he can be.

He gives me a questioning look when he finds me staring at him with an easy smile on my face.

I lift a shoulder. "I'm glad we're friends again."

His answering grin is like the sun coming out from behind the clouds. "Me too, Nutmeg. Me too."

* * * *

Callie was thrilled when I told her about the appointment at Lit. She kept peeking at their website between turns at our game night until the distraction caused her to miss a clue during Monikers and Sebastian asked her to put her phone away.

I manage to get the afternoon of the appointment off, and we all ride together in my car. Callie chatters happily about how well the catering meet went and how sweet Avery is. I'm going to have to thank Silas again for introducing me to her. I can't believe how perfectly things are working out.

I pull up to the address, stopping in front of a nondescript building with a cursive neon sign that simply says *Lit*. Leah and I exchange frowns, but I quickly change mine to a smile. "C'mon. Don't judge a book by its cover and all that."

We get out of the car and walk inside where a stately woman in a pantsuit greets us. "Reservation?"

I show her the confirmation text, and she tells us to follow her. We file down a winding hallway that is ridiculously dim. But when we turn a corner, we're standing in front of a gigantic warehouse with racks of clothes stretching in all directions.

Callie gasps then squeals and bounces on her toes. "I've never seen so many dresses!"

I chuckle at her excitement even as my own bubbles within me.

Another lady appears in front of us and sharply claps her hands to get our attention. She introduces herself as Selena. She's tall and elegant, slender with her dark hair pulled back in a sleek bun—not one strand daring to be out of place. Her thick black frames perch partway down her nose and she peers over them as she asks, "And who is the bride?"

Callie steps forward.

Selena nods. "Very well, let us proceed."

She takes an unlit cigarette from her pocket and rests it between her ruby lips. I wait for her to light it, but she doesn't as she walks away with Callie in tow. Two other attendants approach us. Mine is named Lin, and I don't know how she can walk in heels that skinny.

We all go to different sections of the store. I explain Callie's preference on color, but that we have free rein over style and length. Lin begins placing dresses on an empty dress rack, all of them in varying shades of red, all different styles and lengths.

Then I start the process of trying them on. Once she sees how the first several fit, she discards two from the rack, vetoing that particular cut. She studies me long enough that I'm itching to move before she disappears.

When she returns, I fall in love. Excitement builds in me as I put the dress on and glance at the mirror. It's a perfect fit.

The fabric is a brilliant red that I have the perfect shade of fuck-me lipstick for. The off-the-shoulder neckline emphasizes my cleavage and is decorated with rhinestones that catch the light with my every movement. The fitted material clings to my curves, and a racy slit is lined with a ruffle that runs around the entire hem.

I step from behind the curtain, and Lin gives me a satisfied smile. When I beam my approval, she leads me to the center of the warehouse where Callie is rifling through her dress options.

She gasps when she sees me. "Oh, Meg, that's perfect. You look gorgeous!"

Leah appears from another aisle in a dress that's a shade darker but also off-the-shoulders. The tight bodice shows off her figure, and I love how her hemline is shorter in front. She spins for us, and we take turns gushing over our finds.

We quickly rush to our fitting rooms to get our clothes on, and I can't help taking a few snapshots of me in my dress. I love the slit up my thigh, feeling beyond sexy as I take one picture of just my thigh peeking between the fabric.

I wonder how Silas will like the dress. The thought pops unbidden into my head, but I can't stop it. My imagination takes off as I picture him in a tux, walking with my arm looped through his. Together down that aisle. My mouth goes dry at the image, and I have to yank my thoughts back to the present.

Quickly, I change into my clothes, but I can't shake the lingering wisp of Silas my mind. Even as I sit in front of Callie as she tries on dress after dress, he remains. I keep remembering before, how I used to daydream about trying on my own wedding dress with him as my groom.

Each time I push the past aside and focus on Callie, it pops back in a second later, like a jack in the box with a broken latch. When will my heart learn?

Chapter Eight

Meg

An hour later, Callie dances in front of the mirror, her biggest smile yet brightening her face. The short white dress stops at mid-thigh and is held up by simple spaghetti straps. But the lace makes the dress stand out. It flutters at the tops of her arms, baring her shoulders. It hugs her middle, emphasizing her small waist, and a delicate overlay drapes down to brush the tops of her knees.

This is definitely the one.

While she's changing, my thoughts drift back toward the fantasy of my own wedding. I walk over to a rack of white dresses, unable to resist peeking through a few. Just for fun.

But Selena clicks her tongue. When I glance at her, she redirects me to the other side of the small space and gives me a satisfied nod when I stop in front of the rack she chose. These dresses are much more to my taste and I marvel that she knew.

I pull one out, holding it in front of me as I turn toward the mirror. The fantasy unfolds in my mind, me walking down the aisle in this dress toward my soon-to-be husband. The wedding march plays and I keep time with my steps. Leah is up there, grinning, while my groom stands with his back to me as I clutch the bouquet.

He turns in slow motion and my heart stutters when I see Silas' handsome face. I can't move as his dazzling smile sprawls over his lips then he mouths four little words.

"I love you, Meg."

I jerk back to reality, working to hide my startled expression. A quick glance around shows that nobody else is paying me any attention, and I let out a relieved breath as I return the dress to the rack.

What the hell was that?

* * * *

Silas

Thursday, I leave my internship a little early to go to my first therapy appointment. The moment I step into the office, the therapist greets me warmly and tells me to call her Maria. Her golden skin is smooth and flawless, despite her being at least mid-forties. Her black hair is streaked with gray and I like that she doesn't hide the lighter color.

Her office is as welcoming as she is, with its sunny yellow walls and bright, cheery abstract art. A bin of toys sits next to one of the chairs, all perfect for fidgeting with. I absently pick up a rectangle made of eight connected cubes, loving how it folds and bends at the joints.

My hour passes quickly and I find her quite easy to talk to. This session is mostly a get-to-know-you time, so she can evaluate where I'm at and we can identify specific issues to work on. I leave feeling optimistic and understood.

Next on my agenda is trying on tuxes with my brothers. As soon as Grandpa heard one of us was getting married, he was on the phone to Dad, insisting we get our tuxes at a place called Tony's in the next town over. Evidently, it's a family tradition.

I get home with ten minutes to spare but Shawn and Steven are already standing outside, waiting. I climb out of my car and ask, "Sebastian here yet?"

Steven shakes his head.

"Good. I've got time to grab some food."

Shawn rolls his eyes. "Make it quick."

"And not messy," Steven adds. "I'm driving and if you leave crumbs all over my car, you'll be vacuuming it when we get back."

I snap off a salute then trot inside to raid the fridge. I throw together a sandwich in minutes and stuff a water bottle in the pocket of my jersey shorts before I meander outside again.

"Sebastian's on his way," Shawn says. "He's running a few minutes late."

I nod, then take a big bite of my sandwich as Steven asks me, "How are things with you and Meg?"

Shawn's grin turns sly. "Yeah, is there a 'you and Meg'?"

I'm still chewing so I hold up a finger as I think about what I want to say. It's been one week since Meg and I formed our truce, six days since the high ropes course, and I can't stop thinking about her.

I swallow my food then say, "Not yet."

Shawn nudges me with his elbow. "I notice you didn't have any hot dates this week."

Shaking my head, I take another bite of the sandwich, not sure what else to say.

Steven and Shawn exchange a look, then Steven chuckles. "You're so gone for her."

I plop onto the steps and drop my forehead into my hand. "I can't get her out of my head, guys. It's ridiculous how much brain space she occupies. I'm so fucked."

"Hmm," says Shawn. "That sounds familiar."

We all laugh at that, knowing he went through a similar phase when he was trying to win over Leah a few months ago.

I sigh. "It was almost easier when we were both pissed at each other. At least then we were on equal footing. Now she wants to be 'just friends' while I'm over here pining for her." I shake my head at the irony. "Talk about the tables turning."

Steven pats my shoulder. "Keep at it, Silas. Earning back someone's trust takes time."

Shawn nods. "Yeah, it does. You're doing the right thing, though, starting with friendship. It may suck for you, but it's totally worth it. Gives you a good foundation to start on."

I take another bite of my sandwich, thinking on the words. "Thanks, guys," I mumble around the food in my mouth.

Shawn raises an eyebrow at Steven. "And what about you? Anything new to report?"

Steven shoves his hands in his pockets. "Nah. No one I'm interested in."

"Maybe if you actually went out and looked," I say, tapping my sneaker to his in a gentle kick. I keep my tone light and teasing, though I'm half-serious.

He rarely goes out. The only people he sees are us and his coworkers.

Shawn cocks his head. "You know, Silas has a point."

Steven glares at us, but before he can retort, Sebastian pulls up.

I finish my sandwich, shoving the food into my cheek to mutter, "Don't think this is over."

Steven walks away, calling loudly, "Hey, Sebastian, you ready?"

After we all greet our brother, we pile into the car — Steven driving, Sebastian in the passenger seat with me and Shawn in the back.

Shawn leans forward to wrap his arm around Sebastian's chest, giving him a hug from behind. "I still cannot believe you're getting married, and in four days!"

Sebastian grins. "Me either."

I'm still shocked he's getting married in the first place. He's the last one I thought would get married, and for him to be checking that box off before the rest of us? It stings a little, if I'm being honest.

Steven smiles at Sebastian. "Seb's always known what he wanted. This is no different."

Sebastian nods. "That's true. It may seem fast for you guys, but for me, it can't get here soon enough. I'm ready to start my forever with Calliope."

Shawn pretends to gag as he flops back into his seat, though I've heard him say mushier stuff about Lee. Steven's words pick at the edges of my salty heart. I've always envied Sebastian's laser focus. He knew what he wanted and went for it, with everything he had.

Me? I've changed majors multiple times, dated so many women I've lost track, and jumped from one hobby to another without mastering any of them. Soccer has been my one constant, and I'm not good enough to make that my life's work.

Not that Sebastian's had it easy. I know he has struggles of his own, with his type one diabetes and his recently diagnosed autism. I'm happy that everything is falling into place for him, and I think he and Calliope are perfect for each other.

I just want my happily-ever-after, too.

I have to bite back a groan at the sappy direction my thoughts keep gravitating toward. I'm no better than a lovesick puppy. Grasping for a distraction, I lean forward and ask, "How'd the catering meet go with Avery, Seb?"

He turns toward me with an enthusiastic smile. "She is well-suited to our needs. Calliope was quite thrilled with her, and they seemed to get along nicely."

"Good."

I know Lee's been stressing as maid of honor, trying to get everything done in such a short time frame while still making it nice. That's one more thing off her list, and it'll be good exposure for Avery too.

A wave of grumpiness ripples through me. Here I am making everyone else's dreams come true, but I'm still missing out on the one thing I truly want — a second chance with Meg.

Trying to fight the spiraling direction of my thoughts, I ask, "Did Callie find a dress?"

The girls landed a spot at some hot boutique yesterday because of Avery. I can't count how many times Meg thanked me for introducing them. At least I've got that going for me.

We talk about wedding plans the rest of the drive. Twenty minutes later, Steven guides us into the parking lot of Tony's. We all came last Sunday to get measured, and they did a rush job to have our modifications complete.

Inside, it's fairly quiet. One couple browses the far side of the store, checking out the ready-made suits Tony carries. An attendant helps us right away, leading us to the fitting rooms and hanging each of our suits on a different door.

They have the whole shebang in my bag. Tux, vest, bow tie, and perfectly shined shoes. It's going to look a little ridiculous with the white athletic socks I'm wearing, but I just chuckle to myself as I start undressing.

Several minutes later, I emerge. Steven is already out, and he grins. I have to admit, the people did a great job on fit. I can move without the fabric being too tight, but it also doesn't bag anywhere.

I lift my pant leg. "I'm starting a new trend."

Steven chuckles and shakes his head. "Of course you didn't think to wear black socks."

Shawn bursts out of the dressing room and raises his chin. "Shawn, Agent Shawn." Then he starts humming the *Mission Impossible* theme song as he clasps his hands together, index fingers pointing like he's holding a gun.

"That's two different franchises," I say, throwing up my hands.

As Sebastian steps out, he rolls his eyes at Shawn's antics. "We can't take you anywhere."

Steven walks over to Sebastian and adjusts his slightly crooked bow tie. "Damn," he says, glancing one by one at each of us. "We do clean up nice."

The attendant comes over to check on us, and when they've confirmed we're all satisfied, Shawn holds out his phone, asking them to take a pic. We sling our arms over each other's shoulders and grin. Shawn gets his phone back and sends us the best two pictures, then we head back into the dressing rooms to change.

On a whim, I snap a pic of me then shoot it to Meg, along with the group pic. I set the phone down, only to get an immediate response.

Who are you and what did you do with the Wrighting brothers?

I chuckle before typing out a response.

So Barney on How I Met Your Mother *was wrong? Suits aren't the way to pick up women?*

I didn't say that...

A wave of satisfaction washes over me, but I hurry to ask, *How'd your dress hunt go?*

Good. It took Callie longer than Lee and me, but we all found something we love.

Well, I showed you mine...

The dots appear then disappear, so I set my phone down again as I start the undressing process. A few moments later, it dings, and I eagerly pick it up to see.

One single photo fills my screen and my mouth goes dry. It's her thigh, framed by a perfect slit of red fabric, the hem ruffled and sexy as hell.

I write back before I can stop myself.

Welp, I now have a new screensaver. Damn girl, you're trying to kill me.

Silas!
Red is definitely your color.

You haven't even seen the whole dress...

I don't fucking need to. I know she's going to be gorgeous enough to haunt my already tormented dreams even more. Hopefully, I'll survive.

Chapter Nine

Meg

The day of the wedding finally arrives, and I can't tell if I'm more excited for the wedding itself or to see Silas in his tux. Not that I'll admit that to him.

The past twenty-four hours have been a whirlwind of last-minute details, decorating, and making sure today will be perfect. Us girls stayed at Trent and Judy's last night to get ready today without the guys interrupting. Callie wanted to uphold the 'don't let the groom see the bride until the ceremony' tradition.

Leah keeps thinking of things on her list and stopping to check that they're actually done. After the fourth time, I take her phone away, telling her to chill. She did an amazing job and she needs to have some fun too. Then she finally relaxes.

We have a blast helping one another with our dresses, hair and makeup. Callie is simply stunning and hasn't stopped glowing, not a hint of nerves in sight.

One of my curls keeps sagging from the partially pulled back style I have, and we're out of bobby pins, a feat I hadn't thought possible. I slip out to find Judy, who gives me a handful and several compliments before I head back to the room.

But the guys come trotting through first.

Shawn and Sebastian lead the pack. Shawn grins, telling me how nice I look while Sebastian steps forward, glancing at the closed door.

"How is she?"

I smile, putting all my reassurance into it. "I've never seen her happier."

His shoulders drop and the crease in his forehead smooths. "Truly?"

"She's not the least bit nervous, Sebastian. You two are made for each other." I reach over to squeeze his hand, and he tips his lips up slightly.

"Thanks, Meg."

Steven nods as he walks by, then guides Sebastian toward the sliding door.

Leaving me alone with Silas.

His throat bobs as he stares at me. "I knew the pics weren't going to do you justice. I'm just glad I get a minute to process before I did something stupid, like fall flat on my face in front of everyone." He steps closer, his amber eyes full of awe as he adds softly, "You're gorgeous, Meg. That dress was made for you."

My cheeks warm as I duck my head, the compliment swirling in my mind. His husky voice heats me from the inside out, and I can't stop smiling. "You're not so bad yourself," I manage.

His unruly curls have been somewhat tamed with gel, giving him a more refined air. The suit fits him like a glove, the sleek lines emphasizing his broad shoulders, trim waist and long legs. The red bow tie matches the silk triangle peeking out of his jacket pocket, and I love the addition of the black vest beneath the jacket.

"Yeah? Not that anyone will be looking at me." I frown in confusion as he laughs then adds, "Because I'll be walking next to you."

My cheeks heat even more, and I swat my hand at him, but he catches it, pressing a quick kiss to the inside of my wrist as my blood boils. I can't breathe, focusing solely on the gentle press of his lips to my bare skin.

"See you out there." He drops my hand, stepping back with a wink.

I stare after him, a wobbly pile of goo, even as I remind myself that this can't happen. My chiding does nothing to calm my racing heart which won't slow, even after I finish wrestling the curl into place.

All I can see is Silas staring at me with those heated eyes. All I can feel is the brief brush of his lips on my wrist.

And the wedding hasn't even started yet.

My focus is strained through the final bits of getting ready. When Judy comes to get us, Leah tugs me to one side and asks if I'm all right. I don't have time to explain everything going on in my head or the tug of war in my heart, so I just smile and nod.

"Good, because you're first."

Shit. I hurry to the sliding door, Leah hands me my bouquet, and up steps Silas. He grins, and my knees wobble in the face of his attention. When he offers me his arm, I take a deep breath, then move next to him, looping my hand to rest on top of his forearm.

I can't help taking a few more long glances at him, and he notices.

As we walk across the patio down the slope to skirt around the pool, he raises his eyebrows. "What? Do I have something on my face?"

My cheeks flames again, and I shake my head, then train my eyes forward.

He doesn't let it go, leaning closer to whisper, "Are you saying it is my face?"

I fight a laugh, squeezing his arm. "Silas," I hiss, but my smile is genuine as we cross the lawn and approach the aisle.

The yard came together beautifully. Trey and Judy rented a large tent that now sits in the wide-open space where we usually play volleyball. We'll eat and dance under there, all the tables already set up. Most of the white chairs are in rows to the right of the tent, under the shade of several large oak trees.

At the end of the aisle is a white arch, covered in greenery and red roses. Some from Sebastian himself, the others all grown right on campus. Callie's bouquet is composed solely of roses from Sebastian, an idea I adore.

Sebastian escorts Judy to her seat as we walk past the tent. Then he takes his place in front of the arch, standing tall and stoic. So handsome in his tux. He has a black bow tie, setting him apart from the others. My heart feels like it might burst from an overload of happiness at how everything has come together.

Even the weather is cooperating. Bright blue sky, low seventies with little humidity and just the right amount of breeze. July can be so hot and sticky, but they've been lucky even in this. I'm glad the guys won't be roasting in their suits.

Soft music sways in the background as we approach the aisle, and I can't help another peek at Silas, this time with a pang in my chest. I've imagined doing this so many times, but it was always me walking toward him.

Mrs. Silas Wrighting, that was my goal.

A longing pulses in me, but I shove it aside because we're light-years away from anything in that realm. As if sensing my inner turmoil, he covers my hand with his free one and gives me a soft smile as we pause right before the rows of chairs.

Jess and Steven aren't far behind us, and I turn slightly to glimpse Shawn and Leah together, both wearing the biggest grins. I wonder when I'll get to do this again, when they'll decide to take the next step.

Callie walks behind them, by herself, a choice she made. Trey offered to escort her, but she politely turned him down, wanting this show of her freedom.

The music swells, changing to our cue to walk again, and I fall into step with Silas. There are only fifty or so people here, most of them from the Wrightings' side, but all eyes are on us.

No pressure or anything.

We make it to the end of the aisle without misstep, and Sebastian nods at us. Silas gives my hand another squeeze, then lets me go as we move to opposite sides in front of the arch. The other two couples take their places, and the music changes once more, this time to Pachelbel's *Canon in D*.

Judge Paulson gestures for everyone to rise, and my throat gets thick as I watch Callie walk toward Sebastian. Her blue eyes never waver from his, and the smile on his face is broader than I've ever seen. I have to blink back happy tears as she hands Leah her bouquet and takes Sebastian's hand.

Then my gaze shifts to Silas. His focus is all on me, and to my surprise, he doesn't look away. The tender longing in his gorgeous eyes holds me captive as I suck in a bolstering breath.

My internal tug of war resumes, and I shift my weight, glancing at the arch as I argue with myself.

I have scars from this man. He left me before.

But what if he recognizes that he made a mistake? What if he'll do better this time around? We've both done some growing since we were last together. Can I trust him to be committed?

A part of me scoffs at the thought. *Silas can't even decide on a major. He goes through dates like candy. He doesn't even stick to a hobby!*

He's always played soccer, I protest. *And he's back in law. He left that major before too, but that's what he's settled on, even going so far as to get an internship with his dad. A solid sign of his sincerity.*

What if you two are just as great together, work out all the kinks then he changes his mind again?

What if he doesn't?

I snap my focus back to the wedding, just in time for the exchange of rings. My heart swells as I hear them firmly declare their I dos.

I want that. I want my happily-ever-after.

My gaze shifts to Silas once more, warmth blooming in my chest to find his focus still on me. One thought bubbles up within me, and I give in to the longing, allowing the words to fully form.

I want that with *him*.

For once, it doesn't fill me with fear to admit it, and I smile at the progress. Then clapping sounds as Sebastian and Callie share their first kiss as husband

and wife. I smile wider and cheer along with the others, even as an image of kissing Silas springs to my mind.

If he asked me tonight to be more than just friends, I don't think I could say no.

As we meet together to process out, he leans closer. "Save me a dance tonight."

And his wink has my heart stuttering as we follow the others down the aisle. We give Sebastian and Callie our hugs and congratulations, then Silas and his brothers make quick work of moving the chairs over to the tent as the people walk through the line to congratulate the happy couple.

At the head table, I take my spot next to Jess and Leah while the guys sit on Sebastian's side. Shawn's and Leah's toasts go off without a hitch. We even pound on the table once to get the newlyweds to kiss, which Sebastian does without hesitation. But the best part of being in the wedding party is we're first in line for food.

I heap up my plate, smiling at Avery, who stands to one side. "It all smells amazing," I tell her.

And it tastes even better. She made an array of appetizers from spinach dip to ham wraps, meatballs and the greenest beans I've ever seen. Plus a charcuterie board with meat, cheese, nuts and fruit that takes up one entire end of the table. It's perfect, giving options to everyone.

When the DJ calls the newlyweds to the floor, Shawn says to Sebastian, loud enough for our table to hear, "Since when do you know how to dance?"

Sebastian grins. "Since I started dating a dancer."

He turns to Callie, sweeping her gracefully into his arms, and I marvel at how well they glide through their steps. I let out a wistful sigh, unable to believe Sebastian is married.

When the dancing opens to everyone, Leah and I race to the floor. Callie stays out with us while Sebastian moves off, not surprising considering the upbeat tempo. The people on the floor change, the songs move on, and I have a blast, dancing with all of them.

I take a champagne and water break, pick at a few more apps, then head back to the floor. My heels are somewhere by my chair, and the music calls to me.

Silas swoops in front of me with that dashing grin. "You ready?" He holds out his hand and I don't even consider saying no.

I've danced with Silas before — at school, at prom, at various community weddings. But it's been a while. He's so fun and carefree that we quickly fall into the rhythm and he spins me out, then back.

The song ends and a slower one comes on its heels. *Lady in Red,* of all things. His smile never dims and he raises his eyebrows, a mischievous smirk on his lips.

"You requested this, didn't you?" I say, placing my hands on his shoulders.

"Maybe."

My stomach flips when he steps closer, sliding his hands to rest on my waist. His familiar oaky sandalwood scent washes over me, and I resist the urge to lean in for a deep inhale.

He hums along as we sway together, his eyes never leaving me. The rest of the world falls away as I get swallowed by his presence. Heat flares between us, and I move in, my breasts flush to his chest. He sucks in a breath, his hands flexing on my waist before holding me even tighter.

I toy with the curls at the nape of his neck, for once not worrying about the what-ifs. For once allowing myself to embrace that longing, to bask in his attention.

And it feels so right.

When the final notes of the song begin to fade, he leans in and presses a gentle kiss to my cheek, just outside of my lips. I stare at him as he slowly backs away. My insides are Jell-O, and I want more. So much more.

But he just gives me a soft smile. "Thank you, Meg, for the dance." And he fades into the crowd.

Silas

It took every ounce of my self-control not to drag Meg to the shadows and kiss her senseless. The longing I saw in her gaze echoed mine—just as poignant, just as strong. And when she pulled me closer, I tried not to read too much into it.

I know I'm on the right track, but to jump in guns blazing now would only scare her off. It's like a stray cat you've built enough trust with that it'll eat from your palm—just 'cause they take a bite doesn't mean you can dive in and pick them up.

That's a surefire way to get clawed to bits.

Once I'm back in control, I mingle with the family I rarely see, taking time to kiss my aunts and chat with cousins. But I know where Meg is at all times. Not because I'm trying, but my eyes keep finding her. She's a magnet for my attention, especially in that gorgeous dress.

The party dwindles until only our core group is left, and Leah gathers us all for the surprise she and Shawn organized. We walk Sebastian and Callie to the front of the house where a limo is waiting.

"Surprise," we yell.

Shawn explains about the four-day mini honeymoon we chipped in for, at an adorable cabin in a prime hiking area of Colorado. We all get big hugs before we send them on their way. As they drive off, I notice something glinting in Leah's hand and the conniving smile on her face.

"What are you up to now?" I ask.

She shrugs and holds out a silver key. "Why haul all the presents twice? And while we're at it, maybe we can move the rest of their things. Wouldn't it be awesome for them to come home to a fully moved-in apartment?"

Shawn runs with the idea but Steven hesitates, saying, "I'm not sure Sebastian would want anyone else touching his books."

"Don't worry," Lee says. "I've got a plan."

* * * *

Friday afternoon, I lounge on my bed, thrilled to have a day off. After spending Wednesday putting my parents' place back in order and all day yesterday hauling books and boxes to Sebastian's new place, I'm ready to chill. I'm just thankful everyone pitched in and now it's over with.

Leah had been meticulous boxing up Sebastian's books and taking pictures of his room so we could put everything on his shelves and desk exactly as he'd had it. I hope it'll make him feel more at home.

Steven took the whole week off so I'm not surprised when he knocks on my partially open door. I grin when I see him, until I register the panic on his face.

I shoot upright, wondering what's wrong. "What's going on?"

He holds out his phone, showing me a string of text messages. "She wants to go to karaoke tonight."

"Who?"

"Libby. I met her at the wedding, some grad student friend of Callie's. We've been texting and I asked her out."

My eyebrows raise of their own accord. "For tonight?"

He nods.

"And she wants to go to karaoke?"

He nods again, staring at the screen with wide eyes. "I don't karaoke."

Not only does he not sing, he hates being in front of people. No wonder he's panicking. I rub the back of my neck, trying to figure out a solution for him.

"Wait," he says, snapping his head up and meeting my eyes. "You like karaoke."

"Um, yeah?" What's he want me to do? Take the woman out myself?

"Come with us."

It's not a question, and I frown as I think about the logistics. "And be your third wheel? No thanks."

"Bring a date." His eyes widen then he grins eagerly. "Ask Meg!"

The suggestion takes root and a slow smile spreads over my face. "Now, that's a good idea." A group date would be much less awkward, plus I'd get to spend time with Meg. The more I think about it, the more excited I get.

"So you'll do it?"

"If Meg's available." I grab my phone then pause. "You sure your girl is okay with a group thing?"

"I'll check." He types on his phone and the whoosh sounds when the text sends. A moment later there's an answering chime and he grins. "She doesn't mind at all. Let me know what Meg says."

"Will do."

I haven't seen Meg all day, but I know she has morning classes on Fridays. And she often stays after to study. I send a quick message asking what she's doing, then I set my phone down and wander to my closet to figure out what I'll wear if this works.

The reply comes in a few minutes later as I'm sorting through my clean polo shirts.

Homework. Well, that's what I'm supposed to be doing.

I chuckle at her honesty.

What are you doing instead?

Her response is instant.

Well, I just stopped watching a video of a woman packing everything into one of those bags with all the compartments because she put an unpackaged toothbrush on top of a pair of upside down shoes.

I laugh out loud at the green-faced emoji she adds.

That sounds productive

It was so satisfying until that point.

I snort, shocked at the easy feeling of our back and forth. I quickly ask, *What are you doing next?*

Walking home and deciding how I'm going to get to my room without hearing anything I don't want to.

I frown, not understanding.

What do you mean?

The dots that signal she's typing appear then disappear then pop up once more.

Leah messaged me that she's having quality time with Shawn.

I groan and scrunch my nose, but she sends another response before I can reply.

You asked.

She's not wrong. I smile that she read my mind even though that's not anything I want to think about my brother or Lee doing. So I change the subject to the real reason I started texting her.

What are you doing tonight?

I have this really good book I'm in the middle of that I planned to finish. Why? What's up?

I take a deep breath and type exactly what I want to say. I push send before I think twice.

I want you to be my date tonight.

Just staring at the word "date" has my chest tight. Especially when a response doesn't appear right away. The moments stretch on without any reaction, and I can't take it anymore. I hurry to type out the whole explanation about Steven and his need for help, hoping that will tip the scale.

So if you don't say yes for me, say yes for Steven.

Still no dots appear. I pass several more excruciating moments staring at the screen before I search the room for some sort of distraction. My closet catches my eye, so I reluctantly put the phone down and review my polo options again. The black one is less wrinkled and the collar isn't folded weird. We have a winner. Now for shorts.

My phone dings and I lunge for it.

Don't you have a whole phone full of women you could ask?

I blink at the non-answer.

Probably. But I don't want them. I want to take you.

The dots do their thing several times before her response finally comes through.

Fine. But only if you feed me.

I hadn't asked Steven about times or if they're planning to eat, but I agree anyway.

Deal.

Then I race to Steven's room to tell him the good news.

Chapter Ten

Silas

An hour and a half later, I'm almost ready for our date, dressed in khaki shorts and the black polo shirt. Next I work on taming my curls. A bit of water, a bit of gel and they're fresh instead of frizzy. Then I trim my scruff. I hate having a bare face—I look like I'm twelve without it. But I don't love the feel of a full-on beard either. So scruff it is.

At six-thirty on the dot, Steven and I walk downstairs.

Meg slips out of the mini-suite, earbuds in. She looks hot—as usual—in her bright pink V-neck T-shirt and her ass-hugging jean shorts. I'm still marveling that she said yes to this. Meg Parker is going on a date.

With me.

Steven pushes my shoulder and I realize I'm standing at the bottom of the stairs, gawking like an idiot. I shoot him a dirty look but he just grins and shakes his head.

Pointing at the front door, he says, "I'm gonna wait outside. Our Uber will be here in five."

I nod, then glance over at Meg again. This time she's watching me.

"Hey," she says, taking out her earbuds.

"Hey." I rack my brain for something — anything — to say but everything sounds lame. "You look nice."

"Thanks."

"Not that you don't usually look nice. You do. Actually, I think you're hot. That's what was running through my brain when I walked down the stairs and saw you. That you're so hot — as usual."

She stares back at me with eyebrows high and eyes wide. "You okay?"

The unfamiliar feeling of embarrassment washes over me and my cheeks heat. I need to get a grip. "Yeah," I grunt, shoving my hands in my pockets and staring at the floor.

I hear her walk closer then her brightly painted toes appear in my line of sight. Hot pink, like her shirt.

"Si…"

The nickname has me jerking my head up to meet her heated gaze. A knowing smile tips her lips.

"I think you're hot too."

A thrill races through me and I'm grinning like an idiot before I can check my reaction. Then she reaches up and adjusts the left side of my collar. Her soft fingers brush my neck in a too-quick caress that has my cock twitching. Her lips are glossy and plump.

And right fucking there.

It takes all my self-control not to grab her hips and pull her to me. I want to taste her again. Hear her moan.

"You ready?" she asks.

So beyond ready. But I quickly rein in my runaway thoughts and clear my throat. "Yeah, Steven's outside waiting. Uber should be here any minute."

"Let me just put on my sandals."

We walk outside as the Uber pulls up. Steven gives Meg a wave before he hops in the front seat, leaving the back for me and Meg. I open the door for her and her sweet smile fills me with longing.

I flex my hand as I walk around to my side because I so desperately want this to work. To prove myself to her. I know she probably agreed to come tonight just to help Steven, but I wish it was because she wanted me as badly as I want her.

It only takes a few minutes to get to the High Five, a local bar I haven't been to in years. I didn't realize they do karaoke and I'm excited to sing in front of people again. It's been too long since I had a boost like that.

We hop out and Steven glances at his phone. "Libby will be here in a few. You guys want to go get a table?"

I glance at Meg who shrugs, so I nod and we walk in. A burly guy greets us at the door, his name tag reading Burt.

"IDs, please."

We quickly dig them out and he's validating them when someone calls my name. I turn to find Gina rushing toward us with a black apron over her waist.

"Hey, Silas, Meg. What are you guys doing here?"

I take my ID from Burt and put it away as I answer, "Karaoke."

A woman starts singing in a warbly tone that makes me cringe.

Gina sighs. "It's open mic, so I can't guarantee it'll be good, but people keep coming back so they must be having fun."

"You work here?" I ask.

"Well..." Gina trails off with a little laugh. "My boyfriend owns the place, but I help run it."

"Yeah, you do." A huge brick wall of a man wraps his arms around Gina's waist and pulls her to his side. He's shorter than me, but his chest is huge.

"Liam!" Gina lights up as she gazes adoringly at the man. "Silas, Meg, this is my boyfriend, Liam."

He stretches out a meaty hand, first to Meg who stares at him with wide eyes. Then to me, and I don't hold back on my firm shake, which makes him grin.

"You're Liam Davenport," I say, unable to hide my awe at meeting the former football star.

Gina shakes her head. "No football fan clubs allowed here." She smiles, though. "C'mon, let's get you two a table."

"Actually, my brother and his date will be joining us in a minute."

She seats us at a little booth near the bar and not far from the stage. "I'll be back with menus in a sec."

Meg scoots in first, then I slide in next to her, careful to leave some space between us and not crowd her. I'm happy we have a booth instead of a table. I'll take any chance I can to be close to Meg.

Gina comes back with menus and we put in our drink orders. My phone chimes with a text from Steven, saying it'll be another few minutes but he still wants to meet her outside. I update Meg, then we sit in silence. My knee starts bouncing as tension grows within me.

I glance at my 'date', wondering again why she's here. Gina brings over our drinks. I take my draft beer and hand Meg her vodka cranberry.

"I'll be back when your brother comes in."

We both thank her then taste our drinks. The silence builds, and I want to bounce right out of my seat. The music stops as the singer wraps up their song, and the only sound is the quiet murmur of conversation.

Finally, I can take no more and blurt out my question. "Why'd you say yes tonight, Meg? Was it just to help out Steven?"

She stares at the table for a long moment before lifting her chin and turning to look me straight in the eye. Her gaze is wide and vulnerable but she shakes her head.

Hope bubbles within me, giddy and untamed. "Then why?" I need to hear her say it. I hold my breath as anticipation thrums within me.

"I..." Her lips press together briefly as she twists the napkin in her lap. "I still have feelings for you, Si. I'm not sure I'm ready to do anything about them yet, though." She lowers her gaze to the napkin, which is beginning to shred as she worries it with her fingers. "I'm not sure I can trust you."

Those final words sting, but I can't help the slow smile that sprawls across my lips.

When she glances up, her eyebrows lift. "I tell you I don't trust you and you start grinning?"

I chuckle. "Well, when you put it like that..."

She stares at me, waiting.

"You admitted you have feelings for me. That means I have a chance. *We* have a chance."

She drops her chin, looking at the table before raising her head once more. "I'm scared, Silas."

The tremble in her voice has me aching to gather her in my arms and hold her to my chest until her fear subsides. But I refrain, not wanting to overstep. "Nutmeg, my feelings for you are stronger than ever, but I'm here however you need me. If you want me as a friend, I'll be the best friend you could ask for. If you think you're ready to go on another date, I'm in. If you want a label, stick it on me."

Her wide eyes search mine and I slowly reach over to rest my hand on her busy fingers. She stills at my touch but doesn't pull away. One corner of her mouth even tips up, and I feel more at ease touching her, the way I always do.

I'm an idiot for not realizing it before, but Meg is one of those people I'm just comfortable around—aside from that weird moment in the living room earlier today. I can always count on her to be there, steady and dependable. Even if it isn't easy for her.

It's one of the many things I love about Meg.

This is the first time I've allowed myself to call it that. *Love.* I blink at the realization as my heart races, trying to keep my ridiculous smile toned down so she doesn't ask me what I'm thinking about. She's a part of me, and I'll savor my time with her in whatever capacity I can. Even though she's far from ready, I'll be here as long as it takes. And I want to make sure she knows it.

"Your pace, Meg. I'm not going anywhere."

Her lips curve up and she places her hand on top of mine. "Thank you. That means a lot."

My smile hasn't dimmed when Steven and his date appear a few moments later. He does a double-take at my expression but introduces Libby instead of picking on me. We all shake hands then they slide into the booth across from us.

Libby seems nice, with an easy grin. She dives right into asking Meg where she got the bangles she's wearing. Steven keeps glancing over at his date and I can tell from his upturned lips that he's excited to be here.

She's cute, too, with auburn hair that hangs to her shoulders and a dusting of freckles across her cheeks. She looks good with my brother and I think they'd make an adorable couple. But I'm too wound up from my talk with Meg to sit still much longer.

I bounce my leg as we make it through giving Gina our orders. The moment she leaves, I spring from my seat. "I came here to sing," I say, giving Meg a wink. "Guess I'd better choose my song."

A pretty pink hue tinges her cheeks as she smiles at me. I walk toward the stage as a younger person takes the mic and belts out *Walking on Sunshine*, a song that fits my mood perfectly.

Meg may not trust me but she's here tonight and she admitted her feelings. A perfect start to our second chance.

One I won't mess up.

Meg

Silas leaves and Libby turns to talk to Steven. I feel awkward and want to give them a chance to talk so I excuse myself to the bathroom. Silas is busy chatting with Liam near the book of song choices so I'm not expecting him to talk to me.

But as I walk by, he holds up a finger to Liam and gives me a bright smile. "I'm third," he says.

I can only nod, but my lips are tilted in an answering grin without me even knowing it. He keeps surprising me. First by asking me out tonight, then his awkward rambling in the living room. And finally his quiet question about why I'd come. He'd seemed so unlike his usual confident self that I couldn't help it.

But now I feel like the vulnerable one.

I replay his comforting words as I wash my hands. He hadn't teased me when I said I was scared. He took me at face value and reassured me, putting another crack in one of my walls.

When I emerge, Steven is talking in earnest to Libby. She leans in, her chin propped on her hand. The very definition of interested.

I linger near the bar, despite having most of my drink left.

"You need something, Meg?" Gina asks.

I shake my head even as I go to lean on the smooth, lacquered surface. "Just giving those two some space to talk."

"Ah, I see." She wipes down the bar. "How long have you and Silas been together?"

"Oh we're not—" I start. "I mean, we were once but...um, we're not." I sigh and drop onto the nearest bar stool. "It's complicated."

"Sounds like it."

The microphone squeaks and we both glance at the stage. Liam gives a sheepish wave before grabbing the mic.

"He sings?" I ask, beyond surprised.

His build suggests he'd be more at home on a football field than a stage, but he seems perfectly comfortable as he raises the mic to his lips. Lewis Capaldi's *Before You Go* begins.

Gina stares at him with complete adoration as she softly says, "Oh yeah. He sings." She glances at me. "I see Silas waiting in the wings. Is he any good?"

Liam starts singing and I wait to answer as I marvel at his velvety voice. "Damn, he's amazing!"

Gina just grins.

"Silas' voice isn't anything on that level but he more than makes up for it with his energy."

She nods thoughtfully, looking at Silas then back at me. "You know, Liam and I wouldn't be together if he didn't give me a second chance. From what I know of Silas, he's a great guy, and I can tell he's smitten with you. There's always a risk with opening yourself up, but living all closed off isn't much of a life."

The words hit a bit too close to home but I manage a smile. "Thanks, Gina." I turn to watch Liam finish his song as I mull over what she said.

Relationships do always come with a risk, but I've been burned before, so it makes it that much harder to open up. Why play with fire again when I know it hurts?

Liam hands the microphone to Silas, who wears his usual grin. He adjusts the microphone as the opening chords of *We Will Rock You* start up. Gina gives me a skeptical look, and I can practically hear her asking if he's serious.

"Just wait," I say. She hasn't seen anything yet.

Silas loves his audience. He's great at getting the crowd involved and pumping people up. He lives for the spotlight, and their attention gives him a boost.

His voice warbles a little on the first verse, but his energy and smile never waver. When he gets to the chorus, he's got everyone in the area pounding out the beat as he holds the microphone toward the crowd. People all around us are shouting along, grinning their heads off.

Gina's disbelieving expression turns to one of admiration. When she nods at me, I feel a ridiculous sense of satisfaction from her approval, and I give her a wave as I walk back to the booth. Both Steven and Libby are watching Silas too, clapping along with the beat.

The whole place has a new energy as Silas finishes his song with a satisfied grin. The cheers follow Silas as he struts to our table. He slides in beside me, then starts to sling his arm behind my shoulders.

But he stops mid-air.

His forehead crinkles as he watches me, waiting for silent permission. The gesture warms my heart like a sunbeam. When he's feeling this happy, his need to touch escalates — as if his good mood must be shared. I dip my chin and his dazzling smile returns. His arm lands behind me on the back of the booth, not quite touching me, but so close I feel his heat, and I love his proximity.

The thought trips me up. I mull it over as I notice that the ever-present worry in my chest is gone. I realize it hasn't been there since I laid out my feelings to Silas. Taking a deep breath, I relish how much lighter I feel and glance at him once more, unable to resist grinning too.

His infectious vibe carries over to the next singer, and it energizes our little group. The rest of the evening passes in that fun, easy vein. Libby even convinces me to come up with her and we sing *Man! I Feel Like a Woman!*. When it's time to leave, I give her and Steven hugs, since he's seeing her home.

We hop into our Uber, and Silas lounges in his seat — slouched down, legs spread, one arm on the window, the other between us. The smile on his face is huge as he lets out a contented sigh. "Fuck, I needed that. Thanks for coming with me, Nutmeg."

He reaches over and takes my hand, threading our fingers together like they belong that way. I stare at our joined hands in the passing light of the streetlamps, warmth blossoming in my chest.

Tonight was so easy. Just being with Silas, getting to know Libby, watching Steven relax as we listened to karaoke or sang along. The weight is still gone, and I've noticed the freedom I feel without it constricting my chest. All because Silas and I talked.

I squeeze his hand, then lean over until my shoulder touches his. "I had fun."

His thumb strokes the back of my hand. "Good. Me too."

The words are husky as tension ignites between us. I stare into his heated amber eyes, for once embracing the longing that wells in me. My gaze dips to his lips.

Maybe...

But we pull up to our house and the dome lights flick on. Silas finishes the transaction on his phone, then we both step out. On the sidewalk, he links our hands once again, and we walk side by side to the front stoop.

Except he doesn't reach for the handle. Instead, he turns me toward him, and my breath hitches when I meet his intense gaze.

"Can...? I'd really like to kiss you good night." He reaches with his free hand to brush away a stray strand of hair from my cheek.

I close my eyes at the gentle touch. All the reasons to say no disappear from my mind, leaving me staring into a massive well of longing. I nod as I open my eyes, anticipation fluttering within me.

One corner of his mouth ticks up as delight dances in his eyes. He leans in, touching his lips to mine in a sweet, gentle kiss that soothes the ragged edges of my lingering doubt. I feel safe as he increases the pressure, reassured as he tilts his head and prolongs the kiss.

Then he steps back and I can only gape at him. I want to pull him back to me, to feel his perfect lips on mine again. Yet, I keep my hands to myself.

The gulf between us may be narrowing, but it's still there.

His fingers caress my cheek once more, his thumb touching the edge of my lips. Then he smiles and says, "Good night, Meg." And opens the door for me to go inside.

I walk into the house, feeling as if I'm floating the whole way to my mini-suite. That perfect moment replays in my mind, over and over, searing its way directly into my heart.

* * * *

Silas

I lie in bed, staring at the ceiling long after I should be asleep. That gentle kiss plays on repeat in my mind, the edges of the memory becoming worn in their familiarity. And Meg's look afterward, so awe-filled and trusting…

It's the best gift she could have given me.

Asking for the kiss was a gamble. She'd been accepting of my touch all night, not even minding when I had my arm behind her. Then on the ride home, she'd closed that gap. *She'd* leaned on me.

I would've kissed her right then if we hadn't arrived home. But this was better. I'm not sure my control would have held in the dark confines of the backseat.

I roll over and shut my eyes, begging my brain to turn off. It refuses so I huff and flick on the light next to my bed. Then I grab the latest romance novel I'm reading and lose myself in someone else's problems.

Chapter Eleven

Silas

The next afternoon, Sebastian and Callie stop by to thank us all after checking out their new apartment. Leah met them there and told Sebastian to give it a chance before freaking out. They stay for lunch, telling us about all the amazing hikes they went on. I love seeing Sebastian this happy and relaxed—it's as if being with Callie makes him more comfortable in his own skin.

After they leave, I'm back to pining while I do my laundry. Thoughts of Meg distract me all weekend. I feel like the next move should come from her. I've made my play, shown my hand, so now the ball is in her court. I don't intentionally keep my distance, but I'm not seeking her out either.

A difficult urge to fight.

Monday morning, I have a meeting with my advisor followed by a therapy appointment. I'm already grumpy when I head in to meet Brenda, having had to get out of bed on my day off from my internship. Not that our advisor meetings are ever fun.

I'm dreading telling her that I'm switching majors again. My steps slow as I approach the building and I have to force myself to open the main door. Outside her office, I take a deep breath, then another before plastering on a smile and striding in.

Things go much smoother if I pretend I'm happy.

She glances up from her laptop, her stony expression not wavering as she peers over her half-moon glasses at me. "Silas. Hello."

"Hi, Brenda," I say as cheerily as possible and take a seat. "How are you today?"

"Fine. And you?" She removes the glasses from her nose, letting them dangle from the chain around her neck.

"Great. I know what I want to do now." I beam. "I'm switching back to law, so I want to go back to the poli-science major."

Her eyes close as she pinches the bridge of her nose and some of my energy seeps from me at her usual reaction during our meetings. I hate being a burden. She opens her eyes while her lips press together in a thin line.

"Law? Are you quite sure?"

The doubt in her tone chips at my confidence but I raise my chin. "Yes, this time I am."

"Silas…" She laces her fingers together and leans forward onto her elbows. "You do realize that you'll have to continue here for another full year if you switch your major. Again," she adds with a pointed look that has me slouching in my chair. "If you continue on the communications path I laid out for you, you'll be able to graduate at the end of this coming semester."

My leg starts bouncing as tension courses through me. "I understand that, and I've discussed my track with my father. He advises against a communications major based on the law schools I want to attend."

There isn't one major requirement to get into them, but poli-science is a strong choice.

She stares at me as the moments tick by. I feel like I've been placed on a scale and every single thing wrong with me has been brought to light, weighed, and measured. I want to slink out of the room with my tail between my legs the way I usually do.

Brenda has never been particularly supportive. Her no-nonsense demeanor always makes me feel like any adjustment to my schedule is a huge chore for her. Any questions I ask of her are a major annoyance in her otherwise pristine day. I always imagine that she lets out an exasperated sigh when she sees my name on the schedule.

But I need this change.

"All right. I'll come up with a new plan for you." The words are reluctant and clipped.

I take it, though, popping to my feet. "Thanks, Brenda."

"I'll put you on my schedule for three weeks out at the same time." I nod and start to leave, but she says, "Oh, and Silas?"

I turn, my hand poised on the doorknob.

"Let's make this the last detour, shall we?"

Her condescending tone deflates me further. "I hope so," I mutter before trudging out of the office.

In the hallway, I sag against the wall as every single one of my decisions bounces around my head. Am I doing the right thing changing my major again? Maybe I should just stick with communications.

Why should I think that this time will be any different?

A dark cloud of doubt weighs on me while I walk to my therapy appointment, and I find my energy flagging as I arrive. I grunt out a greeting then plop into one of the overstuffed chairs.

Maria frowns as she leans forward. "Silas, what's going on?"

All my negative thoughts tumble out. She listens intently, the furrow between her eyebrows never disappearing. When I finish, I'm still feeling heavy and unenergetic — miles away from my usual self.

"I'm sorry you're going through that." She turns away to dig through her piles of papers in her cubbies, emerging with a light blue one and handing it to me. "I'd like to try something. Will you go through this with me?"

I stare at the sheet, the title *Grounding* in a bold heading at the top. She leads me through each step. I start with five things I can see, then move to four things I can touch. Next I find three things I can hear, two things I smell. And she hands me a Tootsie Roll for the one thing I can taste.

"How do you feel?" she asks when I've finished the candy.

I take a moment to assess myself, surprised to find that I feel better. When I tell her as much, she smiles.

"Good. Anxiety often goes hand in hand with ADHD. It's easy for negative thoughts to overwhelm us and sometimes they can spiral out of control. Grounding is a way to stop that spiral, to give our minds something else to focus on."

Below those five steps are several other suggestions, like focusing on your breathing, sensory stimulation like music, food, or drink, doing a full body scan and evaluating what each part of your body feels like. I skim the rest of the page, awed that there are simple techniques to stop my brain in its tracks.

"There's one more thing I want to talk to you about, Silas." She hands me another paper titled *Rejection Sensitive Dysphoria (RSD)*.

I frown at it, wondering what this has to do with me.

"People with ADHD can be very sensitive to negative reactions—real or perceived. Whether it be someone saying no to their invitation or a simple criticism, ADHD brains can take this sort of feedback very personally. I believe you are one of these people," she says gently.

My frown deepens. "You do?"

"Overall, you're a happy, cheerful, confident person, wouldn't you say?" At my nod, she continues, "Now think about your meeting today. How did Brenda's words make you feel?"

Some of that weight creeps back in as I replay the memory.

"I can see the negative thoughts edging back in. Here." She hands me another Tootsie Roll and has me focus on the sensation and taste until it's gone. "People with this condition can have heightened sensitivity, emotional dysregulation that causes outbursts of negative emotions, low self-esteem, and can even lead to a person avoiding problematic situations or people."

My mind immediately races to Meg, to how after she gave me the cold shoulder I became bitter and angry. How I avoided talking to her more and shut her out completely.

Maybe I do have RSD.

We spend the rest of my time discussing different tactics to regulate my thoughts. My homework is to try all the grounding tactics on the sheet and journal my reaction to each one. We'll go over them at my next appointment to figure out which ones work best for me.

I leave feeling lighter, but drained at the same time. The emotional roller coaster I've been on took a lot out of me. I glance at my phone, relieved that I have a couple of hours yet before my soccer game. Plenty of time for a snack.

And maybe even a nap.

* * * *

I'm a bit groggy when my alarm pulls me from my sleep. I have to sit there for a moment, images from my dream playing in my mind. Meg had come to me, knocking on my door and asking to talk. She wanted a real date, just us.

Then she sat on my bed and kissed me.

I'm partially hard the entire time I get dressed, and I keep wishing the dream was real. I know giving her space is the best thing, know the next step has to be Meg's so she doesn't feel railroaded into anything. But waiting is agony.

Thoughts of her distract me through warm-ups and more than one of my teammates ask if I'm all right. I keep waving them off, but then the game starts and I can't focus. My three best friends on the team tell me to get my head on straight, one after another, and I try.

It's just not happening, though. My playing never improves, and I never find that focus I usually have on the field. When I miss the one opportunity I have at a goal, I feel awful. Especially when we lose.

I'm trying not to sulk when three of my teammates flank me.

"Somebody had an off day. What were you thinking so hard about?" Remy teases me.

"Nothing," I grunt.

"He just needs to get laid," Aiden says.

Brad smirks. "Not a bad idea."

I concur, but there's only one woman I want and we're going as fast as she'll let me.

"Well, we haven't been out in a while," Aiden says, glancing between us. "What's going on Friday?"

They're all free and turn to me expectantly. I'm often the one to organize these guys' nights, but I've been more than preoccupied with Meg. I could use a night out with my friends.

"I'm free," I say, and we talk about where we want to go, then I add, "I'll even get the first round." Least I can do after playing like ass today.

After we finalize the details, I leave with a smile on my face and something to look forward to in an otherwise uneventful week.

* * * *

Meg

Tuesday morning, I'm heading to work in the same state I've been in since Silas' kiss—a dazed mix of anticipation, hope and doubt. I can't wait to see him again while at the same time I'm dreading it.

The kiss was amazing, and I've replayed the memory so many times I'm surprised I haven't worn it out. But just because we've kissed doesn't mean I'm ready to be his girlfriend. I keep getting in my head about what he expects from me, then his words will echo in my mind.

Your pace, Meg. I'm not going anywhere.

They calm me each time. Even if I don't know exactly what I want right now, he's not going to push me. And he's not going to leave.

My two favorite coworkers are scheduled with me today. I often keep my personal life to myself, but I'm bursting to talk with someone. So when Kaylie and Bekah finish spilling about their weekends, I take my turn.

"Details, girl," Bekah demands as Kaylie nods eagerly.

I tell them all about the kiss and our conversation, filling them in on our complicated history as we set up rooms for patients and look over our charts for the day. It feels good to have someone else to talk to.

"So, are you going to give him another shot?" Kaylie asks.

I lift a shoulder. "I don't know yet. Something's still holding me back." I try not to flinch as the memory of Silas kissing another woman surfaces and all the pain I felt comes flooding in once more. No, I'm definitely not ready to leap off this platform yet. Not when I still don't trust the cable.

Bekah nods. "Totally get it. You gotta be sure, since you've been hurt before. But I'm glad you're keeping that door open. It sounds like he's so into you."

"I think so too," Kaylie says. "On both accounts."

We all smile and I feel a kinship with these two that I haven't felt in a long time. I have Leah, I have Callie, but I remember the other day when they were both busy and I had no one else to talk to. "What are you guys doing this weekend? Want to go have some fun outside of work?"

Their eyes light up and we eagerly start brainstorming. Friday works best for us. It doesn't take long to decide on dancing at the club. Bekah and Kaylie are both single—and looking—and I could use a distraction from Silas, so it's a win-win for everyone.

The morning passes smoothly, and my happy mood elevates even more when Leah and Callie come take me to lunch. I get to hear more details about Callie's honeymoon and all about how great Shawn and Leah are doing. Then it's my turn.

Part of me doesn't want to mention the kiss, knowing Leah might get her hopes up. But I've kept enough from my best friend and I'm not doing that anymore. "Silas kissed me."

"What?" Leah squeals, clasping her hands together in front of her chest. "Tell us everything."

For the second time today, I go over the double date. This time, though, I spill more about my doubts and how in my head I've been since. "One minute I'm reliving that kiss and his sweet words about not going anywhere, then the next I'm wallowing in the past and reliving all that hurt. It's such a roller coaster."

Callie pats my arm. "You've got a lot to unpack. You guys didn't talk about any of this for two years, so I'm not surprised it's all resurfacing now. Give it some time. There's no rush."

I chuckle. "Says the girl who got engaged and married within a couple of weeks." We all laugh, then I nod. "You're right, though. I'm not on anyone else's timetable, and I really can work through this at whatever pace feels right."

"Just make sure you talk to Silas, too," Leah says. "I think your little convo before karaoke was a great start, but you need to keep that going so it doesn't blow up in your face again."

Her gentle words prick at me with their sharp truth, and I nod again. They stay with me for the rest of the day. I stop for a sandwich on the way home, more than ready to eat after our longest shift at work. Once I park and get out of the car, I saunter to the house, happy to be home.

Inside, I glimpse movement out of the sliding door and walk over to investigate. Silas is kicking a soccer ball along the yard. He dodges left, then right, then kicks the ball right into the goal.

I step outside, cradling my sandwich in the crook of my arm as I clap. "Nice."

He spins around to face me, a huge grin on his face. "Hey, Meg! How are you?"

I hold up my food. "Hungry." It's so nice outside that I pull the sliding door closed then plop onto the step and unwrap my meal. "You?"

"Good." He picks the ball up from the goal, then walks across the yard. "Now that you're here? I'm even better." With a playful wink, he drops the ball in front of him and starts dribbling it between his feet toward the goal again. "How was work?" he calls over his shoulder.

We chat between me taking bites of my dinner and him practicing his footwork. It's easy and fun, with a little bit of flirty thrown in. By the time I've finished my sandwich, my smile is permanently affixed to my face.

I stand, crushing the wrapper into a compact ball. "I'm gonna go in."

"'Kay." He props the ball on his hip and grins. "Good talking to you. I missed this."

The sweet words have warmth spreading through my chest, and I duck my head as I admit, "I did too. Night, Si."

"Night, Nutmeg."

And I go upstairs feeling like maybe I'll be ready to try that next step sooner rather than later.

* * * *

Wednesday at work, my phone blows up with texts from my mom. I try to ignore her as long as possible, but the unanswered notifications niggle at me. Finally at lunch, I open her messages.

She wants me to babysit tonight, and I almost put the phone down right then, but a later message catches my eye. How I never see my half-sisters and they're my family too. Guilt weighs on me.

With a reluctant sigh, I check my calendar and find it unfortunately clear. Then I send her a message asking what time.

My dread of going to my mom's hangs over me for the rest of the day. Bekah notices, and asks what's wrong, but I don't want to talk about it. Kaylie is off on Wednesdays, which is probably a good thing because I don't know if I'd be able to evade them both.

I swing by home to change then run to the store to get some Play-doh and coloring books. Maybe some new things will occupy the girls for a bit.

My knuckles barely tap the door before Mom swings it open. I'm still on the front stoop as she pushes past me with George on her heels.

"You're late," she snaps.

Overwhelmed by her abruptness, I stand there for a beat as they rush toward the car. "Wait, have the kids eaten? Do I need —?" But I'm cut off by the slamming of their doors, then the engine rumbles to life and they leave.

I glance at my phone to find that I am three minutes past what she asked for. I've never been able to do anything right in her eyes. Just once, I'd like to hear a *good job* or even a *thank you, I appreciate you*.

Sometimes I wonder if that's why I come back. Because I'm hoping that someday my mom will see me and I'll find that place where I belong.

A shriek from inside has me sighing, then I square my shoulders and stride into the house that I grew up in. I settle an argument between the girls then walk around, noticing how every picture is of Mom and her new family. All the old ones of me and Dad have been replaced.

I peek into what used to be my room and don't recognize a thing. The once pale blue is now a bright pink. The worn tan carpet is also pink, stained and ripped in places. I had shelves with knickknacks and trophies, and I briefly wonder where my childhood mementos have ended up, but I decide I'll never ask.

Because the sinking in my gut tells me they probably ended up in the trash.

Chapter Twelve

Silas

My chat with Meg on Tuesday had hope brimming within me that we could have a few more moments to move us forward the rest of the week. But her sunny demeanor that night has disappeared behind a cloud. I've seen her only in passing and tried to chat, but she makes an excuse or waves me off.

I know I haven't done anything wrong. That doesn't stop my mind from inventing impossible scenarios where I screwed up, though.

By Friday, I'm chomping at the bit to go out with the guys and have a distraction from the endless waiting. The club is exactly my scene — crowded dance floor, loud music, packed bar. We manage to score a table on the edge of the floor, and, true to my word, I get the first round.

My friends begin scouting who they're going to try to pick up. To their surprise, I just hold down the table. I get ribbed a few times, not that I care.

I don't want anyone but Meg.

Remy returns looking grumpy as Aiden comes back with another pitcher of beer.

"What's eating you?" he asks Remy.

"Just got my head bit off."

"By a girl?" At his nod, Aiden grins. "Which one?"

Remy rolls his eyes but leads the way to the dance floor and returns by himself. A minute later, Aiden appears again, seeming a little shell-shocked.

"Told ya so," Remy mutters.

Aiden takes a big slug of beer, regaining some of his color by the time he sets the glass back on the table. Then Brad comes over with a similar expression.

"Not you too," I say, shaking my head. They all exchange stories and my curiosity is piqued. "All right. I need to see this woman."

Remy shrugs. "Your funeral."

I follow him and Aiden to the floor, and he points at the far corner of the crowded area. Where Meg is dancing alone. A tangle of emotions zip through me — elation at seeing her, relief that she turned down my friends, shock that she's here. I'm halfway across the floor before I realize I'm moving.

Meg's back is to me and I can't help admiring her fluid motions. Her ample ass looks amazing in her tight purple mini skirt, and I take a moment to drink in all the bare skin of her luscious legs. She tosses her long dark hair, shifting so I can see her profile. The black corset top almost has me drooling.

No wonder the guys were hitting on her.

I ease behind her so she doesn't see it's me, then grab her waist and yank her flush against me. She goes rigid and I feel her fury as she spins around, hand raised. I quickly catch her wrist before she can smack me and my laughter spills out.

"Hey, Nutmeg." I have to lean close to be heard over the music.

"Silas! That wasn't funny." But she's grinning even as she yanks out of my grasp. "What are you doing here?"

"I owed my buddies a drink for losing the game Monday." I remember my friends then and glance over to the edge of the floor to find them scowling. I bite back a laugh and ask Meg, "What about you?"

"I'm here with my coworkers, Kaylie and Bekah, but they ditched me to hit the bathroom."

"Ah, gotcha." I jerk my head in the direction of my friends. "So I kept hearing about this woman turning my friends down, then they pointed you out." I can't keep the amusement out of my voice. "Want to rub it in their faces and dance with me?"

"Yeah, I can't seem to get a moment's peace tonight." She gives me a sassy look but her tone lacks any heat. Her voice gains a husky edge as she asks, "What do I get out of it?"

"I'll buy you a drink."

She smirks and crosses her arms, drawing my attention to her delectable chest. "The others offered that too."

I step closer, trailing a finger down her bare arm. "One dance and you come hang out with me the rest of the night. I'll make sure you're not bothered by anyone else."

Her eyebrows jump up. "Deal."

The song changes and Dua Lipa comes on. I've heard Meg and Leah singing along to it often enough, and I think it's called *Break My Heart*.

Meg's grin falters. "A little on the nose," she says.

I shake my head. "You've got nothing to worry about from me. Besides," I say, giving her a soft smile, "we're just friends, right?" *Until you say otherwise*, I add silently as I step up to her.

It's enough for her to move closer. We dance—fast and flirty with casual touches that have my heart stuttering and blood rushing to my cock. But I ignore the sensations, focusing on Meg having fun.

At the final chorus, I grab her hand and spin her away. When our elbows are straight between us, I pull her back. She spins in, wrapping herself in my arm, then plants a hand on my chest as she beams at me.

She squeals when I dip her, tipping her head and exposing her gorgeous throat to me. I see her pulse flutter, and I wonder if she's as wrecked as I am but hiding it better. As the song fades and I guide her upright once more, two women rush over, calling her name.

Friends, right. I forgot we both came here with other people.

Meg's cheeks are flushed as she steps out of my arms. "Hey, Bekah, Kaylie. This is Silas."

Bekah is tall and sporty. Her wicked grin has a predatory edge that has me stepping closer to Meg. Her thick black hair is pulled tight into a ponytail atop her head, where a cascade of braids spills out. Each braid has a different shade of neon woven into it and I grin at the riot of color.

"Bekah, nice to meet you. Love your hair."

She beams.

Kaylie is slight and a few inches shorter than Meg, even in heels. Her sunny smile is genuine, making me like her instantly. She sticks out her hand.

"Nice to meet you, Silas," she says, and I like her even more.

"You too." I turn back to Meg. "You all want to come hang out with us? My friends would love that. I go out to dance with one beautiful woman and come back with two more."

Meg laughs then glances at her friends, checking their reaction.

"Friends?" Bekah practically purrs.

Kaylie watches Meg with a hopeful expression.

Meg grins at me. "I guess I'll take that drink now."

I wrap an arm around her shoulders, loose and casual as I guide them across the crowded floor. All three of the guys are waiting at the table, so I get to see their jaws drop as I stride up with my gorgeous entourage.

"Guys, this is my friend Meg." I keep my arm around her, needing the guys to understand she's with me. Then I introduce Kaylie and Bekah before I offer to grab another round. More beer for us, Long Islands for the girls.

Good thing they're on special.

* * * *

Meg

As Silas leaves to get our drinks, Remy nudges Brad. "Looks like we found the distraction."

Remy's umber skin contrasts with the pale and freckled Brad, one of the many differences between them. Brad is short and slight with shocking red hair. Then there's Aiden—tan skin, dark-brown hair, and eyes that are the prettiest shade of sea green.

While the guys chuckle at Remy's comment, I frown, not getting it.

Aiden leans in with a friendly smile and an understanding air. "Silas missed a pretty important goal on Monday."

"His head was nowhere near the game," Remy adds. "Definitely someplace else."

And all five members of our group stare at me as Silas walks back up.

He obviously overheard, slinging a casual arm around me. "Can you blame me? This gorgeous woman lives in the same house as me. We went to karaoke last weekend, and she blew everyone out of the water."

I appreciate the deflection, though I wish I had a drink. At least Silas is keeping this on a fun, flirty level. I adore him for it.

The guys razz Silas a bit more, then the server appears with a tray full of beer and Long Islands. After we pass the drinks around, we clink our glasses together with a hearty "Cheers." As we fall into the polite get-to-know-you conversation, I watch Kaylie gravitate toward Remy, while Aiden and Brad vie for Bekah, who eats up every second of the attention.

After the guys return with our second round—a vodka cranberry for me this time—and another pitcher of water, Brad coaxes Bekah onto the dance floor followed closely by Kaylie and Remy. Silas glances at Aiden.

Aiden sighs. "Go on. I'll keep an eye on things."

Silas grins and tugs me out of my chair. The alcohol flowing through my body makes me more compliant than usual as I let him lead me to the floor. Kesha's *Die Young* begins and we all sing along, dancing in one big group.

The next hour is spent dancing, laughing and drinking. We take turns sitting out to watch our drinks and Aiden is currently on duty again. He and Brad have been alternating dances with Bekah. She hasn't given any indication who she likes better, but no one seems salty over it.

Kaylie and Remy are really hitting it off. Each time they return to the floor, they dance closer. The way she grinds on Remy right now is enough to make me roll my eyes.

I lean over. "Maybe you two should get a room."

Kaylie lights up as a slow smile spreads over Remy's face. He nods. "I know a place." They say their quick goodbyes before disappearing.

Well, then.

Silas eases behind me, slipping a hand along my waist to rest on my abdomen as his lips brush the shell of my ear. "Thanks. I'd rather not watch my friend have sex on the dance floor."

A breathy giggle escapes me, and I find myself leaning into his solid chest. "Me neither."

Bekah and Brad return to the table as the song ends, then she comes back with Aiden. She grins and winks at me before focusing on her new partner. I shake my head, laughing again.

So far, things are still easy between me and Silas, though his casual touches have increased. Each graze stokes the embers of desire stirring within me, and combined with the alcohol, I find myself scooting closer to him, both on and off the floor. He is the strongest magnet for my metallic heart.

Alcohol dims the loud doubts to a mere whisper, and desire rears her head, increasing with each graze or gentle nudge. The air between us becomes heated as the

DJ gives us two perfect grinding songs in a row. The couples around us meld together.

I move nearer to Silas, unable to resist the draw of his heated amber gaze. I reach out to rest a hand on his chest, loving the feel of him under my palm.

His throat bobs as he rests his fingers on my hip, toying with the slice of skin between my top and skirt. Liquid fire runs through my veins at the touch. As a third song begins, the tempo eases, focusing more on a thrumming bass that creates a matching throb low within me.

Silas skirts behind me, dancing close enough so I can feel his heat, but we're only joined by the hand he keeps on my waist. The distance is almost worse than if he pressed against me. The anticipation of each brush of his hips or thighs or chest has my stomach clenching while want laces each of my nerves.

Ava Max's *Born to the Night* begins, even slower yet, and everyone around us dances closer still. Staying behind me, Silas spreads his hand wide on my stomach, his other hand gliding down my hip as he pulls me gently to his firm chest. My breath hitches when I feel the evidence of his own arousal, pressing against me. The idea that I turn him on that much has my heart racing, an answering pulse of desire throbbing within my abdomen.

I reach back, running my fingers along Silas' neck and into his curls. Soft, silky curls that I wish I could touch whenever I want. Every time I see his chaotic hair, I want to bury my fingers in it.

Usually, I refrain, but not tonight. Not with the doubts drowned and my walls paper-thin.

Tilting my head puts my cheek against Silas' and he nuzzles me. His hand leaves my hip, sending a delicious thrill through my abdomen as he slides his way up my ribs, skimming the side of my breast in the barest hint of a touch. I push my ass back against him, feeling wanton.

Everyone else falls away until there is only us, this moment, and the music. The sensations of his body moving to the beat overwhelm me, pushing out all thoughts of consequences or reasons why not. I didn't decide to do this — I had no choice.

His fingers dance along the underside of my exposed arm, and he chuckles when I squirm. "So ticklish." The husky words are murmured against my cheek.

The tension buzzes between us as he continues his gentle gliding over my body, and the heady knowledge of toying with that dangerous line flows through me. But the song ends, fading into *Apple Bottom Jeans*, and reality dumps over us like a cold bucket of water.

I step out of his arms, away from his lips, and don't look at him again until we make it to the table.

Brad breathes, "Finally," then rushes to the dance floor to join Bekah and Aiden.

It's a good distraction from my heated thoughts, and I muse over the three of them, over who she will choose. *If* she will choose. I wonder how solid the guys' friendship is, and just how adventurous she is.

Silas takes a big drink of his beer, and I sip on my vodka cranberry. The silence between us now holds a hint of awkwardness that I don't like. I drink more, hoping it will ease things and bring back the heady bubble I've been in.

"What are you doing this weekend?" he asks.

As we chat about my exciting plans of never-ending laundry and homework, I begin to relax once more, loving that we can just talk like this about everyday things. Brad, Aiden and Bekah return, jumping into the conversation as they take a break from dancing.

Silas puts his arm behind my chair as he takes us on a tangent about his intramural soccer team. The warm fuzzies return with a vengeance at the casual touch. I find myself leaning closer, startled when my shoulder brushes his chest, but he gives me a big smile and tucks me firmly against him, his hand resting on my bare arm.

He continues his story about one of his friends lining up to kick the ball for a winning shot, except the guy got overexcited and completely missed. His momentum was so great he spun in the air before landing on the ground.

"We all thought for sure he'd broken his ankle, but no." Silas chuckles. "He was completely unharmed."

I let out a little laugh. "I wouldn't say completely." Silas glances down, his brows knitted together, and I smirk. "I bet his ego was at least sprained."

The laughter bursting from Silas shakes both of us, and he squeezes me tighter. The warmth inside me turns to a sizzle. I'm thankful I'm not a firework or I'd be shooting into the sky to explode for all to see.

I reach for my drink but it's empty.

Silas finishes his last sip then rests his cheek on the top of my head. "I should probably head out. Do you wanna come home with me?"

I jerk back, wide-eyed at the insinuation as desire and panic war within me.

He laughs sheepishly. "I just meant we could share an Uber."

Relief courses through me along with a prick of disappointment. I sigh, swirling my straw in the remaining ice cubes and wishing the night could go on forever. "Yeah, it's time." It's almost one a.m. and already the tug of sleep pulls at me.

He removes his arm then stretches overhead, his shirt lifting to give me a glimpse of his flat stomach. He smirks when he finds my eyes locked on that bare sliver of skin, and I quickly look away while he checks out Uber.

"They'll be here in five."

"Great."

I make my way onto the dance floor to say goodbye to Bekah, who is happily sandwiched between Aiden and Brad. She gives me a little wave before looping her arms around Brad's neck.

Silas laces his fingers through mine as he leads me through the crowd and outside. The warm night air is heavy with late July humidity. I love that we have our seasons, but I also like it when I can breathe normally instead of sucking in soupy air that has more moisture than a sauna.

The Uber pulls up, Silas' phone dinging with confirmation. He opens my door, and I slide in. When he plops into the seat beside me then lifts his arm, I scoot over happily.

A few more moments in the bliss bubble? Yes, please.

We don't speak the whole ten minutes home. The Uber driver turns up his music after checking with us, and I stay snuggled with Silas, my cheek flush against his chest.

The drive is much too short, and reality crashes back in when we park in our driveway. I begin distancing myself as I fumble with the door handle.

I watch the driver pull away while Silas stands behind me. His presence is like a lighthouse, impossible to ignore with the beam always emanating from him. I wish I could trek safely through the waters to get to him, but I don't know if I can risk smashing against the rocky shores ahead.

He walks me to the stoop where we pause. His longing gaze sweeps over me, as if waiting for some cue from me. When I stay quiet, his shoulders sag slightly, but he says, "I'm glad I ran into you tonight."

"Me too," I say, my throat thick with a sadness I don't quite understand. Was I hoping he'd ask for another kiss?

He opens the door, letting me in first. A part of me wants to grab a fistful of his shirt and bring those perfect lips to mine. To demand he drag me upstairs and we finish this dance we've been in all night.

But I don't.

I know I'd regret it in the morning and blame it on the alcohol.

He pauses at the bottom of the stairs. "Good night, Nutmeg."

My throat is thick but I manage a small smile. "Night, Si. Thanks for a great night."

I stand there, watching him walk upstairs as longing threatens to drown me. Right before he's out of eyesight, he glances down at me. Our gazes meet, electricity crackling between us in our locked stare. His throat bobs as he swallows, then he looks away and disappears from sight.

I watch the spot he just occupied for several long moments before I trudge to my room and give in to the welcoming pull of sleep. At least I can see him in my dreams.

Chapter Thirteen

Meg

The next morning, I stumble bleary-eyed into the quiet kitchen. The coffee pot is full, thankfully. I move on autopilot until the first sip of rich liquid touches my lips then I let out a contented sigh.

Silas chuckles, deep and throaty, from where he leans in the doorway. "You and your coffee."

I'm not awake enough to deal with teasing, but I try. "Not like you're much better."

Silas isn't one to be grouchy, but mornings aren't his strong suit either. It takes a bit for his normal, beaming self to emerge.

I'm nice and pour him a cup. His fingers brush mine as he takes it, sending electricity jolting through me.

That wakes me up.

My mind starts racing to what it would be like to start my morning in bed with Silas. I take another sip as I study him, his unruly curls sticking up every which way, the stubble coating his chin, the huskiness in his voice when he spoke. A heady wave of longing crashes over me, and I hurry to drop my gaze.

Being with him last night felt so good, but I can't help thinking that a second chance for us would be the wrong move. Sure we're great with flirting, good on the dance floor, and we can talk to one another. But I still don't know if he'll stay.

Just friends is all we should be.

Silas rummages through the fridge, emerging with bagels and cream cheese. "Want one?" He has two packs of bagels—everything flavor in one bag, cinnamon raisin in another. When I nod, he grins. "Cinnamon raisin, right? With peanut butter?"

I blink, amazed that he knows my bagel preferences. "Yeah..."

He winks and sets about making our breakfast. I stare after him, finally going over to the table where I slide into a seat. He sets my bagel in front of me, just the way I like it.

"Thank you," I murmur, feeling off-kilter that he knows me so well.

Silence settles between us as we eat and sip until it's broken by Leah's laughter as she trots into the room followed by Shawn. Both of them exude way more energy than I ever thought of having this early. They're dressed in running clothes and wear identical lovesick smiles.

"Morning, Meg, Silas," Lee says cheerily, bouncing to the fridge where she fills her water bottle. A damp sheen of sweat clings to her, a sure sign they've just returned from a run.

We both grunt back to them while I fight the urge to roll my eyes. Running sucks. I'd much rather play a sport or go clubbing or walk all over campus. And all the runners I know love to run first thing. The last thing I want to do after I wake up is go torture myself with exercise.

Silas catches my eye and we share a grumpy, knowing look that endears him to me even more. He gets it.

Once we've finished eating, I excuse myself to start my laundry, then go to my room. Giggling sounds from the bathroom, followed by Shawn's deep chuckle. I wrinkle my nose then grab my book to go sit in the main living room, careful to shut the suite door behind me.

Silas stares at the TV, eyes glazed with boredom, but he perks up when he sees me.

"Whatcha watching?" I ask, plopping on the couch next to him.

He gestures to the screen.

"*Gilmore Girls*?" I start laughing.

His cheeks turn pink before he mutters, "Nothing else was on."

"I love this show, just didn't expect you to be a fan. But you should definitely start at the beginning." I raise an eyebrow and at his nod, flip over to Netflix and find the first episode.

* * * *

Silas

I've heard people rave about *Gilmore Girls*, but never gave it a chance. Now, I get what all the fuss is about. Quips and banter are two of my favorite things in any good romance novel, and this show has both. In spades.

Meg and I are debating if we want to jump right into the second episode when Shawn emerges from their mini-suite looking decidedly relaxed as he whistles a cheery tune on his way by. My stomach sinks as I realize the real reason Meg is hanging out with me.

"You're hiding, aren't you?" I ask.

She ducks her head. "Hiding?"

I roll my eyes. "You know, you could just say something to—"

"I don't *want* to say anything!" Her flashing gaze snaps back to mine. "Lee deserves to be happy. They need their time together. It's not their fault I went and got dumped so I'm home more."

An odd mix of admiration and sympathy washes over me. "You deserve to be comfortable in your space too, Meg."

A heavy sigh whooshes out of her. "I know."

I love her loyalty, how she wants to give Leah this time with Shawn, but I hate seeing her displaced. An idea slowly forms in my mind. "Wait, why don't you move upstairs? We've got room now that Sebastian has moved out, plus Shawn's rarely up there anymore."

She stares at me, wide-eyed, and I can almost see the wheels turning in her mind as she thinks it over. Her gaze drifts toward their mini-suite, her lips tilting into a frown. "I'd be leaving Leah."

I nod. "You know it has to happen someday. She's strong enough now that she can handle it."

Meg's eyes lock with mine. "You and I would be neighbors."

I have to swallow at my suddenly dry mouth before I can respond. "If you chose Sebastian's room, yeah. We would." I hold my breath, waiting for her answer. If she says no now, after that comment... I try to brace myself for rejection, running over my grounding techniques in case I need them.

"What about Steven? Would he mind?"

Hope bounces within me as I wave her off. "Nah. He doesn't care. He never minded having Callie up there."

Shawn waltzes back in, still whistling, and Meg stares at him. Determination settles in her expression then she squares her shoulders. "Okay, let's do it."

A massive grin splits my face. "Yeah?"

She nods, an answering smile tipping her lips. "Yeah."

"What are we doing?" asks Shawn, raising an eyebrow.

She turns toward him, enthusiastically explaining my proposal to Shawn. Her excitement is infectious.

The idea of living so close to her settles on me as images flash through my mind. Us bumping into each other in the hall. Going to and from the shower. If she chooses Sebastian's room, we'll even share a wall. I try not to gulp.

No way am I taking it back now.

Leah steps out of the suite. "What's all the commotion?"

When Meg nods for Shawn to explain, his words come out in an excited rush.

Leah smiles but then her face falls. "Wait, that means…"

Meg lifts a shoulder. "I'll be right upstairs. I'm not moving across the continent." Lee still looks so sad, and Meg laughs at her pitiful pout then pulls her in for a hug. "You and Shawn can have this whole space to yourself. Think about that."

Leah's smile is back when she steps away, her blue eyes locking on Shawn. "Okay, I'm in."

To appease Meg, I send a quick text to Steven, who says he doesn't mind at all and to let him know when she wants to move so he can help. After a quick vote, we decide to move her today. I don't have a shift at the coffee shop until tomorrow after a scheduling mix-up.

Meg stares at us, wide-eyed and slightly panicked. "Today? I'm going to move today?"

I lift a shoulder. "No time like the present."

She takes a deep breath, then nods. "Okay. I can do this."

Leah links her arm through Meg's. "No, *we* can do this."

Meg relaxes, giving her a grateful smile. She decides to take Sebastian's room, saying she likes the color of his walls better. Shawn is thrilled since it means he can take his time moving his stuff. He's been living in two places, upstairs and down, so he still has plenty of things in his room.

We start with Meg's bed, me going backward up the stairs with the queen-sized mattress, Shawn on the other end. Our stairs have a landing three steps up then a curve that's tricky to navigate, but we manage it. On our return, Steven meets us at the bottom with the box spring and Shawn grabs the other end. I ease past them to start taking apart the frame, then haul that up.

The wall that makes the most sense to put the bed against is the one that adjoins my room. Thoughts of Meg sleeping bombard me, my imagination taking off trying to figure out what she does or doesn't wear to bed. I pull my runaway thoughts back and focus on reassembling the frame.

Next is the dresser. Shawn and Steven wrestle it out of the door, leaving me to grab a few of the drawers

Meg pulled out. I take the biggest one, chock full of jeans and pants. Then I nod to the slimmer top drawer.

"I can take that too."

Meg's eyebrows raise, and I think she's questioning my abilities, but before I can say anything she crosses over to grab it. When she places it on top of the other one, I'm confronted with a drawer full of lacey underthings. Shocked, my gaze flies to hers.

She just smirks. "You asked for it."

I swallow, then head out of the room. The riot of color in the drawer keeps drawing my attention, though I valiantly try not to stare. A red thong lies right on top, and I can't stop picturing Meg wearing it. And nothing else.

Fuck. My. Life.

I can't get upstairs fast enough. My brothers laugh when they see what I'm carrying.

Shawn slaps my back after I set the drawers down. "Still think this was a brilliant idea?"

I groan and slump against the wall, letting my head tip back with a thud. "Nope. I'm so screwed."

They both chuckle, disappearing down the hall. I take a second to compose myself then head out for another trip. Books are next—thankfully, she doesn't have as many as Sebastian. Then the desk.

Between our treks, Leah and Meg take armfuls of hanging clothes to her new closet. Then they tackle the bathroom. I show her Sebastian's space in our bathroom, giving her a shelf for her toiletries.

We all get an extra workout with this impromptu move, but it's done before we know it. Meg insists on buying us pizza for our help, and my mouth waters at the thought of dinner.

After the last load is hauled, I linger in her doorway. "Anything else you need help with?"

It's just us, and she turns from her bookshelf to smile at me. "Nope. I'll get things figured out over the next few days, but the layout isn't much different. Thanks again."

"No problem."

"Pizza should be here soon." She gets up from the floor, a pained grimace crossing her face as I watch in concern. She rubs her knee, but stops when she sees me noticing.

"You okay?"

"Yep," she answers cheerily.

But it takes a few steps for her to walk normally. I remember when she hurt her knee playing volleyball in high school. She tore her meniscus and had to sit out for the rest of the season. It took surgery to repair it, followed by physical therapy.

It's been a while since I've seen her favor it, though I know she has occasional flare-ups when she overdoes things. A prick of guilt hits me. Maybe this was the wrong move—for several reasons. She's not the type to complain, though, and she'll push through the pain to not be a bother.

I watch her carefully on the stairs. She navigates them fine, until she gets to the landing.

Her foot slips and her full weight comes down on that leg. I'm rushing toward her as her knee buckles, yet I somehow manage to keep her upright. My heart pounds at how close she came to falling down the stairs.

She clings to me, her fingers digging into my biceps, and I'm not sure if her death grip is from residual fear or pain.

"How bad is it?" I ask quietly, keeping a firm hold on her waist as she gets her bearings.

"Could have been worse." She stares at me, managing a tremulous smile. "Thanks for saving me."

I shake my head. "The move upstairs was my idea in the first place. I didn't think—"

"Silas, stop. I overdid it, then misstepped. It's no one's fault, and the upstairs move was a good idea. It solves a lot of problems."

I still feel bad that I didn't even think about it. I guess it's a testament to how well she's been doing that it's been a while since it's acted up. She didn't even favor it after the ropes course.

Her grip on me loosens, and she gingerly puts her weight on her left leg. She winces, but pats my chest. "I'll be fine. I'll need to rest for a day or two, but then I should be back to normal." She eyes the remaining few stairs as if they are pure evil.

I move in front of her, presenting my back. "Your chariot, madam." I squat down, glancing over my shoulder as I wait for her to climb on.

"Silas, you don't have to—"

"I want to. Come on."

My stomach flips at the gentle slide of her hands as she reaches for my shoulders. Then she hops up, using her good leg and wraps her arms around me. I gently hold her thighs, keeping her in place.

I fight back the heady rush that floods me at the feel of her against me, and I ask, "Good?" Though it comes out a little strangled.

"Yes." Her voice is strained too, and I take satisfaction in knowing I affect her.

"Where to?"

She directs me to the kitchen, since the pizza will be here any minute. When she slides off to ease into a chair, I immediately miss the warmth of her touch. But I push the feeling aside and retrieve a flexible ice pack from the freezer.

There's a knock on the front door as I hand her the pack. "I'll get it."

Her grateful expression is seared into my mind as I hurry away. She's already paid for the pizza, but I tip the guy, then text the others that the pizza is here.

Everyone exclaims over Meg when they come in. She keeps a smile in place, but I know she hates the fawning. I keep redirecting people to the pizza, making sure to get her two pieces of her favorite three meat before Shawn eats it all. The pizza hits the spot, and after we're finished, Steven disappears, leaving me and Meg with Shawn and Leah.

"Who's up for euchre?" Lee asks hopefully.

We all turn to Meg. She'll play sometimes, but it's not her favorite game.

She shrugs. "Why not?"

When we draw for partners, I get paired with Shawn so I'm sitting next to Meg. While Lee and Shawn are taking care of their plates, I lean toward Meg. "Want to prop your leg up? I can grab you a chair or…" I glance at my lap.

She purses her lips then nods. "If you don't mind." And she moves her leg toward me.

Mind having her sleek calf resting on my thighs? Not at all.

She stays that way for all three card games, the weight of her leg reminding me to stay still. I usually bounce or fidget or tap, but with some effort I keep my motions to my upper body, not wanting to disturb her.

Though Lee gives me a reprimanding look for drumming my fingers on the table.

The third game breaks the tie, making Lee and Meg the official winners. We all decide we're done for the night. Shawn thanks Meg again for giving up her room, then ruffles her hair like she's a toddler. I chuckle at her indignant expression and how she shoves his arm away.

Lee gives her a big hug. "Thanks, Meg. Although I'm gonna miss you."

Meg rolls her eyes, but pats Lee's back. "Like I said, I'll be right upstairs. Go have fun with Shawn."

Shawn tugs her hand and their lovey-dovey gaze has my chest tight with longing.

I want that, and I can't help staring at Meg, who watches them go with a smile on her face. But I push the want aside. She's had enough to deal with today.

"You ready to go upstairs?" I ask.

At her nod, I scoop her up before she can protest, grinning when she squeals my name. I love the feel of her in my arms, her hands clasped behind my neck, her soft curves against my torso. Maybe I'll never put her down.

"Give a girl some warning, would ya?" she scolds.

I just laugh. "But I like making you squeak, Nutmeg." Her cheeks get pink, and I have to clear my throat at the rushing memories of other sounds I've made her produce. "So you're officially my neighbor now," I say for lack of anything else.

"Yep."

We reach the top of the stairs, and I can't help telling her, "My door is always open. Need a cup of sugar? I'm your man. Bad dream? I'm there." I'm being too serious, so I add a teasing, "An itch you need help scratching?" And bob my eyebrows.

She smacks my chest even as she giggles. "It's been a minute since I've seen it. Maybe I'd better inspect this illustrious room again to make sure it's worth visiting."

I grin at that and carry her over there, nudging my door open with my toe. And I grimace at how messy my space is.

My room is always chaotic and I have bouts where I clean for a few hours until everything is perfect, but it's been a while. I don't usually notice the clutter until someone else steps in. Then I see everything.

"Sorry for the mess," I say sheepishly.

"It's fine." She waves me off.

I set her down on a clear spot on the floor, making sure she's stable before I shove some of the clothes spilling out of my closet back in. I do a quick sweep for any underwear, finding two pairs that I toss into the closet out of sight.

"Not going to let me inspect your underwear drawer?" she teases.

I let out a bark of laughter. "I mean, if you want. But it's not nearly as interesting as yours."

Her cheeks turn pink again and she looks away, moving to study the game schedule I have tacked on my wall next to the poster of my favorite soccer player in mid-kick. I love the way the mud splatters through the air.

"You're playing Monday, right?" She scans the schedule, although we'd talked about it on Friday at the bar.

I nod, shoving my hands in my pockets.

"You still okay if I come? I'll check with Bekah and Kaylie but I think we're all planning on it."

A thrill zips through me at the thought of her coming to one of my games. It's been a while. "I'd love that." The idea of looking over to see her grinning face as she cheers me on has my heart racing.

She moves to my dresser, smiling at the little dish on top of it—at one item in particular. She picks up the shark tooth, wonder in her eyes as she turns to me. "You still have this?"

I duck my head but nod. "It's my good luck charm."

We were in middle school. I'd been nervous about our music class concert, and her parents had just returned from a tropical vacation with a bag full of shark teeth for her souvenir. Sharks were, and still are, an obsession of hers. The megalodon is her absolute favorite because it has her name in it.

All us guys at school were so jealous, and she became the most popular girl in the class by lending out her shark teeth in return for favors.

Right before the concert, I had stage fright like never before. I'd missed a few rehearsals and couldn't remember any of the words. But Meg had grabbed my hand and pressed a tooth into it, then curled my fingers around the smooth object.

"For luck," she'd said.

It grounded me, and I clung to it throughout the entire concert. My hand never left my pocket, not once. I rushed to her afterward, giving her a big hug and an enthusiastic thanks.

When I tried to give her back the tooth, she shook her head. "You keep it."

I'd beamed and the moment between us grew as we grinned dopily at one another. That was the first time I'd ever thought that maybe I felt a little more than friendship for her.

She spins the black tooth over in her fingers, and I move to stand by her as I say, "I keep it in my pocket most of the time."

And she raises her chin, her awe-filled gaze meeting mine like a sunbeam. "I like that," she says softly before returning the tooth to the dish.

She turns back to face me, the air thick between us, and I'm at a loss as her dark brown eyes linger on mine. She's here in my bedroom, open and relaxed. I don't want to scare her off, and I don't want her to go. But I don't know if I'll be able to keep from kissing her if she keeps looking at me like that.

I close the gap, touching her cheek. "What do you want, Meg?"

Her lips part as she gazes at me. "I don't know, Si. I'm still trying to figure it out."

That's more than she's admitted before, and I try to keep a leash on the hope lunging through me. "Let me know when you do."

She doesn't move away, and the tension builds as we stare at one another. A text comes through on my phone, the buzz breaking the moment.

She steps away. "I should go."

I nod, knowing it's probably best. "Good night."

"Good night." She pauses at my door, glancing back with one last yearning smile.

"Remember, if you need anything…"

"I know where to find you."

I hear her door close a moment later. I shut mine then sink onto my bed, wondering how the hell I'm supposed to sleep tonight.

Chapter Fourteen

Meg

I spend Sunday morning lounging in bed, not wanting to traipse downstairs. Sleep came in fits last night, my knee waking me up more than once, and the thought of navigating the whole flight of stairs makes me want to groan. I'm positive Silas would give me another ride, but I'm not sure I can handle the proximity.

As I lay here last night, trying to fall asleep, all I could see was him and that disarming grin. His sweetness at being my footstool. The fact that he still carries around the shark tooth I gave him years ago. He's wiggling past my defenses at every turn, and if I'm not careful, I won't have anything left between us.

Though that idea is sounding more and more appealing.

As if he knew my thoughts, a tap sounds on my door followed by him asking, "Hey, Meg, I'm gonna head to work soon. Need anything?"

I adjust the compression sleeve on my knee then ease over to open the door. "I've been thinking about going downstairs, but…"

"I'm happy to give you a lift."

That charming smile makes an appearance, and my stomach flips even as I toy with accepting his offer. "You sure?"

"Meg, having you in my arms is the perfect way to start every day."

His teasing wink stills my panic at the heady words. I shake my head at his audacity, then grab my phone, book and charger.

"All set?"

At my nod, he scoops me up, just like last night. My stomach dips as I cling to his neck with my free arm. I feel so safe with him, cuddled against his firm chest as he navigates the stairway. We don't speak as he walks us to the main floor.

"Couch?"

I'll take the extra steps in his arms so I nod again. He sets me down gently, and I trail my hand over his arm as he straightens. Then he holds up a finger.

He disappears into the kitchen, coming back a few moments later with a steaming mug of coffee and a paper sack. "Thought you might be hungry."

Curious, I peer into the bag, grinning when I find several of my favorite snack foods along with a P3 Protein Pack. "Thank you."

He dips his chin and we stare at each other for a long moment as the same tension from last night in his room swells between us. Then he clears his throat, glancing at the door. "I've gotta…"

"Have a good day," I call, my chest feeling both full and empty at the same time.

He thought of me, brought me snacks, carried me downstairs. Warmth spreads through me at the sweet gestures, but he's leaving. And I don't want him to — not just because he's my ride up and down the stairs.

I'm in more danger than I thought.

My stomach sinks as I try to wrap my head around my warring feelings. Eventually I give up and turn on Netflix. *Gilmore Girls* catches my eye, but I can't bring myself to watch more. Not without Silas. And that thought annoys me more.

I swipe to the recommended category and push play on the first series that pops up, settling back as I grab my bag of goodies. While I attempt to pretend everything is fine.

* * * *

My knee twinges as I walk to my car after class on Monday. It's time for another dose of anti-inflammatory for sure. Good thing I drove.

But I'm still doing better than yesterday.

These flare-ups are a pain, though they usually go away in a few days. Wear the knee sleeve, take the pills, keep it elevated when I can. I know the drill.

I have a few hours before Silas' game this afternoon. Bekah and Kaylie are both in, planning to meet me there. I tap on Silas' open door when I get upstairs, shifting my ice pack to my other arm.

"Hey. Can I ride with you to the game?"

Then he steps out from his closet, sans shirt. I'm so glad I got my question out first because I don't think I could speak in the presence of those glorious abs. *Holy shit.* I hate that he always has this effect on me. Whenever we're swimming at his parents', or he gets too sweaty kicking the ball around, or whatever, I get stunned.

"Sure." He saunters over to the doorway and leans his arm on the frame.

He has a good six inches on me, so I have to look up and all I can see are muscles. His carved stomach, the rounded pecs, sculpted shoulders. And above it all, that shit-eating grin that tells me he knows exactly what he's doing.

I pull myself together. "What time are you going?"

"Four-thirty."

"'Kay. I'll be ready."

I start to leave but he asks, "How's the knee?" And nods to the ice pack in my hand.

I steel myself for more conversation, trying to avoid staring at his torso. "Um, better than yesterday. Gonna take it easy and elevate while I do some homework." I shuffle off in that direction.

But he doesn't let me. "What are you doing for lunch?"

I turn to find him hanging out of his doorway, that audacious grin firmly in place as his torso is on full display. Still. "I don't know."

"I was thinking about grabbing a burger from Eat at Joe's. To go. Want one?"

"Sure." If he goes to a restaurant, he has to wear a shirt, right?

"Will do." He winks, lingering.

So I ask, "Is that all?"

"Unless you want to gawk some more."

I scowl, annoyed that he noticed, but I can't be truly mad. Especially when his low chuckles make my stomach flip. I huff to my room, leaving the door open, and he calls out a goodbye when he leaves a few minutes later.

I'm settled on my bed with my laptop to do some reading for our new segment on ADHD for my General Mental Health class but images of Silas swim before my eyes. His cocky smirk, his gorgeous abs, his rumbly chuckle. I flop back against my wall, wishing I had a mute button for my thoughts.

I sit like that for a moment then straighten and open my laptop with a determined grunt. Once I get logged into my portal, I find the assignment, again shoving a lingering image of Silas aside. The reading pulls me in. I devour each word, knowing I'm learning more about how Silas' brain works and I find each new tidbit of information beyond fascinating.

When I finish reading, I lean back once more. Silas ticks so many of the symptoms—his inability to keep still and his impulsive jumping from one hobby to another to name a couple. I remember growing up all the times he'd get scolded for interrupting to shout out an answer or question. I never realized he had a reason for all those traits.

"Special delivery," Silas says, a few minutes later as I finish a quiz.

"Come in. Almost done." I answer the last question, hit submit, then shut the laptop.

"Hey, good timing. You want to eat together or…?" He trails off hopefully.

I wouldn't mind the company, so I scoot over and pat the bed. He bounces down beside me, then hands me a bottle of water. We each get a to-go box and I open mine eagerly, my mouth watering at the massive bacon cheeseburger and still fresh fries. I moan as I chew my first bite.

Silas nearly chokes. "Maybe no sex noise while we're on your bed?"

I ignore him and take another bite and groan. "But it's so good."

"Do I need to take off my shirt again?" His hand flies to the hem of his shirt and he lifts enough to give me a glimpse of those abs.

"Okay, okay, I'll stop." I grin at the teasing as I pop a fry into my mouth. "Thanks for getting lunch. You want any money?"

He shakes his head. "Nah, I'm good."

I don't fight him, and we chew in silence for a few moments. My mind flits back to my reading, and I ask, "How's therapy going?"

We chat about that and my classes as we finish our lunch, then he cocks his head. "What are you doing next?"

I shrug. I hadn't thought that far ahead.

"Wanna watch more *Gilmore Girls*?" And he gives me puppy-dog eyes that are absolutely irresistible.

Excitement flares in me—that he wants to spend more time together, that he's enjoying the show. But I try to keep it to myself and only reply with a casual, "Sure, why not?"

The rest of the afternoon is just as easy. We sit next to each other on the couch so I can prop my leg up. The proximity means accidental brushes and grazes that keep a constant fire simmering in me, but Silas doesn't seem to notice. He loves the show, laughing out loud several times and shaking his head at some of the quotes.

When it's time to get ready, he walks with me up the stairs, waiting patiently as I baby my leg. When we reach my door, he pauses. "See you soon."

The words make my heart flutter as I think about going to his game. Anticipation coils in my stomach, and it hits me how much our relationship has changed as I redo my ponytail. It's been a few weeks since we found out we were walking together at the wedding. I haven't heard a thing about any date he's been on since our talk. Maybe even before.

That's not like him. He's usually out every other night. My mind flits over all our interactions, searching for any hint of his normal behavior, but I come up short.

Even at the club last weekend, the only woman he paid attention to was me. The only one he danced with was me. Same thing at the wedding. He danced with me once, otherwise he was in a group when Lee or one of his brothers dragged him out.

It's only been me.

The heady realization hits hard as I stare at my reflection in the mirror, lips parted, mind racing as I try to figure out what that means. His words at karaoke replay in my head, that he'll be there for me however I need. That he's not going anywhere.

For the first time, I find myself believing him. Maybe he's really sticking around to be with me. Maybe I can trust him not to leave. Maybe the kiss with that other woman truly was a fluke, and not an inevitability.

The cable between me and Silas is strengthening, slowly but surely. Little by little, threads are being added. The chord is thicker now as I picture it, and I suck in a breath at the thought of jumping. Of trusting him that much once again.

Can I do that? My mind immediately recalls the day at the high ropes course and how he helped me every step. How I could only respond to him.

Maybe I already do.

The thought startles me, in the best way. I study my reflection again and decide that while I'm not ready to leap off this platform yet, I could at least wear something cute. It can't hurt, right?

I ease downstairs several minutes later. My favorite denim shorts cling to my hips, showing a patch of skin on my thigh through the frayed hole. I paired them with a fuchsia tank top that hugs my chest, and I topped it all off with some bubblegum-pink lip gloss.

Silas is in the kitchen, and he does a double-take when he sees me. A slow grin spreads over his face. "Hey, you look nice."

"Thanks." I toss my ponytail, taking in his T-shirt with the sides cut out of it. "If that's the standard uniform, I'm gonna need some restraints for Bekah."

"But not you?" His amber eyes fix on me in a heated stare, as if he's dying to know my answer.

I strive for flippant. "Nah, I've had years of practice restraining myself around you."

His pupils blow out as his nostrils flare. I can't move as the air heats between us again, that magnetic pull increasing as my mouth goes dry. I feel as if I'm on one end of a teeter-totter while Silas is at the other. We keep bouncing high or dipping low, but can never maintain that perfect balance where neither of our asses is on the ground.

His throat bobs then he turns away. "I'm packing a cooler for the game, thought it'd make a good leg rest if you need it. I threw in a Gatorade and a water for you. You want anything else?"

I'm tempted to push him further, to tell him I want some ice so maybe I can cool down. But I just shake my head, knowing I'm not quite ready for the consequences. We'll just have to stay in this dance a little longer, until I'm sure.

For both our sakes.

He grabs a camp chair for me and loads everything into his car. The short ride is easy. I check my phone as we get out, but don't see anything from Bekah and Kaylie yet. Silas slings the chair over one shoulder and carries the cooler in his opposite hand.

"We're over there." He points to the field on the left where several players are already on the grassy area, stretching or practicing.

"I'm excited. I think the last time I watched you play was in high school."

He smirks. "And you still don't know anything about soccer."

I nudge him with my elbow. "Hey! I know you're not supposed to use your hands unless you're the goalie or throwing it inbounds."

His dry look makes me laugh, because he's totally right. I didn't know much about soccer then, other than what I'd learned in gym class, and I definitely don't know any more now.

"That doesn't mean I won't be cheering for you," I add, giving him my most charming smile as I bat my eyelashes.

He grins back. "I know." Someone shouts his name, waving him over. He glances at me as if making sure I'm okay, and I nod, letting him know I'll catch up. "I'll save you a spot," he promises before jogging off.

I watch him go, admiring the view of his toned legs and the way the jersey shorts hug his ass. *Yum.*

"Hello," a deep male voice says at my elbow, jarring me from my gawking.

I turn to find a man who looks like he stepped straight off the cover of *Sports Illustrated*. His thick black hair hangs down to his ears, silky and glistening in the sun. He shows plenty of deeply tanned skin in his sleeveless tank, his biceps both decorated with tattoos of an Aztec nature. And his blinding white teeth stand out in a perfect smile.

"Hi," I say, a bit dazed that this handsome man is talking to me.

"Are you here for our game?"

He has an intriguing accent. Spanish, I think, as I try to place it. In answer to his question, I nod, pointing to the field where Silas is setting up my chair.

"You are with someone?"

"I came with my friend Silas. And my other friends Bekah and Kaylie are meeting us here."

"Ah, *friends*." He grins again. "We're always happy to have beautiful women watch us play. I'm Diego."

"Meg." I move to shake his hand, but when he takes mine, he raises it to his lips. My heart stutters at the bold gesture, flattered at the attention. Even as I pull away. "I should get back to Silas."

Diego smirks. "I'll walk with you."

As we fall into step, he asks if I attend SMU and what I'm studying. I don't feel like I should just ignore him — he's Silas' teammate, after all — but I also don't want to give him the wrong impression. So I answer his questions, trying to be polite but not over-friendly.

When we reach the field, Silas trots over, a wary smile on his face as he glances from me to Diego. He gestures to the chair he set up. "Saved you a spot. Front and center."

Diego grins. "This way she will see all the action."

A hint of a storm brews in Silas' eyes, and I fight a sigh because that's all I need. I'm having enough issues figuring out what's going on between us without adding a complication like Diego into the mix.

So I reach over and squeeze Silas' hand. "Good luck."

He relaxes instantly, then his grin widens at something behind me. "Your friends are here." He waves them over, and I let go of him as I turn to greet them.

I start to introduce Diego, but he's already striding away to talk to his other teammates. I frown, trying to figure out his angle, but get distracted when Remy, Brad and Aiden jog over. Brad and Aiden both plant kisses in turn on Bekah's cheeks while she pushes them off, laughing. But Remy is stilted when it comes to Kaylie, polite yet stiff, and I frown watching them.

Silas touches my shoulder. "I gotta get out there. You good?"

I glance over my space, the cooler positioned in front of my chair in case I need a leg rest, then I nod. We share a smile before he and the rest of the guys jog away to where the team is grouping in the center of the field.

"Kaylie, what happened with you and Remy?" Bekah asks, diving into the thick of it as they set up chairs next to me.

Her cheeks go red. "We went back to his place, and..." She sighs. "It was so embarrassing. He has an apartment over the garage of his parents' house and well —" She breaks off, dropping her head in her hand. "His mom didn't know he had company and she barged in to find us, you know, doing it."

"What?" I exclaim, nearly tipping in my chair as I surge forward.

"No way," Bekah adds, both of us gaping at Kaylie.

"Yep. I was sitting on top of him on the couch, going to town. At least my skirt was still on but..."

"Awkward," says Bekah, even as she laughs. "That's one way to meet the parents."

"I'm sorry, Kaylie. That had to be rough."

She nods. "Yeah, I went home after that. We've texted a few times, but I'm not sure I can get over that one."

Silence settles between us as we watch the guys do warm-ups. I can't imagine that happening, or how I'd survive the embarrassment after. It's a relief when Bekah changes the subject to regale us with her night spent with both Aiden and Brad. I'm a little in awe of her and the confidence it must take to be with two guys at once.

The team does a lap around the field, Silas winking at me when he goes by. I can't help noticing Diego's smile too, and so do my friends.

Kaylie asks, "Who was that guy you and Silas were talking with when we walked up?" I explain and she frowns. "How'd Silas take that?"

I shrug. "I don't think he was too thrilled, but I made sure to squeeze his hand and tell him good luck."

"Good for you, girl," Bekah says, but her gaze still follows Diego, now leading the pack. "But damn, is he fine."

I push her shoulder. "You've already got two guys."

"Yeah, and? Who says I can't handle a third?"

We laugh before Kaylie teases, "You've been reading too many reverse harem novels."

Bekah sticks her nose in the air haughtily. "Whatever happened to 'we listen and we don't judge'?"

More laughter spills out of us and we segue into catching up about the rest of our weekend. I tell them about moving upstairs and all that happened with my knee. How Silas was my personal chariot. My chest is filled with warmth as I stare at my friend on the field. He looks good out there—happy, relaxed.

As if he can feel my stare, he glances my way and when our gazes collide, he gives me my favorite charming grin. Then winks. Again. This time, both girls notice. They hoot their excitement, nudging me and smacking my arm.

"Girl," Bekah says, "you better put that boy out of his misery."

"And soon," adds Kaylie.

Chapter Fifteen

Silas

My entire team notices how focused I am, scoring goal after goal today. I'm on fire, and they all pick on me about the reason. But how can I do badly when every time I glance at the sideline I see Meg's smiling face? Whenever I do anything remotely decent, I hear her cheering for me. Calling *my* name.

It's like my own personal energy source and I can do no wrong.

We slaughter the other team, to the point I actually feel bad about the difference in our scores. I prefer things to be evenly matched. Makes it more fun. But I don't let it bring me down for long.

I whip my sweat-drenched shirt off as I turn back toward Meg and her friends. Most of the other guys follow suit and I can't help my satisfaction when Meg's eyes keep coming back to me. Not even Diego can hold her attention.

It worried me at first, seeing her walk over with him. Diego and I are decent friends, but he recently ended a serious relationship and I know he isn't ready for anything serious, just wants to play the field. I also know how charming he can be, especially with that accent. Most ladies find him irresistible.

But Meg grabbed my hand before the game, called my name on the sidelines. It's a heady feeling being the focus of her attention. I jog right up to where she stands, waiting and beaming.

"Great job, Si! I'd hug you but you're all sweaty." Even as she wrinkles her nose, her gaze trails hungrily down my bare torso.

"Eh, you know you like it," I tease, stepping closer.

She squeals and moves back.

Remy smacks my shoulder, grinning at Meg. "So, we need you to attend every game from now on, okay?"

Brad looks over from where he stands with Bekah and Aiden. "Yeah, for sure. He killed it out there, and we all know the reason."

My cheeks are warm as Meg grins at me and says, "Anything you want to add, Si?"

I lift a shoulder, trying to sound casual. "I could get used to having my own personal cheerleader."

We both chuckle, then Diego stops by and says to me, "You played well today." He glances at Meg, with that disarming smile of his. "Though how anyone would do badly with this beauty watching is a mystery."

I tense at the way she melts at his words, but I relax when she moves closer to me.

"You all crushed it," she says.

"Don't forget about my pool party this Friday," Diego says to me and the guys. Then he turns to Meg. "You should come. Liven things up."

A crinkle forms in Meg's brow then she looks at me as if asking permission. When I don't respond, she says, "I'll think about it."

"Good." He nods to Bekah and Kaylie. "Bring your friends. I'm sure we'd all appreciate a change in scenery. Silas can give you the details."

He grins then strides away as I try to control the unease in my gut, my confidence wavering in the face of that invitation. Coming to my game is one thing, but going to a pool party is another. It's taken Meg and me this long to get this far. What if I lose her to my charming teammate now, when things are just getting good?

"Si." She takes my hand, and I gaze down at her. "I came today to watch you. I came with you, and I'm leaving with *you*."

Her understanding and declaration relax some of the tension in me, and I squeeze her hand. "Thanks, Meg."

The air lightens between us as I start to pack up, and she watches me intently. "You know, if you'd told me about the whole thing at the end where you all whipped off your shirts, I totally would have come to a match sooner."

"Oh definitely," says Bekah, laughing as Aiden and Brad vie over who's going to carry her chair.

"Mmhmm." Kaylie eyes Remy, who lights up.

I'd heard about their awkward interruption, but he seems to really like her. I hope they can work things out.

"Y'all could be the next viral thirst trap." Bekah rakes her gaze over each of her guys in turn. "Next time, I'm filming."

We all protest, but we're grinning like idiots too.

"So about the pool party," starts Brad. "You guys want to come?"

Bekah shrugs. "I mean, that's more time I get to ogle you guys in nothing more than swim shorts, so I'm in."

Remy nudges Kaylie. "You busy? I'll have more fun if you're there."

Meg smiles when her friend nods, but her grin falters as she glances at me.

I'm quick to reassure her. "The whole team will be there," I say. "If you don't mind hanging out with a bunch of rowdy soccer players, I'd love it if you'd come."

She beams and I know I said the right thing.

"Well, I don't have any other plans, so yeah, I guess we're in."

Now I'll just have to figure out how to keep my dick under control while I spend the day with Meg in her swimsuit.

The seven of us walk toward the parking lot, laughing and chatting as we rehash highlights from the game. I feel light and easy as I slip into the car to find Meg staring at me.

"Hi," I say, acutely aware of my lack of shirt. I reach for the spare one in the backseat then pull it on.

"Hi." Her smile holds a hint of shyness, letting me know I'm not imagining her extra attention.

Heat flares in me, but I try to keep the easiness going. "Home?" At her nod, I put the car into gear. "Feel free to play some music if you want." Maybe that'll help cut the tension.

She flips through a few stations, settling on a pop one that plays some upbeat music she sings along to. As we pull out onto the road, *Born to the Night* comes on, the song we danced to at the club. Memories of her in my arm wash over me, and I grip the steering wheel tighter.

When we get home, neither of us has spoken in several minutes and the air is thick between us. "I'll meet you inside," I say roughly.

She scampers out of the car and into the house before I can blink. I take my time putting away the camp chair in the garage. Then I go in and unload the cooler, bringing a Gatorade with me. I need a shower.

Preferably a glacial one to douse the fire still roaring within me.

I head to my room, tossing my gross socks into the hamper. I take one more swig of Gatorade before I set it and my phone on my nightstand, then move into the hallway. Only to find Meg leaning on her doorjamb. Her warm gaze trails over my torso, and I wish I'd taken off the shirt.

"Still needing your eye candy fix?" I ask, striving for a lightness that I don't feel. I want nothing more than to pull her into my arms and show her exactly how riled she's made me.

"Are we good?" she asks, startling me with her train of thought. "Between Diego and the pool party thing, I wanted to make sure."

I find myself stepping closer when I should truly maintain my distance. I can't help brushing back a piece of hair that slipped from her ponytail. "Meg, we're fine."

"Good." She stares at me, adoring and trusting. "I feel like we're starting to turn a corner at being something...more, and I hoped I didn't ruin anything."

Her words have my heart soaring and twisting at the same time—elated that she feels like we're moving closer while also hurt at her lack of confidence in me.

"Nutmeg, if you think another guy flirting with you is going to ruin things between us, you'd better think again. I'm all in."

Her breath hitches as she stares, her eyes locked with mine.

"I mean it, Meg." I can't stop my explanations now that I've started. The words tumble out. "There's a reason every girl I've dated over the past two years looks like you."

She starts shaking her head, but I need to say this, need her to hear me.

"I didn't realize it until Steven laid it out for me, but I've been looking for *you*. I didn't think you were an option, so I've been trying to find a replacement." I graze my thumb over her skin as her muscles tense then relax under my hand.

"Silas…"

"I'm an idiot because no one can hold a candle to you. You're it, Meg. I'm done looking anywhere else for the person who's been right under my nose the entire time." I inch closer, needing to eradicate the distance between us. "I'm not going anywhere unless you tell me to. I'll do everything I can to earn back your trust. I'm here. Whenever you're ready."

I don't know who moves first, but we're both reaching for each other as the ripples of desire grow into crashing waves that overtake us. Our lips meet in a ravenous kiss as I grip the back of her neck and her hip, holding her steady. Her hands roam across my shoulders, over my chest, down my abdomen and back up.

Liquid fire consumes me as I'm overtaken by my need for her. I pull her flush to me, grinding my instant erection against her as she rocks her hips and moans into my mouth. I feel her nipples peak beneath her shirt.

A throat clears, and I wrench away to find Steven watching us with raised eyebrows. He says with a wry grin, "You have two perfectly good rooms right there. Maybe consider using them?"

Meg and I hurry to step away from one another as he disappears down the stairs. The moment is broken, and I'd do anything to get it back. Though maybe it's for the best. I don't want to rush this or scare her off. While I'd love to hear more about how she feels, it's enough right now that I got to tell her what's in my heart.

I should give her some time to process.

"I'm going to go shower." I want to end on a good note, so I walk back to my room and toss my shirt in on my bed. "Don't need that," I say with a cocky wink in the face of her gaping.

She chuckles as I strut by. I duck into the bathroom, then quickly remove my shorts and boxers.

Standing to one side, I open the door and fling them at her. "Don't need those either."

"Silas!" she yelps indignantly, but I hear her laughing and I smile.

Then I turn on the water to the coldest setting, and I step in. *Maybe this will cool me down.*

* * * *

Meg

In bed that night, I stare at the ceiling with Silas' declaration rolling on repeat through my mind. Followed by that delicious kiss.

I'm not good at speaking my feelings. Not that Silas has had the best track record either. The only one I'm remotely comfortable with is Leah, and it took me a long time before I could respond to her saying "Love ya" without feeling like an idiot. Still, sometimes I can't manage more than a "you too."

My parents weren't super affectionate people. I had occasional hugs and the good night kiss, but "I love you" wasn't common. If someone was upset, they held it in until they exploded. And there were a lot of explosions before my dad left.

Mom and my stepdad —

Another example of stellar communication.

Silas was brave today, laying it on the line for me. He wants me, he's all in. The thought makes my heart soar — this gorgeous man that I've crushed on forever can easily be mine. I just have to claim him.

For once, the thought doesn't send panic spiking within me, and I smile as I let my mind picture it. Imagine taking that last step off the edge of the platform. Imagine the cable between us holding.

It just needs to be a little thicker first.

* * * *

I make it through my long day of work on Tuesday. My knee is improving, though still not one hundred percent, and the patients keep me hopping. Bekah and Kaylie help as much as they can, letting me sit more than usual, but I'm worn out by the end of my shift. I grab dinner on my way home and hole up in my room.

Wednesday is pretty much the same. Except I go out to a movie after work with Bekah and Kaylie, *then* I hole up in my room. I'm not ready to face Silas yet because I don't have a response for him.

My brain isn't as easy to convince, though, and I dream of him both nights. Particularly the feeling of his lips and hands.

Thursday, I wake up horny as hell, but also late for work. In my dream state, I somehow snoozed my alarm so I'm already ten minutes behind. Not enough time to relieve the ache between my legs.

Images of him in real life and my dreams keep popping into my head all day, making the hours feel like years. Luckily, my boss leaves early in the afternoon and gives us the rest of the day off as well, so I get home around two p.m. and have the house to myself. I hurry upstairs and shed my scrubs then lie back on my bed. I feel like I'm about to explode with the tension.

Slipping my hand between my legs, I bite back a moan as I picture Silas' beautiful face. The memories of dancing the other night combined with our kiss Monday wash over me, and I sink into them. The way his hands felt on my hips. His growing length digging into my ass as I writhed against him. The passion in that kiss as he held me tight to his erection.

It won't be the first time I've gotten off to thoughts of Silas, and I doubt it'll be the last. The tension builds within me, so strong I think I catch a whiff of his scent.

Then a knock on my door startles me, and I freeze.

"Meg?" the embodiment of my thoughts calls through the closed door. "I have a package for you."

Yeah, you do. I recall the press of his eager cock, and I swallow a groan, wanting to hurry back to my fantasy.

But he knocks again. "Meg? You can't avoid me forever."

With a frustrated huff, I sit up to yank on my silky, lightweight robe, tying it tightly at my waist before I crack open the door. Leaning my shoulder against the doorjamb, I grip the door in my right hand as I glare at him then the brown package he's holding.

"Don't you look…comfy?" he asks with a tantalizing smirk as his gaze eases over the V neck of my robe.

I avoid the question, responding as casually as I can, "What are you doing home already?"

"I got out early. Saw this and took it as I sign that we needed to talk."

I shift and my robe slips, baring more of my shoulder. "You're not in your suit."

His eyes darken. "I changed. You gonna let me in?" He leans forward, a teasing grin on his lips as he pushes against the door. His eyes widen as his nostrils flare, and he inhales deeply next to my fingers.

The ones I just had between my legs.

My cheeks go hot under Silas' intense stare as a longing smile crosses his lips. "I guess you *were* busy."

Fighting embarrassment at being caught in the act, I shove open the door, yank the package out of his hands, then storm back into my room to set it on the dresser. He follows, shutting the door behind him.

"Meg," he whispers, then walks up behind me. He runs a hand down my arm, slipping over the silky fabric and giving me delicious goosebumps. "What were you thinking about?"

I give in to the urge to lean back against his torso, craving his closeness. My shoulders touch his firm chest as he sucks in a quiet breath. Speech fails me, and my lips won't form the words that stick in my throat.

"Were you thinking of me?"

His fingers dance back up my arm as his left hand eases to my hip. His right hand skims the line where the robe meets my bare shoulder, and he follows it down. I gasp when he stops just above the swell of my breast, the ache within me desperate to be satisfied.

His breath is warm on my cheek as his lips brush my ear. "I could help," he offers in a husky voice that has my stomach flipping.

His fingers glide along my waist, then dip between the two edges of fabric until he touches the bare skin of my abdomen. A hiss of breath slips between my teeth as a thrill of desire races through me. He presses his growing erection to my back and traces a finger over the swell of each breast.

"Meg?" he asks again, wanting my permission.

"Yes," I whisper.

I lean into him, tilting my chin and exposing my neck. His right hand dances down my chest, pushing the fabric open even more. His delectable lips trail along my jaw, then he nibbles on my ear.

"Yes, you want me to help? Or yes, you were thinking about me?" The gravel in his voice has my thighs clenching as he toys with the tie holding my robe shut. But he waits for my answer.

"Silas, please."

"Use your words, Meg."

His heated mouth plants kisses along my neck, creating fire in my veins and combining with the searing warmth of his fingers on my chest. I need him. I need this. And I surrender to that sensation. "Touch me, Silas. I need you," I gasp.

"That's it, Nutmeg. Let me help."

He quickly undoes my robe, and the cool air feels delicious on my overheated body. He slides his hand over my abdomen, the languid touch making me groan.

He chuckles, the deep sound rumbling between us, and he guides me with him as he sits on my bed. With my back still to him, he positions me between his legs then tugs me down to sit in front of him, nestled between his thighs. He pulls me back until his thick erection presses against my ass.

I tip my head to rest on his shoulder, giving him full access to my front. He touches my chin, guiding me until our lips meet as his fingers glide down to roll my aching nipple. I grip his legs when his other hand skims over my hip to dip between my thighs and run along my seam. I open wider, craving his touch with a desperation that startles me.

His deft finger slips inside me, and his palm rests against my swollen clit. He sucks in a sharp breath. "So wet. Just how close were you?"

I don't answer, resting against his firm body as he guides me toward that peak. I have to close my eyes when he tweaks my nipple again, the electric jolt shooting straight to my core.

"Look at how gorgeous you are," he commands.

When I open my eyes, I collide with my own stare in the full-length mirror on the wall in front of us.

His amber gaze fixes on my reflection. "All splayed out, just for me."

I can't look away from his finger pumping in and out of me, the way he toys with my breast, his unruly curls bobbing as he swirls his tongue in the divot where my neck meets my shoulder.

"I woke up this morning thinking about dancing with you," he whispers. "And I thought about you the entire time I stroked myself. The way you felt in my arms, that luscious ass rubbing against my cock, your gorgeous tits against my chest."

He slips another finger in, and I groan. The image of him jerking off with my name on his lips is enough to send me tumbling over that edge. I grip his thighs tightly as I shudder on his hand.

"You're so beautiful, Meg. I love watching you come."

He doesn't stop until I'm done clenching, and I sag into him, his impressive erection digging into me. The thought of returning the favor has my mouth watering.

Chapter Sixteen

Meg

I stand and push my robe back as I spin to face Silas. Our mouths collide in a fervid kiss as I settle next to him on the bed. I ease my hand down his torso, wishing his T-shirt wasn't between us, but too impatient to remove it.

He yanks his mouth away. "Meg, you don't have to—"

"I want to." I ease onto the bed, lying perpendicular to him. My robe hangs open so he can see my breasts as I rest on my side and let my hand drift over the track pants he wears, caressing his length through the straining fabric.

My name is a plea on his lips and I glance up, loving how close this man is to coming undone just from my simple touch. I ease down the elastic band of his pants and boxers, grinning as his eager erection bobs out. The tip is damp and leaking.

But I take a moment to stare at him. Our two previous encounters were quick and heated, not giving us much time to explore. I know he understands when he trails his hand down my shoulder to cup my breast again.

We both want this time to be different, and the thought settles in me. *This time.* We're really going to do this.

I lean over his thigh, my breast pressing to his warm skin and making him groan before I take him in my mouth. I wrap my hand around his base as I lap the tip with my tongue then hollow my cheeks and glide down his length. He hisses my name as his hips buck and his free hand tangles in my hair.

I take him deeper, loving each of his moans and pleas, keeping my pace even as my hand and lips meet over his thick shaft.

"I'm not going to last long, not with that fantastic mouth."

I hum at the praise, making him let out a guttural moan that has my stomach flipping. The salty taste of his pre-cum dances on my tongue.

"Last chance, Meg, I'm going to come."

In answer, I grip him more firmly and take him even deeper into my mouth. His release floods me, spilling down my throat as I swallow it all. Then I sit up with a satisfied smile.

"You…" His gaze is tender and full of awe, then he grips the back of my neck and crashes his mouth to mine, uncaring that his cum was just on my tongue. "Holy fuck, that was amazing."

I grin against his mouth, then kiss him once more before leaning back to say, "Better than your hand this morning?"

His cheeks get red. "Hey, it made you come."

I nod. "That was a delicious image, though I'm glad I got to witness it in person."

He shakes his head then pulls on his pants. "And here I just wanted to make sure you were okay from the other night. I kind of poured my heart out and I know it took you by surprise."

He caresses my cheek, and I lean into his touch. "I'm glad you told me. You've given me a lot to think about, and yes..." I pause, shooting him a wicked smile. "I *was* thinking about you earlier."

He grins, a wide, preening grin, like the cat who ate the cream.

"I want to keep going like this, Silas. Moving forward, but little by little." I stare into his tender gaze. "I'm hoping this cable holds, but I'm not ready to make that leap into being your girlfriend yet," I say, hoping he gets the high ropes analogy.

His grins drops but understanding crosses his face as he nods. "Take all the time you need. I promise I'll be here."

"I'd like to date, though. No labels, keep hanging out?" I feel beyond vulnerable as I say what I want out loud. "I do want more."

His eyes darken. "Whatever you need from me, Meg. I'm yours."

I still hesitate, feeling like I'm leaving him as a booty call when it's so much more than that.

He shoots me a knowing look and shifts closer. "I know it's not easy for you to tell me what's going on in your heart, and I appreciate you telling me all you have today. Not just with your words." His gaze drifts lazily over my breasts, down my abdomen, then back up to meet my eyes. "I know you wouldn't be able to open up to me like that if you didn't trust me, and that is a precious gift that makes me so freaking happy."

I swallow at the lump in my throat, knowing he's right and appreciating that he knows it too.

He kisses me gently then pulls my robe back together and ties the ends. "All set?"

"For now," I answer, the words soft and full of promise.

"Well," he says, standing up. "I look forward to whatever happens next."

* * * *

Silas

I step into the hallway and lean against the wall next to Meg's closed door. Then I let out a gust of breath. *Holy shit.* When I knocked on her door, I never dreamed we'd do anything close to that. Sure, she told me she wasn't ready for a label, but it's still a step forward. One I'll gladly take.

After I hit the bathroom, I glance at Meg's closed door and wish we could hang out more. I'm not ready to be alone. Then I notice Steven's door is cracked open, a sure sign he's home. I go over and tap on it. He calls for me to come in, and I find him sitting at his desk working on his laptop. His high-school yearbook sits on the desk next to him.

A dead giveaway that he's thinking about Bianca.

"Hey, wanna kick my ass in chess?" It's a guaranteed way of cheering him up, plus I'll get the company I crave.

He takes one long look at his computer, but eventually nods.

"You hear anything from Libby?" I ask as we go through the familiar motions of dragging his nightstand to the center of the room. I grab the chessboard then perch on the bed and open the board.

"Dropped her off that night. Didn't hear from her over the weekend. Texted her that Monday and she'd gotten back together with her ex."

The terse words have my shoulders slumping. "I'm sorry, Steven."

He lifts a shoulder, and we finish arranging the pieces. I feel bad for the guy. No wonder he was thinking about Bianca. He wheels the desk chair over, but the back catches the corner of the yearbook, sending it flying through the air to land at my feet. I can't resist picking it up and flipping to his class. I was in middle school at the time, so I'm not even in this one.

There he is, looking the same but not. His face has lost its baby fat, but his hair is still styled that way. Right next to him is Bianca Wakley, a constant in our home while Steven was in high school. Her and her other best friend, Colt.

"You ever hear anything about Bianca?" I ask, wanting to give him an opening if he needs to talk.

He glowers. "Nope."

I can also take a hint. I shut the book and toss it back onto the desk, then we rock-paper-scissors to see who gets to be white. He wins. As he takes his turn, I mull over my memories of Bianca. Her blonde hair and blue eyes garnered a lot of attention, but she was always sweet. Always kind.

Even to annoying younger brothers like me.

Mom had always wanted a girl. Sure, she loved us and had Leah to dote on, but Bianca didn't have much.

Mom was thrilled to help her with her hair or take her dress shopping for dances.

I vividly remember Steven's first prom, seeing him in a suit. It was the first time I saw Bianca in a dress. I was all of eleven and told her I thought she looked like an angel.

We start playing, and I push the memories aside as Meg takes the center stage of my thoughts once more. I don't even realize I'm smiling until Steven comments on it.

"What's with you today? I mean, your mouth is permanently tilted up. Even though you're losing." He gestures to the board. "I just took your queen."

I only grin wider, and he shakes his head.

"Something more happen with you and Meg after that make-out session I interrupted?"

That puts a scowl on my face. "Yeah, what was up with that? You could've kept walking, minded your business."

"Brother—" He reaches out and puts a hand on my shoulder. "No one needed to see that."

I roll my eyes, but I know he's right. "She avoided me after we were so rudely interrupted. So when I saw her car was here already, I decided to not let her ignore me."

When I don't say more, he raises his eyebrows. "And...?"

"I interrupted her, um, 'me time'." I put those last words in finger quotes. "Which actually turned out to be good because then we had some *us* time." I beam, images of our interlude dancing in my head before I can get a grip on myself.

But Steven's frowning. "Did you talk?"

"Yeah, some. Afterward." I rub the back of my neck and move my remaining rook to take one of his pawns.

He swoops past me with his bishop and announces, "Checkmate."

I tip my king over and sigh.

"So what'd she say?"

"Well, I'd kind of spilled my guts to her before you caught us in the hallway. I told her exactly how I'm feeling, that I'm willing to do whatever it takes to earn her trust again." When he nods, I admit, "She told me today that she's not ready for a label like girlfriend."

"Yet you're still grinning like an idiot."

I chuckle. "Yeah, because she said she wants to keep moving forward. Baby steps, man. Meg would never let me touch her if she was truly over me." I think of my friends at the bar, how she'd shut them down so fast. "The fact that I've danced with her, kissed her and all we did today, well…" I smile even bigger. "That door is still open."

His answering smile is small, but genuine. "I'm happy for you. Make sure you keep that communication going, though. You guys don't have the best track record with that."

"Yeah, yeah."

We start resetting the board, and he lets out a long sigh that has me glancing at him in concern.

"Mom still sends Bianca Christmas cards," he says quietly, and it's my turn to frown. "I saw one last year, her name, her address." He stares past me at the wall. "I knew they were close, but I thought after she left like that…"

She'd disappeared after they graduated, and so had Colt. Just gone. No goodbyes, no notes, no nothing. A wave of sympathy washes over me. It's been hell having Meg here, day in and day out. In my face when all I wanted was to avoid her.

But I think not seeing her would have been worse.

"We were going to elope after graduation."

The words drop like a bomb between us as I gape at him. I've never heard the details. I know he loved her but this… "Seriously?"

He nods, putting his last piece down and shooting me a wry smile. "Don't tell Mom."

"Steven, I…" I'm lost for words.

He lifts a shoulder. "It's done now. Can't go back. She chose him and I have to live with that." He moves his first piece, but I'm too shocked to respond.

"Did you wait for her?" The picture of him standing alone in the dark, scanning for Bianca, pops into my head and my heart breaks for him.

"Yeah." His brown eyes are full of pain as he glances up. "Right after graduation, I said I was going to a party, but I went to the train station. Bought two tickets to Vegas and she never showed."

Brutal.

"I never saw her again."

I push to my feet, bumping the board but not caring as I rush over to hug my brother.

He lets out a half-laugh. "Silas, it's okay."

Reluctantly, I go back to my spot on the bed and begin righting the pieces I knocked over. "But that's…awful! I never thought she'd —"

He holds up his hand. "Thanks for listening, but don't repeat it okay?"

He's not one for the spotlight, ever. Much preferring to be in the background, helping people backstage.

My mind begins to race as my brain pieces together the similarities of how Meg and I broke up. "What would you do if you ever saw her again? What if she moved back? Would you give her another chance?"

He stares at me, long and steady, reading all my insecurities. "Hey, what happened between us is nothing like what happened with you and Meg." He reaches over to place a hand on my shoulder. "You made a mistake and you both said things. But you're here, you're working it out."

I relax a little. He's right. A drunken kiss is not on the same tier as promising to elope then running off with another man.

He drops his hand. "I don't know what I'd do. There's a lot of bitterness there, you know? I've never found someone that even comes close to how she made me feel."

And I understand that because it's identical to how I am about Meg. I stare at the chessboard, then shake my head, unable to stomach the idea of sitting anymore right now. I stand up. "Come on. Let's go to Eat at Joe's. You need a fucking milkshake, my treat."

He blinks at me, a mixture of amusement and exasperation on his face. "Fine. But you owe me another game. One where you actually pay attention."

"Deal."

* * * *

Meg

I wake Friday morning with a vise gripping my chest as the weight of my interlude with Silas yesterday hits me hard. It's like my heart took the lead with Silas then, so now my brain is demanding compensation. Big time.

The tug of war is too much and I need an outsider's opinion. I quickly text Leah, who is happy to have lunch with me after her shift at the library. Maybe I can get a handle on my doubts before the pool party with Silas this afternoon.

Fuck. I can't even think about that right now.

I decide to go for a walk since my knee is feeling great, then I shower and organize my shoes to pass the time until I can talk to Leah. Finally, I can leave. I meet her right on campus as she saunters out of the library, waving when she sees me. I give her a much-needed hug and she holds me until I let go.

"Thanks for meeting me," I say, feeling bad about the concern in her eyes.

"Of course. It sounded like you needed to talk. What's up?"

I stare across the parking lot. "Um, first, where do we want to eat?"

We go over our options then decide on Chinese and start walking. I haven't had an in-depth talk with her since our lunch with Callie a week and a half ago. So much has happened since then.

She listens intently as I fill her in. My head spins from it all and, on one hand, Silas and I feel like we're moving at the speed of light, but on the other? It's slower than molasses in January.

She's all caught up by the time we reach the restaurant. We put in our orders—Pad Thai for her, broccoli chicken for me, and crab rangoon to split. I sip on my water, needing something to cool me down.

"It's sounds like Silas is really in this." She tilts her head, studying me. "So what's holding you back?"

Relief hits me at her curious tone. No judgment, no resentment. And I realize then that part of me has been worried about what she will think. "You're not mad?" The question spills out before I can stop it.

Her eyebrows jump up. "Mad? What would I be mad about?"

I swirl my straw in my glass, the ice cubes clinking against the sides. "It feels weird, you know? You're my best friend and the Wrightings… They've always felt like yours." Doubts well in me — doubts I've had so long I haven't even noticed them in years.

"Meg…"

I shake my head, staring down at the table. "Lee, I've always been the tagalong. The Wrightings are *your* family. You take care of them, they look out for you. But me? I'm *your* best friend and cousin, so I get brought in by proxy. Sure I'm in, but only just." Silence hangs between us as I feel her stare.

"I want you to listen to me."

Her fierce tone has me jerking my head up in shock. Lee rarely gets angry, and right now she sounds beyond pissed. The glower on her face confirms it.

"You *are* part of this family. Sure, you and I share blood, but more than that, we share history and memories. I've never thought of you as separate. The moment we heard about the mini-suite in that house, the guys brought up how perfect it would be for me" — she pauses, raising her chin — "*and* you."

I blink at the sting of tears and swallow at the lump in my throat.

"I know you had a shitty childhood, but that doesn't make you being my friend — my *best* friend — any less valid. I've done everything I could to include you, to make you feel loved. But you have to accept it." Her brow crinkles as she tries to explain. "It's like a present, you know? I could put it on your doorstep and you have the choice to walk over it every day, knowing it's there waiting."

The truth of her words squeezes my chest and twists my insides.

"Or you can pick it up. Open it. Make it a part of your life."

My ability to breathe halts as I gape at her, my vision tunneling as I glimpse my half-lived, walled-off life.

"You have to choose."

And the world restarts again.

I have a choice. These amazing people want me in their lives, choose to include me, and have over and over again. The only thing separating us is the walls *I've* put up.

Our food arrives, and I watch our server set my plate in front of me through the daze I'm still in. Leah's words are spot on. Not just with the Wrightings as a whole, but with Silas too, and me accepting what I deserve.

As hard as that is to wrap my head around.

"You okay, Meg?" she asks, watching me in concern.

I nod. "Yeah. That was a lot, but…" I pause, smiling to convey my gratitude. "Lee, I really needed to hear that. Thank you."

The furrow in her brow smooths as she smiles back. "You're welcome." She reaches over to grab my hand. "I love you, Meg. Always have, always will."

I squeeze her hand. "This is why I asked you to lunch. I knew you'd get it."

She beams, moving back to her own space and cracking open a crab rangoon then blowing on it. "What are best friends for? You've given me some hard truths before. It's not always easy to wrap your head around, but sometimes a different perspective can really help."

"I've got a lot to think about." I use my fork to spear off a part of the complimentary egg roll. "Lee?"

She glances up.

"Thanks for loving me. For including me, and not giving up on me. I know I'm not always the most vocal about my feelings, but I love you too. So much."

"I know, Meg. I know."

We finish our lunch, changing the subject and chatting easily, the air between us much lighter. As is the weight on my chest.

Chapter Seventeen

"You ready?" Silas asks from my open door as I scramble to find my sunscreen.

"Almost." Most of my room is in order after the move, but a few things still aren't in the right place. I throw my hands up in frustration. "I can't find my sunscreen!"

"That sunscreen?" He points to the closet shelf where an orange tube sits next to a shoe box and a pack of batteries.

"Yes!" I hurry to grab it, then tuck it in my teal-and-melon-striped bag that matches my melon sundress cover-up. "Thank you." I hurry over and press a kiss to his cheek.

He grins. "Maybe I'll start hiding your things if that's going to be my reward for finding them."

I laugh, excitement zipping through me at the thought of spending the rest of day with him. A far cry from the way I felt this morning.

The nerves are still there, twisting in the background of my gut, but I know it's time. I need to step off that ledge and test this cable, trusting that it will hold me. Trusting Silas to catch me.

Trusting that I'm making the right move.

Silas takes my bag from me, slinging it over his shoulder to join his backpack. Then he stretches out his free hand, and my heart soars as I lace my fingers with his. His grin is easy and the light mood stays with us for the fifteen-minute drive.

We stop in front of a decent-sized corner house with cars lined up in every direction. Silas has to circle around and park on the opposite side of the road. The whole yard is surrounded by a six-foot privacy fence, painted a pristine white.

"C'mon," he says, leading me along a stepping stone path to the side gate.

A hint of pesky nerves flutters in me, mostly at being with Silas' team — Diego, in particular. I'm not ready for more of his intense attention, especially when it puts Silas on edge. But Diego is the host. I know I won't be able to avoid him, so I square my shoulders and hurry after Silas.

Music fills the air, a heavy, enticing beat pulsing from the far corner as we approach the gate. The hum of chatter reaches us, broken by an occasional laugh. Silas gives me a reassuring grin before pulling open the gate.

It leads right into the pool area, a cement pad that abuts the sliding door to the house with the aqua in-ground pool as the focal point. A grill stands next to the house in one corner of the fenced-in area, and people mill everywhere. There must be at least thirty —

standing by the grill, draped in lounge chairs, sitting on the edge of the pool, lounging in the water.

"This is bigger than I thought it'd be," I say, loudly enough to be heard over the din.

But he doesn't get to answer as Bekah and Kaylie barrel over—bikinis on, drinks in hand, and squeals bursting from them. I'm caught in hugs and an endless stream of chatter. I stare helplessly at Silas who laughs, then mimes getting a drink. I nod that I'll take one before trying to decipher what my friends are saying.

We move to a few lounge chairs where they have evidently set up shop. Bekah fills me in on how doting Aiden and Brad have been. Kaylie spills that she and Remy had sex last night—without interruption—after he took her to a nice dinner at Club 42.

Silas appears, handing me a hard seltzer and my bottle of sunscreen. "Want help?" He nods to my back and my mouth goes dry at the thought of his hands on me.

My friends give me knowing grins before making themselves scarce.

"Sure," I answer.

He sits behind me on the lounge chair as I tug off my cover-up. I swipe my ponytail to one side, waiting for him to do my shoulders. But nothing happens. I glance back to find him staring at me over the top of his sunglasses. I look down, making sure nothing is out of place. Everything seems fine.

"Damn, Meg. New suit?" His voice sounds hoarse.

I nod, even as a slow grin tips my lips. "You like?"

He leans closer. "You trying to get me laughed off the team? I can't go walking around here with my mast flying."

I sling my hand back to smack his arm. "Stop."

"I can't believe I offered to sunscreen you, too. Is it too late to get a replacement while I go jump in the pool?"

Now, I'm laughing at his flirtations. "Silas!"

"Fine. If I have to die, this is the way I want to go." He sighs, playing up his resignation before pulling his shirt over his head. "You can do my back next."

My laughter dies in my throat at the gorgeous sight of him and a smirk plays on his lips. He grabs the bottle of sunscreen, nudging me to face forward, and it takes me a moment to tear my gaze away from his chiseled torso. Then I close my eyes as he glides his hands over my shoulders.

"You're right," I say softly back to him.

He leans in to hear me.

"This is the way to go."

His motion stills for a moment before he begins rubbing again. I can't focus on anything beyond his touch. Fire dances under my skin, the flames following the smooth glide of his fingers as he coats me in lotion.

I'll be a needy pile of mush if I don't pull myself together.

I open my eyes and hurry to grab the sunblock. I methodically start at my face, then work my way down. Silas groans when I do my chest, tall enough to peer over my shoulder as I make sure to get all my bits.

"Fuck, Meg." He leans closer to whisper in my ear. "I want you so bad right now. Can you imagine making love, all slick and slippery like this?"

A delicious shudder racks me as my imagination takes off. I whisper fiercely, "You're *not* helping."

He chuckles as he finishes the lower part of my back. "Don't freak out, but I'm gonna do under your strings in case they move."

I freeze as his hand dips beneath the straps, along the flat of my back then skimming one side, almost to my breast. "Silas," I hiss.

He laughs again, but moves to the other side where he behaves. "Sorry, couldn't resist."

When he's done, I bend down to do my calves and shins, only to feel his incessant fingers swoop in along the elastic holding my bottoms up. I fly upright, glaring back at him.

He holds his hand up, all innocence. "You bent, I saw un-sunscreened skin. I was just helping."

I don't even know what to say in the face of his innocent, adorable expression. "Just…hands off while I finish my legs? Please?" He nods and I quickly rub the rest of the lotion in, then turn around. "Your turn."

"You're going to finish me?"

"Shut up and turn around," I say, though laughter seeps through my exasperation.

I steel myself as I slide my hands over him. I try to be quick and efficient, but Silas still grabs his towel out of his bag, dabs his face, then drops the fabric over his lap. My mouth goes dry that I affect him that much and I really want to play it up. To see how far I can push him.

But I don't think I can handle it.

When I'm done, he leans back in the chair, knees up, arms behind his head. "I'm gonna…chill here for a few, okay?"

I tuck the sunscreen in my bag then lean forward, giving him a perfect glance at my cleavage. "Need anything?"

He bobs his eyebrows. "Like you and me finding an empty bedroom?"

I gawk at his audacity then quickly shake my head. "Not happening."

He snaps his fingers then waves his hand. "Then how about you disappear for a bit and at least give me a chance of settling down?"

My gaze drops to his lap, and his throat bobs.

"Meg?"

I jerk my head up.

"Not helping."

My cheeks heat, but he just smirks again before I hurry over to the shade where Kaylie and Remy are twined together, watching Bekah and her guys dance at the end of the cement pad, far away from the slippery edges of the pool.

Kaylie shoots me a knowing smirk. "You two were putting on quite the show."

I take a drink of my seltzer but don't say anything.

"Hey, chica," Diego says, sidling closer to me with an overly charming grin. "So glad you could make it."

I resist the urge to cross my arms over my chest when his gaze lingers a bit too long. "Thanks for having us," I say, and pointedly glance back at Silas, who beams at me.

"No problem. You hungry? Let me show you where the snacks are."

He doesn't give me much choice, so I follow him to the table near the grill where there is a massive spread of snacks. I am a little hungry, so I help myself to some veggies and dip along with fruit and a few crackers with slices of cheese. Diego stays with me, chatting and asking me questions. I relax slightly when he doesn't flirt, surprised to find myself enjoying the conversation.

When my plate is empty, I toss it in the garbage can and scan for my friends. Kylie is now in the chair Silas was occupying, Remy sitting at her feet. I search for a few moments before I spot Silas in the shade with some of his teammates. He raises his beer at me, and I smile back.

"Have you been in the pool yet?" Diego asks. "I'm about ready to go cool off myself."

The bright blue water beckons. It's a perfect day for a pool party, relentless sun, humidity, and no clouds in the sky. The water would be a welcome relief.

"Sure," I say, "if you don't mind staying in the shallow end."

I'm not a good swimmer. I grew up going to the Wrightings' pool and I can dog paddle if needed, but I much prefer to lounge in the shallow end on a floatie where the water won't go above my waist. Especially with my recent knee flare-up, I need to play it safe.

"Whatever you want."

We walk in, and he immediately goes under. Diego looks like a model as he emerges, tossing his hair back as water sluices over him. I can't help noticing how cut he is, but at the same time, it's like seeing a gorgeous picture in a museum.

I can appreciate the art without wanting to take it home.

The water is refreshing, and I'm happy not getting my hair wet. I snag a free circular floatie sitting on the edge of the pool then put myself in it as gracefully as possible. There is no way to hop on one of those without feeling like an oversized hippo. But I land it in one try and pick up my drink from the side of the pool.

"Good?" Diego asks.

I tip my head back and soak up the sun. "This is great."

He smiles as if I gave him the world's best compliment. The fawning makes me uncomfortable so

I ask him about his tattoos. He launches into an explanation that I tune out partway through as I survey the people around me.

Everyone is clumped off in little groups. Some rowdier guys horse around at the end of the pool, splashing a group of girls and making them squeal. I make sure I stay close to the edge, alternating which foot I prop up to keep me in place. No need to get sucked down by someone else's carelessness.

When Diego pauses, I ask, "How deep is this pool?"

"Twelve feet."

My eyes widen. "That's deep."

He grins. "Some people like it that way."

The innuendo crawls over me, and I resist the urge to wrinkle my nose. Instead, I tip my can, draining the last drop.

"Would you like another?" he asks eagerly.

"Sure, thanks. And a water too?" I smile when he nods.

He pushes himself out of the water at the side of the pool, next to where my foot is propped. The waves from his exit slosh my tube and I turn away, trying to avoid getting splashed.

Then my foot slips.

His momentum pushes me out deeper, and I try not to panic. It's not that far to the edge, so I grit my teeth and begin to paddle myself to the nearest one.

"Meg?" Silas asks. "You good?" He peers at me over his glasses, his brow furrowed in concern.

"Yep," I say between gritted teeth. I've almost got this, and I don't need him hopping in here when he hasn't even gotten wet yet.

His eyebrows jump and his mouth drops as he starts to point. Someone splashes in next to me, a cannonball gone wrong. Their wave crashes over me and their arm hits my tube, the combined force toppling me.

I tumble into the water, panic fluttering at the edges of my vision as I try to keep calm. Holding my breath, I allow my body to plunge down, hoping to touch the bottom and propel myself back up. I stretch my toes, but nothing's there. My eyes pop open, and I ignore the chlorine burn as I try to figure out which way to swim.

But all I see is churning water.

Someone dives in next to me, their strong arm wrapping around my waist as they shoot us up. I gasp as soon as my head clears the surface, clinging to Silas. His lips are pressed together in a furious frown as he keeps one arm around me. His powerful legs and free arm work together to get us to the edge, where I cling and cough.

"You okay?" he asks, still holding me.

All I can see is him. Those amber eyes, that worried gaze, the love peeking out behind it. My lips part as I nod.

"Let's get you dried off."

I'm still dazed from the whole experience. I allow him to guide me to the ladder, and he waits for me to get out. Then I stand there, staring at him as he steps onto the concrete next to me. Water runs off his chiseled body and I can't look away.

He hurries me over to the lounge chair and grabs my towel, draping it around my now trembling body. Then he pulls me to his chest, wrapping me in those strong arms as I shake with the terror and adrenaline coursing through me.

Silas saved me. He caught me. I can trust this cable. I'm making the right move by trusting him. He's just proven it.

Again.

Silas

My heart pounds as Meg shakes in my arms. Anger washes over me at Diego, even as the rational part of my brain tries to tell me it was an accident.

I saw the whole thing. How her foot slipped when he got out of the pool. How she drifted into the deep end. The panic disappearing as determination took over. Then that guy had jumped, way too close for comfort.

And she disappeared.

I hadn't thought twice about diving in after her. My relief when her head broke the surface and she gulped in a breath was unparalleled. I rub her back, waiting for her to calm. Happy to have her in my arms, unharmed.

Finally she looks up at me with those beautiful eyes. "Thank you."

I nod, not trusting myself to speak. Kaylie and Remy watch us from their perch on the lounge chair, wide-eyed and curious.

"Everything okay?"

Diego's voice breaks all the fragile threads I hold on my self-control and I whirl around to face him. "No, it's not. Meg asked to stay in the shallow end and you were too busy showing off to not notice that your antics shoved her into the deep. Then some careless jerk jumped in way too close and toppled her over. She's not a strong swimmer *and* has an injured knee." All my anger and panic unleashes on him. "She could have drowned!"

Diego gapes as he stumbles backward, hands up. "I-I didn't know," he stammers.

I'm still seething when Meg grabs my arm, spinning me to face her as Diego stutters out an apology. I ignore him when Meg steps in front of me, letting her towel drop. I swallow hard at the delicious view of her, but the intense yet tender expression on her face is what stops me in my tracks.

"Take me home, Silas," she says, running a hand up my bare chest.

Goosebumps appear in the wake of her touch. Her fingers have no resistance as they glide over my damp, heated skin, reminding me I haven't even dried off. I can't answer, can't move as the red haze in my vision starts to ebb.

She gives me a tempting smile then glides her other hand along a parallel path. "Silas, please. Let's get out of here."

The words break me from my trance, and I grab our bags as I stride away with her on my heels. I don't stop until I'm next to the car where I drop the bags and pin her between me and the car door. She mouths my name as I cup her face with both hands.

Then I bend to crash my lips onto hers, pouring the depths of my feelings into that kiss. She clings to my shoulders, meeting me motion for motion as I try to show her exactly how terrified I was for her. How very relieved I am that she's okay.

How much I love her and want her in my life.

That one emotion trumps all. *Love*. It's stronger than ever, an all-consuming, never-ending love for this beautiful, smart, sassy woman in front of me.

When I finally break away to suck in a breath, she stares at me, wide-eyed.

"Meg," I breathe, cradling her face in my hands. "I love you."

Her eyes widen even more, then I notice the panic dancing in them.

I swallow, realizing how impulsive that was. I step back, running a hand through my wet hair. "Sorry, if that was too much. I...well I've wanted to tell you for weeks now and if anything had happened to you..." I trail off, my heart thundering in my chest at the thought.

She brushes her fingers along my jaw. "I'm okay, Si. Really."

I study her, forcing myself to hear the words and process them. Some of the tension drains from me.

"But I'm not ready to say —" She stops as I press my fingers to her lips.

"I'm not asking you to say anything you're not ready for. I didn't tell you so I could hear it back. I just needed you to know, all right?" I let out a deep breath then rest my forehead against hers as more of the tense energy drains from me.

When I move away, she frowns. "Are *you* okay?"

I nod, and even manage a smile. "I am now." I glance back at the house, music drifting toward us. "Still want to head out?"

"Really?" Her eyebrows jump up. "You're going to kiss me like that, tell me you love me, then ask if I want to stay?"

Startled laughter spills from my lips at her indignation. Satisfaction floods me that I've affected her so thoroughly, and I lean one arm behind her against the car, loving how her gaze drops to trace over my bare chest.

I give her a moment, then touch her chin, guiding her focus back to my face as I smirk. "Do you have a better idea?"

Meg's stare is hungry and wanton. "Take me home, Silas."

But I want to hear her say it. "And do what?"

"Me," she whispers.

Chapter Eighteen

Silas

Somehow I get us home in one piece, a feat in itself when all I want to do is make Meg mine. She tries to stop and grab the bag from the backseat, but I growl, "Leave it."

I can't resist kissing her again as I shut the car door, then I wrap my hand around her wrist and lead her into the house. Luckily we don't see anyone else as we race upstairs where I pause. *My room or hers?*

But she bites her lip, hesitating. "Silas?"

Concern flashes through me. I know she's been through a lot. We both have, and I wouldn't blame her if she'd changed her mind. "You all right?"

"I just..." She keeps her gaze trained on the floor. "Can I have a bit to get ready? I want to shower off the chlorine and..." She leaves the rest to my imagination.

"Of course." I've waited this long, and I want her to be comfortable. My skin is already feeling tight from the pool, making me add, "Maybe I should rinse off, too." Heady images of her lips on my skin have my dick twitching, but I try to keep my self-control.

She blinks at me, and I realize how my words sounded.

"I meant separately. Just also!" At her chuckle, I relax again. "Maybe I should go first. I'll wait for you in my room, then you can take as much time as you need."

Her warm smile is full of gratitude. "That sounds great."

I lean down to kiss her cheek, then straighten, not trusting myself to speak. I head for the bathroom where I take the quickest shower of my life. Wrapped in a towel, I hurry back to my room and text her that the bathroom is free.

Indecision hits me. Do I stay in my towel? Go totally nude? In the end, I pull on a pair of briefs then toss my sheet over my lower half, not wanting to seem desperate. Or presumptuous. I lie on my back, scrolling through my phone to pass the time. I don't even know what I'm looking at and my foot doesn't stop jiggling.

Twenty minutes pass. Each one feels like an hour, before a tentative tap sounds on my door.

"Come in," I call, setting my phone on my nightstand and turning onto my side.

Meg peeks in, only walking into the room when I wave her over. I prop myself up on one elbow, grinning as I drink her in. Her long hair is damp, creating darker spots on her silky robe from the moisture.

That robe will be the death of me. I itch to feel its smooth fabric beneath my fingers again, but I need another peek at what's under it more.

She walks over, nibbling at her lip as she stops at the edge of the bed. I wait, not wanting to push her. She sits gingerly, tucking both legs to one side as she leans on her hand. The neckline of her robe shifts, giving me a tantalizing glimpse of teal lace framing her cleavage. My mouth goes dry at the sight.

"I'm not any good at this," she says, her voice just above a whisper.

"At what? Perching on my bed like a fucking snack?" I scoff. "It's taking all my self-control not to devour you whole right now."

She giggles, some of the tension easing out of her shoulders as her posture relaxes. "I meant the whole telling you my feelings thing."

I freeze, every nerve in my body wound tight with anticipation. And hope. I hadn't assumed that this was more than sex. Meg holds all the cards, and I'm along for whenever she wants to deal me in.

She's still staring at me, and I know I need to reassure her. I sit up, crossing my legs under me, but that makes her suck in a sharp breath because the sheet no longer covers me or my erection straining against my briefs.

"Is it easier with the sheet?" I ask gently. Her cheeks tinge with pink as she nods, so I cover my lower half once more. Then I reach for her hand. "I'm listening. Whatever you need to say, however long it takes you to say it. I'm not going anywhere."

She dips her chin, studying our joined hands. "I had lunch with Leah today."

Tension in her voice sends a jolt of fear through me, but I push it aside. She's here, in my room. She asked to come home. With me.

"I told her about…us."

My lips tip up at the word, warmth bursting through my chest. *There's actually an us.*

"I also told her how I've always thought of you guys as hers. That I was worried she was going to be upset if we were together."

I frown, hardly able to keep up with the whiplash of my emotions. Meg didn't feel included? I tighten my grip on her hand. "You've always been ours." *Mine.*

She flashes me a small smile. "That's what Leah said too. She told me that love is like a gift. She can give it to me, but I'm the one who has to open it." She pauses to swallow, staring down at our hands once more. "That hit me hard."

My heart breaks for this amazing woman. I know she hasn't had it easy, but to not know she's loved? By all of us? Her scars run deeper than I thought.

"I'm the reason I've felt apart, because I won't let anyone else in." She takes a deep breath and squares her shoulders then meets my eyes. "But I want that to change, Si. I want you in my life. When people ask who you are, I want to tell them something besides you're my friend."

My breath stutters at her fierce declaration.

"Can I call you my boyfriend?"

Her name flies from my lips, and I can't get close enough. I shoot to my knees, dropping her hand to cradle her face. "You can call me whatever you want, as long as I get to call you mine."

Delighted awe blossoms in her beautiful eyes as she gazes at me. "Mine. I like the sound of that."

"Me too." I lean in, brushing my lips to hers as heat churns between us. "Mine," I whisper again before kissing her soundly.

"Silas?" When I hum in answer, she pulls back. "Prove it? Now?"

"Of course. Over and over, as many times as you need." I stroke her cheek with my thumb. "Like I said, I'm not going anywhere."

And I mean it with every fiber of my being.

Meg

I shouldn't be nervous.

I've known Silas most of my life. I just poured my heart out to him, and he reacted without flinching or bolting in the opposite direction. Plus we've had sex before, but this feels different. Bigger.

Especially because he called me *his*.

His hands frame my face and I stare into his amber eyes, searching for any hint of doubt or reasons to back out. There aren't any. All I see is love, acceptance and reassurance.

He closes the gap and touches his lips to mine. The air crackles with electricity, the gentle feel of his mouth unlocking the deepest part of me. The one that's been holding back.

And I dive off the edge.

I need him like oxygen. As if I've been pushed to the bottom of the pool and he is the breath I've waited to take. I close the distance between our bodies, kissing him hungrily as I launch myself at him. My enthusiasm has us toppling but Silas grins against my lips, catching us and lowering us to the bed. He hovers over me, his hand skating down the edge of my robe.

"As much as I like this robe," he murmurs, "there's one way it could look better." When I raise my eyebrows, he grins. "On the floor."

He deftly unties the knot at my waist, easing the fabric over one shoulder. His intense look devours every inch of my skin as it's revealed, his gaze so fervent I can feel the weight of it. Like the most poignant caress.

I'd taken my time getting ready, wanting to look good. Wanting to feel good. The matching bra and panty set I chose is teal, lacy, and accentuates my curves in the best way.

Silas traces a finger between the swells of my breasts before reaching for the other side of the robe to ease it back. Impatient, I sit up and fling the thing to the floor. His throat bobs at the proximity of my breasts to his mouth.

"I'm going to taste every inch of you," he promises. "Starting here."

My nipple hardens as he runs his finger around it, his heated touch searing me through the lace. I collapse onto the bed, desperate to feel his lips on me.

He kisses me again, and I moan as his hand cups my breast. I arch into his palm, feeling his smile as his lips leave my mouth to scald their way down my neck. I take a moment to run my hands over his shoulders, his biceps, his pecs. Then skate back up to thread in his hair as he kisses me through my flimsy bra.

His hand snakes behind me, expertly undoing the clasp. I raise my arms and he tugs the bra off to join my robe on the floor.

He hums his approval as he hungrily surveys my breasts. "I could spend all day on these."

Silas ducks his head, taking my peaked nipple into his mouth as I close my eyes at the pure jolt of pleasure shooting to my core. We have time now, time to explore and find out what the other likes. He takes advantage of that, living up to his promise as his talented mouth teases every inch of my breasts.

My hips buck, needing a release from the tension climbing higher with each nibble, suck and lick. He pauses to grin at me, a wicked, cocky grin that tells me he knows exactly what he's doing.

And loving every minute of it.

He shifts to nudge his leg between mine, and I open for him, gasping when his firm thigh rests against my pussy. I grind on him, my hip pressing into his hardened length that strains his black briefs.

The friction feels so good. All our interactions throughout today have wound together, stringing me tighter. I fist Silas' hair, keeping him locked on my breast as I seek my release. His other hand comes up, rolling my opposite nipple between his thumb and forefinger.

When he pinches lightly, the sensation sends me over that edge and I cry out as I shudder under him. My breaths come in rapid pants. I stare into his awe-filled eyes as he rises above me and licks his lips.

"That was fucking hot," he says.

I laugh, feeling free and unhindered in a way I never have. Silas lets me be myself, lets me find my own way, in my own time. And is right there to catch me if I fall.

My heartbeat slowly returns to normal, but Silas eases down my torso. Kissing my ribs, my belly, my hip. He slips his fingers between my legs, his breath hitching when he collides with my heat.

He's only tasted me there once, our second time together. During that fateful party. He dropped to his knees in my room, hitched up my dress and... I've never forgotten the feeling of his passion as he devoured me.

Anticipation makes me squirm as he continues kissing along my inner thigh. His breath passes over where I need him most, but he just continues on his path.

"Silas," I beg. "Please."

He glances at me, his gaze hungry and provocative. I've dreamed of him in this position, fantasized about it, and I take a second to memorize every bit of the delicious image before me.

"You going to come all over my face, Meg? Let me taste your sweetness again?" He runs a finger along my seam, over my soaked panties as I nod frantically.

He hooks his fingers in the waistband of my underwear then drags them down my legs before settling between my thighs. I whimper when his breath cascades over me again. He's so close. That wicked grin appears once more and I want to grab his hair and shove his face—

Then he licks me and I drop my head back to the pillow as I hiss, "Yes."

One of his hands cups my hip while the other slides along my inner thigh. He keeps licking and circling as his fingers ease closer, then he pulls his mouth back and slips a finger inside me. I welcome the intrusion, especially when he returns his tongue to my sensitive clit.

Ecstasy is within reach as he stokes that fire with me. I can't help weaving my fingers into his unruly curls as my hips begin to buck in rhythm with his ministrations. I grip the sheet with my other hand as my inner walls clench.

The first wave of pleasure blindsides me as I cry out. He keeps licking and pumping, prolonging the bliss as the waves continue to crash over me. I drop my hand from his hair as the tremors finally subside.

He gives me one last lick, then sits up on his heels, a beyond satisfied grin on his face. "Look at you," he says, leaning forward to slide a hand along my abdomen. He leaves it there, his fingers spreading wide over my stomach. "All laid out for me like my favorite meal. I could stare at you all day."

The words and his hungry gaze flip that switch once more and all I can think about is how empty I am. "Si, I need you."

His smile is tender as he puts on a condom then eases his weight on top of me. I welcome it. Our lips meet in a sweet kiss as he lines his eager cock up with my slick entrance. When he slips inside, joining us together, I can't help my gasp.

I feel complete and full—a feeling I haven't experienced since we were last together.

Only now, when he pulls back to stare at me, I add another sensation. Loved. I inhale sharply at the depth of emotion swirling in his gaze, and he holds my stare as he rocks his hips, sliding almost all the way out then thrusting back in.

We've never been able to take it slow. Both our interludes were rapid bouts of need that escalated quickly and were over much too fast. I thought I'd be just as impatient today. That Silas would be anxious to reach that peak.

But he takes his time.

Our gazes stay locked as his left hand slips beneath my shoulder, cradling me and anchoring himself as he finds a rhythm. His right hand caresses my cheek then glides down to take my hand, threading his fingers through mine.

The intimacy of this moment is more powerful than any I've experienced. I feel raw and exposed, entwined like this with him. With my heart on the table.

A spiral of fear wends through me, but I push it aside, clinging to Silas. His steady presence comforts me even as he nudges me up that cliff for a third time. I rock to meet him, willing to let him be my guide.

"Meg," he whispers, his voice strained. "I never thought… I've never felt…"

"Shh," I croon, using my free hand to cup his face. His stubble grazes my palm and I revel in the rough sensation, juxtaposing his gentle movements. "I'm here."

His need grounds me, and I tilt to take him deeper. He groans, closing his eyes while his hips begin pounding faster as he loses himself in us. I stroke his cheek, my gaze never leaving his face so I get to see the awe when he opens his eyes.

His lips form my name again, even as the sensations overwhelm me. The gliding of his cock into my depths, the friction of his abdomen pressing on my clit, the smoothness of his chest on my sensitive nipples. A ripple is all the warning I get before my vision explodes with stars and my orgasm rockets through me.

I cry out, clenching around him as he thrusts home and finds his own release. We quiver in each other's arms for a long moment, then he exhales and pulls out of me to flop on the bed. My arm is under his head and he nuzzles me.

I turn on my side, staring at this man as warmth and bliss flood my being.

How did I wait so long to claim what has always been mine?

* * * *

Silas

I'm not one for naps but after we clean up, I pull Meg against my chest, needing to hold her. Then I crash out. Between the excitement at the pool and the rawness of our lovemaking, I need a reset. We both do.

An hour later, I wake to her stirring in my arms. She lifts her head and blinks at me. I grin sleepily at her, my grin widening when she sits up and stretches.

Still completely naked.

I can't help reaching out to run my hand over her abdomen, then up to cup her tit. She raises her eyebrows but doesn't stop me. My cock starts hardening all over again.

She notices. "Already?" But her smirk tells me she's teasing.

I grab her arm, pulling her so she lands on my chest, then I bring her mouth to mine. "Mmhmm."

The heated kiss turns frantic. There is nothing slow or sensual about this round, as if we're making up for lost time. As if we need an outlet after all that intimacy. When we're both finished, she rolls off me and we lie side by side, panting. I take care of the condom and clean myself then lace my hands behind my head.

"I could get used to this," I say.

"What? Fucking me?"

The crass words stab at me because what we did today was the farthest thing from fucking I've ever done. But I see the wariness in her smile, know this is how she reacts when someone gets too close. So I let it slide.

Rolling onto my side, I prop my head on my elbow as I run my fingers down her arm. "Taking our time.

Chilling afterward. Not hiding." I smirk. "That's what I can get used to."

Understanding lights her face as she relaxes and gives me a real smile. "Yeah, this is nice."

I raise her hand to my lips. "What's next? Dinner?" It's a little after seven p.m., and I'm ready to eat real food. Not just my delectable girlfriend.

"Mmm, food." She climbs over me, standing then grabbing her robe and her discarded underthings.

"Order pizza? Eat in, watch *Gilmore Girls*?" I can't believe the words are leaving my lips.

It's a Friday night. When do I ever want to stay in? But the idea of snuggling with her on the couch, just us, seems like heaven.

Especially when she rewards me with a bright grin. "That sounds perfect."

The evening *is* perfect, at least in my opinion. We watch back-to-back episodes while stuffing our faces and sipping beer. The best part is that she sits right next to me, always touching, instead of leaving her usual carefully cultivated space. Like she knows I need that right now.

When we're done eating, she picks up my arm and curls against my chest. I cuddle her to me, basking in her warmth. Steven comes home in the middle of our third episode and he grins at us.

I pause the show. "Where have you been?" My curiosity is piqued because he rarely goes out, even on Fridays.

"I went out with some guys from work." He seems happy, and I'm glad to see it. He glances between us. "Movie night in?"

I nod while Meg's cheeks turn a bit pink. "It's been an eventful day, but I'd like to introduce you to my girlfriend."

His grin widens. "Aw, that's great, guys. I'm thrilled you worked things out." He gives me a pointed look. "Maybe this one will quit moping so much."

I duck my head even as Meg lets out a delighted laugh. He waves before disappearing upstairs, leaving us to our show.

"You've been moping?" she asks, grinning.

"Maybe a little."

She settles in at my side again, resting her hand on my abdomen. "Well, I'm glad to help."

Our episode wraps up right before Shawn and Leah come in. They can't keep their hands off each other as they remove their shoes, but Leah stops when she sees us cuddled together on the couch. Her eyebrows pop up as she glances expectantly between us.

Meg laughs. "Yes, Lee. We're official now."

She squeals and races over to give us both hugs. Then she frowns when she notices Shawn hanging back. "Come on, Shawn. Isn't this exciting?"

He grins at both of us but pins her with his pointed stare. "Sure, just not as exciting as what we'd planned to do."

Her mouth forms a little O, and she scurries back over to him. "Night, guys. Meg, tomorrow, details." That's all she gets out before Shawn hauls her off to the mini suite.

"Now we just need to tell Sebastian and Callie," Meg says, yawning.

"Maybe we should try for a game night tomorrow or Sunday," I suggest, mulling it over. "I've got to work at the coffee shop tomorrow from noon to six, but I'm free after."

"I'll text everyone. Tomorrow."

"And what do you want to do in the meantime?"

She tilts her head as she thinks. "I think I'm done with *Gilmore Girls*." At my nod, she runs her hand over my chest. "Maybe we could go back upstairs?"

I will never turn that down. I quickly shut off the TV and hop to my feet, offering her my hand. She takes it, our fingers joined together as I lead her upstairs.

Where all my sweetest dreams are about to keep coming true.

Chapter Nineteen

Silas

The next afternoon, I'm busy behind the counter of Not Your Average Joe, taking orders, making coffee, and calling names when Meg walks in. Despite the line of five people at my register, I notice her immediately.

It's always been like that. Her presence has a direct connection to the radar of my heart. I give her an easy grin, then focus once more on the customer in front of me.

At last, it's Meg's turn. "Wow, you're busy today."

"Yeah, it hasn't stopped. What are you doing?"

"Well, I kind of thought I'd come to a coffee shop and," she lowers her voice to a conspiratorial whisper, "order a coffee."

I feign a gasp and she laughs, then puts in her usual order. I wave off her card, happy to treat her again. We have game night after my shift, and I wonder what she's up to until then. "You sticking around?"

She pats the strap of her backpack hanging on her shoulder. "If you don't mind me taking up a table."

I jerk my chin toward a booth in the back corner that happens to be empty. "Saved one just for you."

She beams and steps off to the side as I help the next customer. An hour later, things have slowed and it's time for my break. I'm due for my own coffee. I also grab a sandwich for myself, plus a refill and a muffin for Meg. Chocolate chip — her favorite.

After I pay the difference of my daily shift allotment, I weave my way to her table. She's so deep in thought that she doesn't notice me until I perch on the seat beside her, totally crowding her space. She seems affronted until she realizes it's me, then she laughs and scoots over.

"Here." I give her my offerings, loving how her face lights up. "Thought we could both use a break and some sustenance."

"Thank you."

My thirty-minute break goes by too fast, but I relish the time with her. After I return to the counter, I keep stealing glances in her direction. Each time my gaze lands on her studious form, one thought echoes in my head.

Mine.

I can't believe she's finally my girlfriend, though that seems too small a word to encompass all I feel for her. She is my planet and I'm her moon, revolving around her as her gravity pulls me in. I love her.

And I told her and she didn't run.

Being together is so new, so fresh, and to give it a weight like that... But at the same time, we've danced around each other for years, and this feels more than right to me. I've always felt tethered to her. I just wish I'd realized earlier how much she means to me. I could've saved us both a lot of heartache and strife.

The end of my shift draws closer and she's still here when I clock out. I lean on her table until she notices me again. She blinks, taking in my lack of apron, then glances at her phone.

"Six already?" she says, then straightens and stretches, her back and neck popping.

"Must have been some good reading."

"Mostly studying. I've got a Trauma Care test on Monday and I keep getting some of the treatments mixed up." She rubs her temple.

"Hmm, sounds like you need a brain break. Maybe I can dream up something else for you to focus on." I give her my most flirtatious wink.

She peers at me through lowered lashes. "What did you have in mind?"

I've resisted the urge to kiss her all day, but I can't hold back any longer. "For starters..." I draw her into my arms and press my lips to hers as she melts against me with a contented hum.

When I let her go, she looks a little dazed but grins. "I'm listening."

I lean down to nibble at her neck, then whisper in her ear, "To be continued at home."

She hums again then quickly packs her things. We hurry back to the house hand in hand, me still marveling this beautiful, smart woman is mine. In my room, I show her just how much I care, and by the end of our interlude, she lies in a contented heap on my bed. Exactly like I'd imagined.

* * * *

Meg

Game night is a success. When Silas proudly tells them I'm his girlfriend, Callie gives me a big hug and Sebastian smiles at me, several times. I almost feel like one of them now. I'm not sure if it's because I let my walls down after my talk with Leah or because Silas draws me in like never before.

He's always made sure that I'm included, but now, it's like I'm an extension of him. I move and he adjusts. I speak and he responds. The attention is heady, and his need for touch only adds to it all.

My test Monday goes well enough. I get a solid B, which I'll take. Then I go with Kaylie and Bekah to Silas' game, where we cheer them on. Ogling my hot boyfriend running around in his sleeveless shirt and jersey shorts? The perfect way to spend an afternoon.

I stay in his room Monday night, but Tuesday I go back to mine. After my long work day and having an early morning Wednesday, I need the space to decompress. Thankfully, Silas understands and doesn't pressure me at all.

Wednesday, after work, we go on our first official date. I dress in my favorite wedge sandals with a cute frayed-denim skirt and a flowy pink top that matches my lip gloss. He picks me up at my door, even bringing me a small bouquet of wildflowers in a vase.

I gasp at the gorgeous bouquet. "Thank you! I can't remember the last time someone brought me flowers." I rest my hand on his arm, pushing onto my tiptoes to kiss his cheek before I take the vase from him.

"You're welcome," he says. "Beautiful flowers for a beautiful woman."

I duck my head at the compliment, dancing over to set the bouquet on top of my dresser. The flowers brighten my room so much, and I adore them.

"Where are we going?" I ask, grabbing my purse and meeting him at the doorway.

He zips his lips. "You'll see."

We drive one town over, and I pepper him with questions the entire ride but he doesn't give me so much as a hint at his plan today. When we pull into the parking lot of their local museum, I gape at the huge banner on the side of the building. A massive shark spans its length, proclaiming below that the shark exhibit is now open.

"Sharks?" I exclaim, turning excitedly to Silas.

He runs his thumb over the back of my hand. "I thought of you the first time I heard about it. I've been wanting to bring you ever since."

I throw my arms around him. "Thank you!"

Museums are always fun, but an exhibit solely dedicated to sharks? I can hardly wait. Silas insists on buying my ticket, and we saunter in, meandering to the shark section as we pause at anything that sparks our interest.

Finally, I see the sign for the new exhibit. The doorway is ringed with a mock shark's mouth, arching over the entrance with huge sharp teeth. I fight an excited shiver that may be tinged with the smallest hint of real fear. I adore sharks, but that doesn't mean I'd want to swim with one.

I walk under the menacing arch, grinning the whole way. Silas' hand still grips mine. He hasn't let go the entire time, and I'm not complaining.

As we step in, a massive model of a whale shark fills the majority of the space. I stare at it in awe, then tug Silas over to inspect it up close. I point out the nearest plaque, soaking in all the information. Like the fact that the whale shark is currently the largest in existence, growing up to forty feet long.

"That's almost half a football field," Silas murmurs, eyes wide.

"Thank goodness they only eat little things."

We move down the winding hallway to find a glass case containing a whole array of shark replicas in line from largest to smallest. After that is another case containing a whole slew of different sharks' teeth. I study Silas, wondering if he has his now, and he pulls it out of his pocket with a knowing grin before tucking it away again.

The fact that he still carries it adds another strand to our cable. One more piece of proof that he can stick with something, that he does care. I cling to it, hearing his declaration of love once more, and my lips tip in a secret smile.

Because I believe him.

As we wander along, I get to touch several different shark scale replicas, comparing them. I marvel at how it feels smooth if I run my hand from front to back, but if I reverse my touch, the skin feels like sandpaper.

When we finally get to the end, my mind feels like it might explode if I try to process one more bit of information. "I don't know how Sebastian does it, cramming in all those facts," I say as we leave, and Silas laughs.

"Well, not all of us have a photographic memory like him." A wicked grin spreads over his face.

"What?"

"Just thinking that you could give him a run for his money about sharks, and I would love to see that."

I shake my head, even as I chuckle.

On our way out, we pause in the huge shark jaw for some selfies. A kind passerby takes several pictures of us while we pose in fake terror. After I get my phone back, warmth spreads through me when I see an extra one of us laughing afterward. The adoring looks in our eyes is sickeningly sweet in the best possible way.

"You up for more? I had another idea and" — he pauses to check his phone — "we can make it if we hurry."

I shrug. "Sure, I've got no plans other than hanging out with you."

We share a grin as a zing of excitement zips through me at the idea of spending more time with him. We drive back to our town and into the movie theater parking lot twenty-five minutes later. My eyes widen in delight at the poster with a massive shark chasing a diver's swim fins.

Silas glances at me eagerly. "You haven't seen it yet, have you?"

"Oh, I've been dying to, but haven't had time. You?"

"Nope. I was waiting to go with you."

The simple declaration has me melting. We go to the movies often enough — with or without one another, but sharks are *our* thing. This movie sounds incredibly intense with underwater miners being hunted down, one by one. And the idea of snuggling with Silas in the theater, grabbing his arm when I jump from fright, has me smiling even wider.

It hits me again that he's mine, and I stare at him in amazement until he raises his eyebrows. A hint of embarrassment washes over me.

I duck my head as I explain, "I'm kind of excited to do this movie thing as a couple." I sheepishly glance back up, loving how he lights up.

"Hey, you're right. I don't just have to pretend you're my date."

The teasing statement stabs. How many times have I done that? I know the answer is more than I can count, and I shove the warped longing aside, reminding myself we have now and we're going to make new memories.

Truly together.

We are the only ones in the movie theater, not surprising on a Wednesday evening. We load up on all the goodies — popcorn, pop, Reese's Pieces for me and Buncha Crunch for him. Our seats are prime real estate, four rows back and in the middle. Far enough that we're not craning our necks the whole time, but close enough to be engulfed in the action.

The recliner seats are luxurious. They even have little trays that swivel in front of us, plus heated seats. Which might come in handy if they blast the air conditioning.

When the previews begin, the first thing I do is prop up the armrest and put the popcorn between us. I take a handful, tossing it into my mouth, then adjust my footrest. I glance at Silas, only to find him staring at me intently.

"What?" I mumble around my food.

He smirks, slowly reaching toward my chest. I glance down to find a stray piece of popcorn resting on my boobs. His fingers graze over the swells of my breasts before he sensuously pops the kernel into his mouth.

He leans over until our shoulders touch. "We do have the whole theater to ourselves," he whispers, his voice low and husky enough to make my stomach flip.

Not that I don't want to play, but I do actually want to see the movie. I waffle for a second. "I don't think this movie is quite the right one to ramp me up like that." I keep it flirty though, and give him a teasing wink.

"Not true," he continues. "I know exactly what a good shark movie does to you."

I smack his shoulder, unable to believe he brought up the one time I made out with another guy during a shark movie. "It was *Sharknado*!" I protest. Although I'm not sure which one.

He laughs, sitting back in his seat. The space between us yawns impatiently, and I wonder how long he'll be able to refrain from touching me. I begin counting, not even reaching ten in my head before he yanks the popcorn onto his lap and swings his arm around me until I'm nestled against his side.

Staring at him, I chuckle because it is kind of adorable. "Miss me?"

His grumbling is silenced when I tilt my chin, wanting a kiss. Our lips meet tenderly as a thrill runs through me. I'm actually allowed to do this—make out with Silas in public. The heady feeling lingers as the movie starts and I snuggle against his chest.

Exactly where I want to be.

* * * *

Silas

Friday rolls around, and I'm still riding the high from Meg being my girlfriend and our perfect date. It's usually my day off, but we have a big case coming up. I've volunteered with two other interns to spend the morning highlighting phone records. Not super exciting, but I get free bagels and coffee out of the deal.

After we've made it through the stack, it's a little after noon, so I pop up to Dad's office to say hi. When I tap on his open door, he waves me in.

Maren Jenner

"Hey, son, didn't expect to see you today."

"I'm helping on the Reading case."

He glances at his watch and his eyebrows lift. "After noon already?" He shakes his head as if unable to believe it. "Want to grab a bite?"

My smile widens. "That sounds great."

I expected to see more of my dad when I started this internship. I thought we'd go to lunch, have coffee breaks together. But I rarely see him. He does more of the corporate cases while I'm helping with the civil ones — divorces, trusts and the like.

A few minutes later, I'm sitting in the passenger seat of his Mercedes as we catch up.

"I've got a girlfriend now," I say, loving how the word sounds on my lips.

Dad grins, waiting. I don't tell him about women often, since they don't usually stick around.

I add, "It's Meg."

"Our Meg?" At my nod, he shakes his head. "I always thought there was something between you two. Good for you." His phone dings with a text and he glances at it at the next stop sign. "Do you mind if we run a quick errand? I've got a present for your mom that's ready."

"Sure, no problem." I've got no plans for the rest of the afternoon.

I'm a little surprised when we pull into the parking lot of a local jewelry store at the edge of town. Dad's not one to usually buy Mom sparkly things.

"Special occasion?" I ask as we fall into step.

"Our anniversary is at the end of September. Thirty years already." A wistful expression crosses his face. "I wanted to get her something special, so I planned ahead."

We walk inside, and I'm impressed with the warm feeling of the place. So many jewelry shops feel sterile or cold, but this one is done in welcoming colors with fun art on the walls. Dad starts to explain to the woman behind the counter what he's here for, but another man hurries out of the back.

"Trey, good to see you."

"Paul! My wife's necklace ready?"

I leave them to chat as I absently peruse the cases. I saunter along the edge of the room, scanning the selection of necklaces and bracelets. Then I get to the rings.

I've never thought much about jewelry or proposals, but I try to imagine it now. Me, standing in front of a crowd filled with my friends and family, outside, like at Sebastian's wedding. I look down the aisle, watching my brothers and the women they've chosen walk toward me, one after another.

The music changes and my chest gets tight as I wait for my bride.

She appears from behind a tree—a vision in white with a simple dress that touches the grass. Her long, dark hair flows behind her and she carries a bouquet of red and white flowers. But her chin is down and I can't see her face.

I wait in excruciating anticipation as she lifts her head, my heart skipping a beat when I see her familiar features. Of course it's her. Meg stands before me, and she is all I can see as her face lights up in a radiant smile.

My bride.

The vision takes my breath away and I have to lean against the nearby wall as I stumble back to reality. My mind races as my heart pounds, the realization settling over me. It all makes sense. I love Meg, promised I'd be there for her no matter what. I meant it then, and I mean it now.

An awed smile spreads over my face as I turn back to the rings. Meg is it for me. I don't want anyone else to join me at the end of that aisle. Not that I plan to buy anything today.

But it never hurts to look.

Most of the rings are the standard silver or gold with a decent rock in them, but to the far left I find a whole tray of unique ones. A gold one with a red stone catches my eye. The band starts solid then splits to wind around two small red stones with a delicate leaf pattern before connecting around the main gem.

All I can think about is how perfect it would be for Meg. It's bold and unique, just like her. And it's her favorite color.

"Can I help you with anything?" the cheery employee from earlier asks. "I'm Yasmine, by the way."

"Yes, thank you." I point to the ring. "Can I see that red one?"

She pulls out the tray, setting it on the counter. "This one?" At my nod, she picks it up and offers it to me. "The stones are garnets. And that's twenty-four-karat gold for the band."

A rightness settles over me as I take the ring, holding it between my thumb and forefinger as I study it in the light. I can see it now, me on one knee offering the black velvet box to Meg as her hands fly to her mouth in delighted surprise.

"You find some—?" My dad stops abruptly when he sees what I'm holding. "I didn't realize things were that serious."

I glance at him, noting the concern in his gaze, and I understand it. I'm not known for committing to anything or anyone. But it's always been Meg, and it's not like I'm planning to propose tomorrow.

They'll understand eventually.

"Just browsing, but this one jumped out at me." I glance at Yasmine. "How much?"

We talk options, how I can put a hold on it if I want to think about it for three days, then that money will be applied to the purchase. Or if I change my mind, I can use it for credit on a future purchase. I nod. That will give me time to think it over, so I hand her my card.

Dad and I walk in silence as we return to the car.

"Silas…"

"I know what you're thinking, Dad," I say quietly. "It's not like I'm going to propose right away. It's just…I know Meg is who I'm meant to be with. She was right under my nose, and I thought I had to find someone like her. But I didn't— I need *her*."

"Just…" He trails off, pressing his lips together for a moment. "Don't go jumping into something you'll regret, okay?"

Annoyance flares within me. "Is that what you told Sebastian when he said he and Callie were getting married?"

"Sebastian is a completely different person from you. He's singular in his goals, and once his mind is set on something, there's no stopping him."

All the things he doesn't say echo between us. That I'm not like that. That I change my mind every five minutes. That it's taken me years to settle on my major and he's still not sure I'll stick with it.

The weight of his judgment presses on my shoulders, and I shift in my seat. "You know what, Dad? I'm not very hungry and I just remembered some other things I need to do this afternoon. Could you just drop me off?"

The short ride is spent in a tense silence full of disappointment and unspoken expectations. The weight only grows heavier, pressing me further and further down until I can barely stand when the car comes to a stop. I say a terse "see ya" then head for my own car, thankful for the freedom of fresh air.

Chapter Twenty

Silas

My need to move makes the drive home excruciating. Frustration and hurt swarm within me, needing an outlet, and I pop the car into park, leaping out before it even stops rocking. Maybe I'll go for a run. Or practice goals in the backyard.

Kicking a ball as hard as I can sounds like a perfect option for my dark mood.

I remember my grounding techniques as I storm upstairs. I go through several of them, but they don't touch the maelstrom brewing within me. Getting some movement and a change of scenery will help, so I make a plan to change. My stomach growls but it can wait, then I open my door and all I see is chaos.

When did my room get this messy? I can't believe I let Meg come in here.

Each pile that once offered me comfort in its familiarity now screams failure. I can't even keep my own space neat. Tossing my jacket onto my bed, I loosen my tie and chuck it on top of the jacket. Then I roll up my sleeves and get to work.

An hour later, my closet has been sorted, but everything is piled into the center of the room, creating one large mess even more daunting than before. I dump another armload of clothes onto it, then step back as the pile comes into focus.

Shit. How am I supposed to get all of this done? My energy drains in a snap. *A break, I'll just take a little break.*

I zone out and scroll through my phone until a tap sounds on my door. "Come in," I call.

Meg peeks in, her eyes wide when she sees the rearranged chaos. A concerned frown furrows her brow when she finds me on the bed, my phone in hand. "Whatcha doin'?" she asks, cautiously.

"I started cleaning, but then…" I hate the defeat in my voice yet I can't help it.

"Ah." She turns a full circle and puts her hands on her hips. "What'd you have for lunch?"

Sheepishness makes my neck heat as I remember that I never did grab anything. "Um, I got sidetracked and—"

She clucks her tongue, shaking her head. "I'll be right back."

I'm not one to forget to eat. Sure, there are occasions when I get caught up in something, but that happens to everyone. I'm usually the one in the group asking when the next meal is coming. Just another tick in my list of failures. I drop my head back to thud against the wall as I sigh.

Meg returns with a plate of cheese, crackers and meat, along with nuts and grapes. A perfect mini charcuterie board. Then she hands me a Gatorade and tells me to drink.

She perches on the bed near me and we share the food, chatting about her study session this morning and other lighthearted topics she comes up with. When the plate is gone and my Gatorade is almost empty, I start to feel...more normal. The weight on my chest isn't so heavy, my limbs aren't entrenched in cement.

"Better?" she asks. When I nod, she grins and stands up. "Okay, let's do this."

"Meg..." I shake my head. "You don't need —"

"Silas, I'm helping." She surveys the chaos then says, "You bring me any clean clothes that need to be folded and put the dirty ones in the hamper. That's a good start."

I glance around the room, my gaze catching on each article of clothing strewn about. But it's only clothes. I don't have to tackle the card house in the corner or the wood carving mess on my desk. I don't have to sort through all the trash scattered around the garbage can. Just the clothes.

I can do that.

Once the clothes are sorted and folded, Meg stacks them neatly on the closet floor and tells me to put them away. When I'm done, she's picked up all the bits of trash and broken pencils and odds and ends that were scattered about on my floor. It's starting to feel like a room again.

We go through each of my previous projects. The wood carving kit is put back into its case while my half-done eagle gets tossed because it looks more like a camel. And just like that, I have my desk back.

The card house is disassembled, dominoes are put away, the items I'd set up to make my own Rube

Goldberg machine are dismantled and restored to their correct places. Then we grab the cleaning supplies. She vacuums while I dust and take care of cobwebs.

For the final act, we strip the bed and put the dirty shirts next to the overflowing hamper. As we remake the bed, I sigh. "Guess I have more laundry to do this weekend."

"Just make sure you put those clean clothes away and don't live out of the clothes basket." She grins, though, telling me she's teasing.

Once the comforter is on, I flop onto my back and she eases next to me. I ask quietly, "How'd you do that? I was so overwhelmed before you came in then you showed up and broke it down into smaller bits..." I trail off, turning toward her for an answer.

She won't meet my gaze, instead studying the comforter and tracing her finger along the seams.

"Meg?"

She lifts a shoulder. "We did a segment on ADHD in my General Mental Health class. It made me curious so I did some research. I, um, I wanted to know more, to see if I could help you with your new diagnosis. I'm sure it has to be overwhelming."

My heart warms as I picture her reading articles and watching videos. For me.

"There's a really cool YouTube channel where a teenage boy documents his journey with his ADHD diagnosis. He reminded me a lot of you." She pauses to shoot me a gentle smile. "David had a new hobby every week. He'd find some YouTube video about something and throw himself into collecting cards, tin punching, karate, you name it. Only for his interest to fizzle out in no time."

I try not to duck my head, knowing that she's not judging.

"His room was always a mess. So was his locker at school. Teachers would have to order him to clean it out because it'd start to smell from a forgotten orange or carton of milk. He had a hard time keeping track of his assignments. If they weren't in his bag, he had no idea where they were."

I can relate to that. I'd floundered in middle school, when the teachers wouldn't let me hand in my assignments right away. When I was forced to use their binder system with a folder for each class. I'd done much better in high school when I was allowed to manage myself. I had a whole system that relied on my backpack.

"One of the episodes is him cleaning out the spare room where he kept all his projects. He reacted like you did, shutting down in the middle of the job." She gestured to my now pristine room. "Task paralysis is a common symptom. ADHD can make it super difficult to start or finish tasks because they feel overwhelming as a whole."

I push myself upright, crossing my legs under me, needing to know more.

"The buddy system is one way to combat that. Even having someone in the room with you, to talk or sing or whatever, can help you feel not so alone and give you something else to focus on so the task isn't as daunting."

Which is why having Meg here helped so much. I blink at the realization.

"Breaking one big task into smaller parts helps too. Makes your brain think it's more manageable."

I remember how focusing only on the clothes gave me space to breathe.

"And eating right is definitely helpful."

I nod. "My therapist and I have talked about that, the role nutrition plays in our brain's performance. We've been mainly focused on grounding techniques when I feel out of control." I look around the room again. "Task paralysis hasn't come up."

"I could show you the YouTube channel, if you'd like? Maybe you can learn some other things you don't know yet."

Gratitude washes over me and I reach out to take her hand. "Thanks, Nutmeg. I appreciate this, more than you know."

She squeezes my hand, giving me a sweet smile. "Of course, Si. You're important to me, and I want to understand how your brain works, just as much as I want you to understand yourself."

I pull her in for a hug, needing the contact as my throat tightens at her words. I'm important to her. She cares about me. Knowing it and hearing it are two different things and I needed to hear that today.

The image of that perfect ring appears in my mind, and I grin before holding her even tighter. Meg rarely talks about her feelings. I'm taking this as the sign I was hoping for.

Tomorrow, I'm definitely going back to buy that ring.

* * * *

Meg

Silas works Saturday and Sunday while I spend my time studying for my finals. After his shift, Sunday evening, we take over the living room and put on *Gilmore Girls* while we snuggle. Between episodes, Silas checks his phone and immediately tenses. He pushes play on our show but seems distracted, not laughing like usual and his knee keeps bouncing.

I grab the remote and hit the pause button. "What's wrong?"

He jerks like I startled him.

"You're tense, your knee's bouncing." I nod at his phone. "Whatever you saw before we started this episode upset you. You don't have to tell me, but I'm here if you want to talk."

His shoulders slump. "Sorry. I…" He sighs, glancing at the blank screen of his phone where it rests on the arm of the couch. "I have a meeting with my advisor tomorrow, and I'm kind of dreading it."

I frown. No one likes meeting with their advisors. It's boring and mundane, but this sounds like more than that. Silas genuinely seems uncomfortable. I start to ask more but he sighs.

"She doesn't like that I keep changing majors."

My frown deepens. "You're allowed to change your mind. It's your life."

"I know…" But he still looks dejected.

"Silas, you can request to change advisors you know."

He nods. "Yeah." Several seconds pass before he sighs once more then sits up. "I'll be fine. It's just a meeting." When I hesitate to push play, he grins. "Seriously, I'm fine."

But his smile doesn't quite meet his eyes.

* * * *

I have a difficult time focusing at the start of my class, but I dial in enough to feel like I do decently. The second class is more difficult, knowing that Silas is going to his advisor's soon. I promised to have lunch with him afterward, hoping that would give him something to look forward to.

My phone shows no notifications when I finish with my test, so I decide to walk over and meet him. I push open one of the big double doors, unnerved by how quiet it always is in here. They have a waiting area at the end of the advisor's hall, so I make my way over there.

I have to walk by Brenda's office. Of course, I glance in the big window that takes up half the door, but I stop short when I see Silas.

His shoulders are hunched as if he's trying to make himself smaller. He clenches the hem of his shorts in one tight fist beneath the desk, and his leg jiggles so fast, I'm surprised his chair isn't moving across the floor. I frown, glancing at Brenda. Her mouth is tight as she sneers imperiously at Silas, then she begins speaking.

I only make out part of what she says, but it's not nice. Her tone is judging, and her next words set my teeth on edge.

"Again, Silas, I don't think you're making the right choice."

I even don't think before I grab the door handle, waltzing in before I know what I'm doing. I quickly put on my sweetest smile. "Sorry I'm late," I say.

Silas gapes at me.

Brenda's frown deepens. "Excuse me, young lady, we're in the middle—"

I hold up my hand. "I'm here as Silas' advocate."

"His what?" She blinks at me over her thick frames.

"His advocate. He obviously needs the support." I take the seat next to Silas, focusing on him. "Are you all right?"

He blinks, then sits up. I watch his strength return as he stares back at me. No longer cowering, no longer so tense.

He takes a deep breath, then his lips tip up. "I am now."

My heart breaks. If I hadn't come along... Anger swirls within me as I face Brenda once more. "Silas has recently been diagnosed with ADHD. Your job is to make sure he can meet his requirements for his major as well as be a safe space for him to talk to about any issues with his classes. You are obviously failing at the safe part of this job."

She gapes for a second then starts to protest, but I ignore her, standing and offering my hand to my boyfriend.

To him, I say, "We'll get you switched over to someone who understands what you're going through and supports you, instead of judging. Come on."

He gazes at me with awe in his eyes, then takes my hand and gets to his feet. We stride right out of the door, down the hall, and outside before he tugs me to a stop, facing him. He studies me for a long moment, then pulls me into a tender embrace. "I don't think I've ever loved anyone more than I love you at this moment. Thank you for standing up for me."

I hold him tight, running my hand over his curls. "I've always got your back, Si. I'm in your corner. And you deserve so much better than that."

He lets out a shaky breath, then grips me even tighter as he whispers, "Thank you."

I don't move until he does, knowing he needs this. When he does pull away, I make sure to lace my fingers through his. "Now, how about some lunch? I'm dying for a good burger."

His normal smile appears unhindered, like the sun moving from behind a cloud. "A burger sounds great."

* * * *

I get through my work shifts Tuesday and Wednesday, making sure to give Silas a bit of extra attention each evening. He seems to be doing well, though. I talked him into sending an email to the dean, who followed up with him personally and assured Silas that Brenda's behavior will not be tolerated. Silas has already been assigned a new advisor and is optimistic about his first meeting next week.

Thursday drags—our patient load lighter than usual—and I start talking to Bekah and Kaylie about plans for the weekend. Neither of them are doing anything.

I grab my phone, checking the weather. The August heat is in full swing and it's going to be a scorcher. The one place it's always cooler pops into my mind and out of my mouth. "Maybe we should go to the beach."

They both light up at the idea. Kaylie asks, "Just us or want to invite the guys too?"

Bekah protests at the idea of inviting the guys. She's going through a rough patch with Brad and Aiden, but she eventually gives in. The guys leap at the invitation and we make a plan.

The rest of the day flies by. Silas and I have dinner with Steven, Shawn and Leah after work, then I stay over in his room where I sleep soundly after we make love. Friday morning we can't keep our hands off each other, finally emerging from his room to get a late breakfast. Then we watch *Gilmore Girls* until it's time to get ready.

The sun is out in full force and not a cloud mars the deep blue sky when we pull into the state park on the shores of Lake Michigan. A gentle breeze helps cut the humidity as I step out of the car. It's a perfect day for the beach.

We're the first ones there and we walk along the expanse of light sand that extends from the parking lot to the massive lake. I grin as I study the horizon line where the water meets the sky. Lake Michigan is always moving but her waves are on the gentle side today, her waters a deep blue reflecting the pristine sky.

Silas grabs a sheet from our beach bag and we spread it out close to the water. I tuck the edges under the sand, weighing it down so it won't blow away. I've just sat down when I hear my name, turning to find Bekah with Aiden and Brad in tow.

I give them a big wave, popping to my feet again when I see Kaylie and Remy behind them. I'm so glad I stepped out of my comfort zone and became friends with these women. I greet them with hugs, feeling beyond excited that we all get to hang out today.

Silas grins at me, and I can't resist going over to hug him too.

"What was that for?" he asks.

I push onto my tiptoes to kiss his cheek. "You make me happy, Si. I'm so glad you didn't give up on me."

His smile turns tender. "Love you, Meg."

And I beam because the words warm me completely. He leans in to touch his lips to mine, then Remy calls his name. I give him a gentle shove, watching him run toward the guys. Aiden kicks a soccer ball at him and they're off, racing along the beach.

Bekah settles on the sheet, and I plop down next to her, facing the water. Kaylie unfolds her beach chair, setting it on the other side of Bekah. Kaylie and I share a grin, but Bekah sighs and digs her toes into the sand.

"What's wrong?" I ask.

She wrinkles her nose. "Aiden and Brad aren't getting along lately. They've been picking at each other over stupid things and not wanting to share. I don't want to give either of them up. They're both great. But I'm not sure this is gonna work out long term."

Kaylie tilts her head. "So would you choose one or break up with both of them?"

Bekah thinks for a long moment. "I think I'd have to break up with both of them. I don't know how I could choose one or the other without feeling terrible about it."

I can't imagine being in that scenario, trying to balance two guys and work out all our schedules. I'll stick with Silas. But I do feel bad for Bekah. They'd all seemed so happy together and to go into that thinking you're all on board only to find out they're not... Well, that just sucks.

"If you need anything," I offer, "let us know."

"Thanks. I'm glad I have you guys." She leans over to bump my arm with hers and smiles.

The rest of the day passes in a blur of laughter, squeals, sunshine and waves. We walk the shoreline, play soccer and Frisbee, talk and have a wonderful time. Aiden and Brad butt heads a few times, but otherwise everyone seems to be in a good place.

As sunset nears, the others head out, leaving me and Silas to watch the orange orb descend toward the water. I sit with my legs stretched in front of me, heels in the sand. Silas lies on his side, facing the water with his head on my thigh, his hand resting above my knee.

I run my fingers through his wind-blown curls, loving that I can play with his unruly hair whenever I want. "Today was fun."

He hums his agreement.

"You all set for school starting up again?"

"Almost. I'll see my new advisor next week and we'll finalize my schedule." He lets out a long sigh. "I hope I'm making the right move here, going back to law."

My heart twinges at his lack of confidence. "I think you are. You've really seemed to enjoy your internship. I haven't heard you complain at all about it."

One corner of his mouth tips up. "Yeah, it's been pretty cool actually."

"See? That's a good sign that you're going in the right direction."

He squeezes my leg. "Thanks, Nutmeg."

We stay quiet for a few beats, the lulling sound of the waves providing a perfect backdrop. "Have you been able to see much of your dad this summer?" I knew Silas had hoped to have lunch with him, maybe see him at the office, but I hadn't heard much one way or the other.

A frown crosses his face. "Yeah, I went out with him last week after I got done with my volunteer shift."

The terse words have me concerned, and I wait for him to tell me the rest of the story. "Did he say something?"

"He made a comment about me rushing into things, but it was more what he didn't say. I'm not like my brothers. Sebastian has always known what he wanted to do and he went for it. He's living his dream. Steven stumbled onto his path right away and stuck with it. Even Shawn took a year off and is still farther ahead than me."

Now I'm frowning. I rest my hand on Silas' shoulder, waiting for him to glance up before I say, "Just because you didn't take the same path as your brothers doesn't mean you're wrong or failing. You're allowed to try different things. You're allowed to take time to explore. I think you're smart for doing what you've done. Now you know what you really want, and you'll never wonder what if you'd done this or that. Not many people can say the same."

A true smile tips his lips. "I like that."

"And you know your dad loves you, Si. Maybe he had a bad day, maybe his words came out wrong. I've never known him to judge any of you guys, or compare you to one another. I'm sure you'll work this out sooner than later."

He relaxes a bit at that. "I hope so."

We turn our attention to the magnificent sunset. Several lines of clouds linger above the horizon, turning vibrant shades of gold, red and purple as the sun begins to disappear.

A beautiful show, just for the two of us. A perfect end to a wonderful day.

Chapter Twenty-One

Silas

My meeting with my new advisor goes well the following Friday and I walk out of that building with a smile for the first time in, well, years. I knew things weren't great with Brenda after seeing my therapist last time, but I'd still written it off. I hadn't realized how bad it was until Meg stepped in.

Why would I let someone treat me like that? My only answer is that it had been gradual, Brenda's behavior becoming a little harsher on each visit. Her impatience made me second-guess myself, and as my advisor, I believed she knew what she was talking about.

I was obviously the one with the problem.

The memory of that last meeting with Brenda replays in my head. When I reach the end with Meg stepping in, the warmth in my chest grows. She believes in me. That heady knowledge hits me again, and it feels like nothing else in the world matters. Even if everyone else sees me as a flaky, mind-changing slacker, Meg doesn't.

And that's good enough for me.

I get to spend the afternoon with her, having lunch together after her classes and hanging out. We go our separate ways to get ready for tonight.

A bunch of my teammates are getting together at a bar outside of town to watch a big soccer game. Remy and Kaylie are coming, so Meg decided to tag along to keep Kaylie company. I pull on my Brazil jersey, then attempt to tame my hair. It doesn't want to cooperate so I eventually give up and sit on my bed to wait for Meg.

Not long later, she knocks on my open door. "Hey, you ready?"

When I glance up, I'm mesmerized by the sight of her. Her strappy heels do amazing things to her calves and, paired with her barely there denim shorts, make her legs look a mile long. The shorts themselves draw my attention—the frayed edges resting on her creamy thighs, the dark material hugging her hips.

It's all I can do to remember to breathe when I notice the band of skin showing between the shorts and her fitted crop top. And her silky black hair is pulled back into a sleek ponytail.

"Damn, Meg," I groan. "How the hell am I supposed to focus on the game with you looking like that?"

She smirks and leans against the doorjamb. "Maybe I wanted to make sure I had some of your attention tonight, too."

I jump to my feet, eating up the distance between us in two long strides. I rake my gaze down her body once more, leaning closer until our faces are a breath apart. "I assure you, you have it."

Her lips part as I pull her in for a claiming kiss. She loops her arms around my neck, her hungry moan making my cock stand at attention. It's too much, and I drag her into my room, kicking the door shut before pressing her against it.

She tears her mouth away, staring at me with hungry eyes. "I guess we had two different things in mind when I asked if you were ready to go."

"With you, I'm always ready to go," I growl, a delicious idea popping into my head. "Turn around, Meg. I want to see this outfit from every angle."

She blinks twice, her chest rising as she sucks in a startled breath, and I wonder if she'll oblige me. A second later, she spins around, presenting me with another gorgeous view. I run a hand down her back, over her ass, along her frayed hem just below her ass cheeks. The shorts barely cover that delectable bottom, and she squirms when I dip my finger under the fabric to caress her.

"Silas!"

But I'm just getting started. "Let's see if you're right there with me."

Her heat calls me as I glide my finger inward, along the edge of her lacy panties, already drenched. My cock twitches in my shorts when she writhes, silently begging for more.

"Fuck yeah, Meg. So wet." I spin her around to face me again, then pull her in for another searing kiss before I ease her back until her ass hits the door. I drop to my knees with a gentle thud.

I nudge her legs apart, salivating at the sight of her smooth thighs spread for me. I run my finger along the edge of her panties once more, grinning when she bucks her hips. Craving my touch. I pull her stretchy denim shorts and soaked panties to one side in a swift motion. I'm starving, and not for food. We both groan when my tongue finds her molten center.

She grips my hair when I hum against her. "I love the way you taste." Then I devour her, proving my words.

I'm relentless in the pursuit of her pleasure, loving how she writhes when I lick her swollen clit. How she starts to pant when I alternate delving into her channel with sucking on the sensitive bud. My free hand is clamped onto her hip, holding her steady.

Her arousal grows, coating my nose and chin as I work to lap up every drop she gives me. She shudders, biting out my name as release finds her.

I stand, wiping my mouth before I ease my hands along the curve of her hips, along the swell of her stomach, then undo her fly. Her shorts and panties slip to the floor after I give them a gentle tug. She kicks them aside, but her heels stay on. A sight which turns me on even more.

"Turn around," I say, tapping her arm.

She hesitates, but obeys.

"You ready for me, Meg? You want this?" I need to hear her say it.

"Silas..." She wiggles her hips, swaying that gorgeous ass in front of me. "Please. I need you."

I grab her sides, pressing my jean-clad erection against her. Then I step back, shucking my shorts and briefs. Her ass calls me, and I can't resist nipping it lightly.

"Mmm, I could just eat you up."

"You just did," she teases, and for that, I nip her again.

I pop to my feet, grabbing a condom from the nightstand. I hold her again, leaning in to whisper, "Brace yourself."

Her palms smack against the door as I snap her hips back to meet my front. She gasps at the sharp motion, but presses into me so I know she's loving it. I line up my aching cock to nudge her entrance, and she moans my name. So ready for more.

She gasps as I thrust fully in, and I bite back a groan at the delicious sensation of her tight walls squeezing me. I don't give her time to adjust, don't have the restraint to take it slow.

I pound into her, anchoring myself with one hand. The love I feel for this woman consumes me as I find my rhythm. How quickly she turns me on, how helpless I am in the face of her beauty and sass. She meets me stroke for stroke, moving with me in perfect harmony. As she always does.

My release is barreling forward like a freight train, and I'll be damned if I shoot my load without her coming again. I keep up the pace, slipping my right hand around to play with her clit. I keep teasing and toying and pumping as she gasps and pants, leaning her forehead against the door.

If I let go, I wonder if her knees would hold her.

I'm not going to last much longer, so I pinch her clit and she shudders as she cries my name. She clenches me so tight, I see stars as I thrust fully into her and find my release. I pulse into her as she trembles in my arms.

After I ease out of her, she turns around and sags against the door, a gorgeous picture of satisfaction. I throw away the condom and clean up, then take a moment to drink her in—the languid grin on her face, the way her eyes are almost closed, how she doesn't even move.

I lean forward to kiss her cheek, and she leans into my touch as her lips part. I bend to rest my forehead against hers. "Love you, Meg."

"You're pretty amazing, Si. I'm lucky to have you."

I can see the adoration in those brown eyes, know she cares about me even if she can't say the words. And it's enough for now.

Her ponytail brushes my arm as she turns, and I give it a gentle tug as a picture pops into my head. "This could be a fun handle, if you're into that sort of thing."

"Silas," she breathes, staring at me with lowered lids. "I'm into whatever you want to give me."

My cock jumps again at the words and I pretend to glare at her before I reach for my shorts. "We're never going to leave if you keep talking like that."

She laughs and we both get dressed. She takes a few minutes to smooth her clothes, right her hair and make sure her makeup is still decent. I watch her intently, loving how she moves. Loving the quiet confidence she gives off.

Loving her.

* * * *

Meg

After Silas is out of work Saturday, we go for a hike in the dunes near Lake Michigan. It's a perfect evening, and we have a wonderful time. We're on the last hill, heading back to the car, when I misstep and twist my bad knee just wrong.

"You okay?" he asks, as I cling to his arm.

I grit my teeth, berating myself for being so careless. I was so close to making it without a mishap. "Yeah, I will be."

"You need help to the car?"

Gingerly, I put my weight on it, relieved it's holding me up. But the thought of walking down that last hill has me wincing.

At my reaction, Silas steps in front of me and bends, offering me his back again. I manage to hop up, feeling annoyed with myself for ruining our perfect day. When we get to the car, he lowers me to the pavement, then spins to face me.

I'm startled by the wide grin on his face. "What're you so happy about?"

"Having you on my back, your arms around my neck, gorgeous thighs wrapped around my waist? What's not to be happy about?"

My cheeks heat and my annoyance ebbs as I mutter, "I guess that's one way to look at it. I really didn't ruin our outing?"

"Nutmeg," he whispers, running his fingers along my jaw to cup my face. "Any time with you is well spent. I'll take whatever I can get."

I stare at this man as a wave of emotion crashes into me so hard, it makes my good knee wobble. I'm not ready to say the words yet, but what I feel for Silas is stronger than anything I've felt before. I'm no longer hovering on that edge with my heart on the line.

I've already fallen — hook, line and sinker.

The thought unnerves me, but I push it aside as I focus on getting into the car. The ache in my knee sets my teeth on edge, as does the thought of climbing those stairs at home. I don't want to deal with another flare-up and I wallow the entire way back.

"At least I can relax tomorrow." I hobble to the front door, holding onto Silas' arm.

"No watching *Gilmore Girls* without me," he chides, giving me an imperious glare that lightens my sour mood a bit.

"Who's going to stop me?" I tease.

He's working tomorrow, a double shift to cover for a friend. "I'll sic Leah on you."

I roll my eyes. "Oh, no. Not Leah." Though I do wonder what she's doing tomorrow. Maybe her and Callie want to hang out. It's been a minute since the three of us got together.

Silas carries me upstairs, right to the bathroom, where we have a quick shower. His full mast has me wishing my knee wasn't bugging me, but he ignores it as we take turns washing and hogging the spray. We look each other over, inspecting for any sand we missed, then we step out to towel off.

Wrapped in our towels, we go to our separate rooms. I pull on some comfy clothes then flop on my bed and sigh. My phone buzzes.

You staying in here or am I coming in there?

My knee throbs and I want to lie still for a while with it propped on pillows. I picture trying to do that with Silas and grimace just thinking about it.

Not sure I'm up for that.

A moment later, there's a tap on my door, and Silas peeks in after I give him the all-clear. "Everything okay?"

I nod from my position on the bed.

"Then why...?" He waves his phone as he steps into the room, a frown furrowing his brow.

"With my knee, I...um, need to lie still for a while." I say the last part in a rush.

Hurt crosses his face as he studies me, which is exactly what I wanted to avoid. It's not his fault or mine, but he always seems to take it personally when I'm not in the mood to cuddle or be intimate or stay with him. He sighs as his shoulders droop. I press my lips together, trying to think of what I can say to help.

To my surprise, he asks, "Can I talk to you about something?"

Confused and a bit concerned, I nod.

He grabs the wooden chair in front of my desk, pulls it closer to the bed, then straddles it, resting his arms on the back. "There are so many things I'm learning that go hand in hand with ADHD. One of the common companion issues is called rejection sensitivity dysphoria or RSD."

He glances at me, as if gauging my reaction, but that's not a term I'm familiar with. I tilt my head, waiting for an explanation.

"I've always been motivated by people liking me. That attention fuels me, like at karaoke the other week."

I smile, remembering how he'd been so wired after his song.

"But the reverse of that is true too. If I'm left out or shut down, or sometimes even when I'm told no, it feels like a personal rejection. Like whoever I'm with no longer likes me as a whole person. It drains all of my energy, and I feel...depressed, I guess?"

His words click in my brain as I think again of times in the past I told him no. How when we fought, he'd seem even more upset.

"My therapist has given me some grounding techniques and we've been slowly retraining my brain to not take things so personally. But it's still a work in progress."

"Silas." I sit up, reaching out to rest my hand on his forearm. "This is not me rejecting you on any level. I overdid it today and I'm hurting. I wish I could do more, but this is just because of a stupid, physical obstacle." I glare at my knee, then peek at Silas. "I still want you."

He nods, meeting my steady gaze with a tender one of his own. "I get it, Meg. I was fighting that rejection just now, even though I know you still care about me, and I wanted to explain. Please know that I'm just excited to spend time with you. I'd never leave your side if I had my way." His lips twist in a wry smile. "But that's just 'cause I love you so damn much."

We grin at each other for a long moment, and I'm relieved to find him happy and smiling once more.

He pops up off the chair, returns it to the desk, then snaps his fingers. "I'm gonna get you an ice pack. Need anything else while I'm downstairs?"

I shake my head at his enthusiasm, but I won't turn him down. "Ibuprofen? Maybe some chips and a Gatorade?"

"You got it." He bends down to kiss my cheek. "Back in a flash."

"Si?" I say, and he pauses at the door. "Thanks for explaining."

His grin grows impossibly wider as he dips his chin then disappears, and I settle once more on the bed, smiling at the ceiling like an idiot.

* * * *

The following week is fairly uneventful. Silas is my personal chariot on Sunday, before and after he goes to work. Monday, I'm able to hobble up the stairs by myself, and I baby my knee at work Tuesday through Thursday. Each night, Silas dotes on me, and I find myself falling for him more and more. Which I hadn't thought possible.

Friday, my knee is almost one hundred percent. I plan to meet Leah and Callie at Callie's apartment for lunch. She's finally finished setting it up and asked us over to show it off. I'm looking forward to seeing my friends again. I miss hanging out with them as much.

I pull into the parking lot of the apartment building and walk to the second floor. Leah is standing in the hall when I arrive and we say hi as Callie opens the door.

"It looks so nice," Leah marvels, walking around and taking everything in.

"It really does," I add.

Callie beams, guiding us through the full tour. We've seen it before, but now we get to admire the finishing touches. Sebastian has a breakfast nook area turned into an office with his desk arranged just so. I chuckle at his precise desk, a far cry from Silas'. Even after we cleaned, his still has haphazard books and broken pencils.

"And this is my dance studio," she says, pushing open the door to the second bedroom.

I gasp at the sunlight streaming into the beautiful room. A bar runs along the back wall beneath the big picture window. A few shelves rest below a TV, holding DVDs, shoes and some weights. A mat sits in one corner, and I wonder if she does yoga too.

We finish the tour and head back to the dining table off the kitchen, where we each pull out the food we brought. As they get their food, I study a small shelf above the sink next to the window. A delicate butterfly sculpture sits in the middle of the shelf, made out of impossibly thin, iridescent metal. The details are exquisite.

Flanking the butterfly are two rather plain-looking rocks. I frown at the juxtaposition of their simpleness with the sculpture's ornate craftsmanship, then glance at Callie, only to find her grinning at me.

She walks over and picks up the brown one with the lacy pattern. "Sebastian's favorite animal is a penguin, and they mate for life. When they find their mate, they give each other a rock." She offers me the stone. "This is a Petoskey stone Sebastian found on Mackinac Island. He gave it to me when I gave him that one."

I glance at the other stone, loving the story, loving the significance of these two plain, ordinary rocks. "That's so sweet." I gently put the stone back, my mind wandering to Silas and our future.

As I make my plate of food, I try to picture it. Not just the fantasy of a perfect wedding like I've imagined so many times before but our actual future. Both of us graduating, having our careers, waking up each day with each other and going to bed each night in his embrace.

The panic and doubts I expect to rush in never come. Instead, a sense of rightness settles over me and I feel like I'm glimpsing the path I should be on. I smile to myself as I sit down.

Leah asks Callie, "How are things with you and Sebastian?"

"I've never felt more like I'm where I'm supposed to be," Callie gushes, a huge grin on her face.

She goes on about how easy it's been to adjust to living with Sebastian. How considerate he is, and so supportive of her teaching dance. Her classes have expanded so she teaches almost every afternoon, though she'll have to pull back a little when the next semester starts.

"I'm so happy for you," Lee says.

"Me too." I never would have pictured Sebastian settling down first, but I'm so glad that this is working for them. I turn to Lee, smirking. "And how are things with you and Shawn?"

She gives me a bright smile. "You moving upstairs has been the best thing for us. We barely use the extra room. I love having him in my space all the time."

Her blue eyes sparkle and peace washes over me. I'm thrilled to see her so content, back to her normal self, complete with spark. I want nothing less for my best friend.

"How about you, Meg?" Lee asks and Callie nods eagerly. Lee lifts a pig in a blanket from the tray before tilting her head. "How are things with you and Silas?"

"Great," I tell them honestly. "He told me he loves me."

They both beam at that, and I launch into the story of the pool party.

"Have you said it back yet?" Lee studies me, knowing me too well.

I stare at the table. "No. I'm just not sure…" Saying those three words to him feels like the last jump, the biggest one of all. Once I tell him I love him, there's no going back. We're at such a good place right now, and I don't want to change a thing.

"Do you, though? Do you love him?" Leah presses.

I lift a shoulder. "I care about him a lot and we've been able to have some really good talks this time around. I feel like we're in a lot better place than last time. But love? That's a big step." *Especially for me.*

Lee touches my arm. "I know it is, Meg. And I'm not trying to push you. I just want to make sure you're being honest with him and yourself, that you're not holding back out of fear."

A ripple of tension rolls through me as I question myself. Is that what's happening? I thought I'd been making such great progress, but maybe I'm still keeping that last wall up. Just in case.

The idea leaves a sour taste in my mouth, and I shove the thoughts aside, not ready to examine them any closer right now. "Thanks, Lee. I'll keep that in mind." Then I change the subject. "What classes are you all taking this semester?"

Callie is in her third year at SMU, studying genetics, while Leah is starting her Master's in anthropology this year. We chatter about what we're looking forward to, what we're worried about, and how we're going to juggle everything else in our lives.

I leave feeling content and in a good spot, ignoring the pinprick of doubt that Lee's words opened in me. *I'm fine. Silas and I are more than fine.*

We're doing great.

Chapter Twenty-Two

Silas

September barrels in, starting with Labor Day on Monday. Everyone is going to my parents' house as usual. Dad never misses a chance to grill, and it still feels like August weather-wise, so the pool will be open. Meg and I leave a little early because I'm hoping to talk to Dad.

I've been avoiding him since that day at the jewelry shop. We've said hi in passing at work, but we haven't actually *talked*. He's not much of a texter, or even one to chat on the phone.

The way he judged me really hurt. It also opened my eyes to how the rest of the world sees me—flaky, indecisive, and perfectly happy to keep it casual. No wonder it took Meg plenty of time to trust me again. I'm determined, though, to show her and everyone else that I'm in this for the long haul.

I know what I want, and I'm not changing my mind. I have the ring to prove it, sitting safely at home in my drawer.

We're the first ones at my parents' house. When we get out of the car, Meg takes my hand with a reassuring squeeze. Mom's inside cooking, and Meg sets down the fruit bowl we brought. I give Mom a quick hug, then leave them to chat while I step out onto the patio to talk to Dad. He smiles at me as I shut the sliding door.

"Hey, son." A hint of wariness hangs in the words.

"Hey, Dad." I shove my hands in my pockets. "How are you?"

"Good. You? Been working hard, I know. Keep seeing your name on files at meetings. You've been doing a great job, everyone is saying so."

"Thanks." The praise has me smiling and feeling more at ease. "Um, about the other day..."

He doesn't let me find my words, just puts down his scraper and crosses over to rest his hands on my shoulders. "Silas, I'm sorry about that. It took me by surprise, that's all, but I know you've got a good head on your shoulders. You've always loved fast and hard, giving your all. If Meg is it for you, then congratulations. She's a fine woman."

His outright acceptance has me stunned, and I let him pull me in for a hug. "Thanks, Dad. That means a lot."

He smacks my back then steps away. "So how are things going with your ADHD diagnosis?"

I grin at the question, loving that he cares. "Pretty good. I'm doing some cognitive therapy to retrain my brain away from negative patterns."

He opens the grill to flip the burgers. "I meant to tell you, I think Jason went through something like this a couple years ago. Pretty sure he was diagnosed with ADHD too."

Uncle Jason? I run through some of the interactions we've had with him at family parties. I always felt a kinship with him, the overly loud, affectionate uncle who smiled constantly. He has a fun vibe that puts people at ease.

"You do remind me of him."

I chuckle at that.

"Well, if you need anything, we're here."

I can only nod, overwhelmed by his love and support. I jerk my thumb toward the slider. "I'm just…"

He waves me off, and I step inside. Meg and Mom pause their conversation as Meg watches me, waiting. When I smile, her shoulders drop and she smiles back.

"Need any help, Mom?"

She shakes her head. "But you can stay here and tell me all about finally landing this young lady. Last I knew, you were at each other's throats and now here you are, together." She arches an eyebrow. "I need details, young man."

So I pull up a chair and tell her the story, with Meg's help. When the others trickle in, she shoos us outside to make room.

I grab a beer, Meg gets a seltzer and we sit on the edge of the pool, dangling our bare feet in the tepid water. I press my cold can to the side of my face. The humidity is killer today. We'll all be sweating buckets before we know it.

"How'd it go with your dad?" she asks, cracking open her seltzer.

"We're good. He offered to help if I needed anything with the ADHD thing, too."

"Of course he did." She gives me a wistful smile. "They love you so much. You're very lucky."

I am, and I don't take it for granted. "Speaking of parents," I say, "when are you going to tell your mom?"

I know it's a tense subject for her, one she doesn't talk about often. She rarely visits, and most of what I know, I've learned from Leah. But I'd like to meet the rest of her family as her boyfriend.

Meg's gaze drops as she lifts a shoulder. "Maybe after we start the next semester. She's going to want to have us over for dinner and..." She sighs. "That's always work."

I lean over to bump her shoulder. "Well, I'm happy to go with you, whenever you're ready. You don't have to go alone."

Her smile is tight, but it's there. "Thanks, Si."

I glance at my brothers and friends gathering on the patio. Dad holds court at the grill, leaning against the railing that stretches from the house to protect Mom's flowers. Steven steps outside with a woman I don't recognize.

"Who's that with Steven?"

Meg raises her hand to shield her eyes, squinting in that direction. "Did he bring a date?"

We both stare at each other in shock, then hurry to join the crowd.

"Okay," Steven says loudly, bobbing his hands to quiet us down. "Everyone, this is Anastasia. Anastasia, this is everyone."

The woman stays unruffled, appearing almost bored. Her tawny skin stands out against her pale-pink top. Her thick black hair is piled on top of her head in a bun of intricate braids, and when she stretches out her hand to shake Leah's, I notice her long, perfectly done nails.

Meg leans over. "That takes skill, having nails that length. I wouldn't be able to function."

I nod my agreement as we wait our turn to introduce ourselves. She seems nice enough, except her voice has a piercing pitch to it that grates on me. As we move off the patio, I hear Steven ask if she wants to play volleyball.

"With these?" she scoffs, glancing at her nails. Then she looks around and asks in a voice filled with disdain, "Is this all the people who are coming? I thought you said this was going to be a party."

We do get a game going, me and Meg against Shawn and Leah, and it's a relief to get away from Anastasia's shrill tone. Then we switch it up to play guys against girls. After our third game, I'm more than ready to go chill in the pool.

Callie and Sebastian are sitting with Steven and Anastasia in lounge chairs. Callie's smile has a desperate edge to it as we approach. "What are you guys doing?"

"I'm changing into my suit then jumping in." I point to the deep end.

She lights up. "That sounds great." Sebastian joins her as she stands.

Steven turns to Anastasia. "Up for a swim?"

She sighs, and I don't stay to hear her reply. We all head to our rooms to change, and Meg darts out to use the bathroom. I almost run into Steven when I emerge from my room, but his date isn't anywhere in sight.

"Anastasia coming?"

He shakes his head, looking dejected. His mouth is tight, shoulders drooped, hands in pockets. "She left."

"What?"

He nods. "Yep. Said this wasn't her scene, ordered an Uber, and I walked her to it."

I clap a hand on his shoulder. "I'm sorry." I hesitate to ask, but curiosity wells in me. "What'd you see in her anyway?"

Surprised laughter spills from him and he finally smiles. "I don't know, Silas. Honestly, I'm tired of being alone at these things and she flirted with me so I leaped at the chance."

"Steven…"

He waves me away. "I'm happy for you guys, but it's hard being the only one not paired up. Plus, I'm the oldest. I should be leading the way, and here I am straggling so far behind…" He trails off with a sigh.

"I'm sorry," I say again. "But there's no rush, you know? You'll find her." Meg's words from the beach echo to me, that we all have our own path. I guess it's true in more than our careers.

"Thanks, man. I hope so."

I head down the hallway, glancing back to watch him duck into his room. I do wish he'd find someone, sooner rather than later. It'd be nice to see him truly happy again.

Meg emerges from the bathroom, and I take a minute to drink in the sight of her. Her bright green two piece hugs her curves in the most appealing way. I glance over at Steven's closed door and wish that he could find even a sliver of the joy that I feel being with Meg.

I reach out my hand, grinning when she takes it. I walk out of the door with her at my side, marveling at how lucky I truly am.

* * * *

School starts the next morning, and I have classes on Tuesday, Thursday and Friday. I'm still going to intern at the office on my off days as well as some afternoons.

Meg is taking two courses again this semester. She had to adjust her work schedule because the classes meet

Monday, Wednesday and Friday mornings. I admire her tenacity, juggling classes, homework and work.

We make it through the week, and I take her out to lunch Friday after our classes are over. I'm dying to go out tonight, to blow off some steam and celebrate making it through our first week of school.

"What do you think about karaoke tonight? Maybe some of the others want to come."

Her mouth twitches before she laughs. "Sorry, was trying to picture Sebastian at karaoke."

I can't help chuckling, but I don't dismiss the idea. It seems like anything is possible now that he has Callie.

"Yeah, I'd love to. The High Five again?"

We make a plan while we eat and text everyone the details. After we walk home, we spend the afternoon on homework. By the time I need to get ready, I'm so antsy, I can't stand still. I blast music while I'm changing, dancing around the room as I pull on clothes and work on my hair. I'm so ready for this.

Steven, Shawn and Leah meet us in the living room. Sebastian declined since Callie is teaching a dance class tonight. The five of us cram into Steven's SUV, the only one big enough to hold all of us, but he loves to drive and he's happy to be DD.

The bouncer, Burt, grins at me and Meg, evidently remembering us from last time, and waves us in. I don't see any sign of Gina or Liam as our server, Kane, leads us to a round table not far from the karaoke stage.

Shawn bobs along with the Aerosmith song the current singer is nailing. We put in food and drink orders then everyone looks at me.

I grin. "Okay, I'm going." To my surprise, Steven walks with me. I lean in to say, "You singing or just browsing?"

He lifts a shoulder. "Not sure yet."

We flip through the songs together and I settle on Justin Timberlake's *Can't Stop the Feeling!*. Steven puts one in too, but won't tell me what it is. Then we go back to our seats to wait our turn.

Leah raises her glass and says, "Cheers." We all clink our glasses together, then take a sip. She glances around, frowning. "Why don't we come here more?"

"They've got good food, too," I tell her, Meg and Steven nodding their agreement.

My turn to sing comes before our food arrives, and I hop on stage, feeling at home. Energy buzzes in the air, all good, easy vibes that I breathe in like a wine connoisseur inhaling the bouquet from a vintage bottle.

The moment the song starts, I lose myself in that energy, hyping up the crowd, getting them to sing along. By the time I'm done, I'm out of breath, but the cheers are deafening and my cheeks hurt from how wide my smile is.

I hand the mic to Steven who pats my back, then takes the stage. I hurry to my seat, slinging my arm over Meg's shoulders as she tells me what a good job I did.

The familiar notes of Bob Seger's *Turn the Page* float through the air. Dad listened to him all the time while we were growing up, especially in the car. I've heard Steven sing plenty, but never seen him do it in front of a crowd. He nails the slower song and returns to the table amidst cheers and catcalls.

Although most of the catcalls are from Shawn.

I shake my head at my brothers. Steven comes up, head-locking Shawn and rubbing his knuckles in his hair before sitting down. Right before the food comes.

The wings I ordered are the perfect mix of spicy and sweet. I make a mess and Meg refuses to kiss me when I try to lean in, but my heart is full as the night moves on. And I know I'm right where I belong.

* * * *

Saturday morning, I wake to Meg's phone ringing. She looks at it and sighs, then answers it.

"Hey, Mom."

I hate how instantly tense she is. She paces near the window in nothing but a tank top and sleek panties that hug her curves. I'm getting hard just watching her, though I know now's not the time.

After nodding and murmuring, she says, "Hang on, I'll ask." Then she covers the phone and turns to me. "Dinner at Mom's tonight?"

I rack my brain but can't think of any other plans. "Sure."

She goes back to the conversation, wrapping it up a few moments later. Setting the phone down, she stares out of the window, and I hate the way her lips press together. The rigid line of her shoulders and her stiff movements scream how uncomfortable she is.

I climb out of bed and wrap my arms around her from behind. "What's so bad about this, Meg?"

"Well, I texted Mom on Monday that I have a boyfriend, and she's just now getting back to me. I was beginning to think she didn't care."

Indignation zings through me.

A lengthy sigh leaves her as she leans against my torso and rests a hand on my forearm. "My family isn't like yours, Silas. Dinner isn't going to be, well, fun. George is basically a lump on the couch, more entranced by the TV than his family. My half-sisters run around screaming at each other most of the time and Mom…" She pauses to take a deep breath. "Mom says she's happy but she just looks tired."

I rub her arm, wishing I could do more for her.

"I keep thinking one day we'll reconnect. Maybe when my half-sisters are grown up and she has more time and energy." She lifts a shoulder. "I don't know. I guess I should be grateful she invited us over at all."

"I'm sorry," I whisper. I can't imagine a family like that, not involved or supporting one another.

She turns in my embrace and smiles, but her eyes still hold a weight that makes my stomach sink. "It's okay. We don't have to be there until this evening, so we've got all day. Maybe we can think of something to do." Her voice drops for the last part and she runs her hands down my bare chest.

"Hmm. I had thought about going to the library for a book I need," I tease. At her indignant glare, I chuckle. "Or is that not what you had in mind?"

I kiss her pouty lips then tug her back to bed and show her exactly how much she means to me.

Chapter Twenty-Three

Meg

Dinner with Mom and George hangs over me all day like a black cloud, though I do my best to ignore it. When it's time to get ready, I settle on a dark pair of jean shorts that don't show too much leg and a higher-necked top. My stepdad, George, is a stickler for modesty in women and I'd rather avoid his snarky comments. This is going to be stressful enough.

Silas wears an open button-down over a white T-shirt, paired with khaki shorts. His curls are gelled, somewhat tamed, and his grin is infectious as he takes my hand to kiss it. "Hey, gorgeous, all set?"

I lace my fingers through his, thankful for his easy manner. "Yep. Let's get this over with."

The ride to Mom's house passes quickly with Silas blasting the radio and singing along without a care in the world. I know he's doing it for me, and I appreciate it. The ball of tension in my gut is forgotten until we pull into the driveway, then my stomach turns to knots again.

Once upon a time, the house felt like home. Before Dad left. Before I knew Mom wanted her next man more than she wanted to take care of me. Now the dilapidated place has chipped paint, an overgrown lawn, and a dangling shutter, a perfect metaphor for my relationship with Mom.

After knocking on the door, I stand awkwardly waiting. We can hear Mom yell for the kids to be quiet and George to turn down the TV. Silas gives me a sympathetic look and rubs my back. I lean into him for a brief moment, then move away, not wanting to be entwined when Mom meets him.

The door swings open and there stands Mom. Her wrinkles are more pronounced than last time I saw her, her thin hair circling her in a frizzy halo. Even her "Come in" is frazzled.

"Hey, Mom." I ignore her lack of greeting and kiss her cheek.

She pats my arm, then I hold up the bottle of wine we brought. Her eyes light up and without so much as a thank-you, she rushes off to the kitchen. I bite back my sigh, taking Silas to the living room where I know I'll find George.

There he sits in the ragged blue recliner, his feet kicked out in front of him. His left sock has a hole in the heel, matching the others that dot his dingy wifebeater. If I showed that much skin, it'd be a crime.

"Hi, George."

He grunts, not looking away from the TV.

"This is my boyfriend, Silas."

Still no reaction. The girls come tearing through the space. The older one holds a baby doll above her head, glancing over her shoulder as the younger one wails on her heels.

"Georgina, Naomi, keep it down. I'm trying to watch the game." His brusque order holds no room for disobeying and they leave as quickly as they came.

Silas presses his lips together, staring at me as if wondering what to do next. At least he likes sports.

I nod to the couch. "Have a seat. I'll see if Mom needs any help."

He does, gingerly, and I hurry to the kitchen where I find Mom struggling with the corkscrew. I offer to take over, wishing I could be more important than a glass of wine. She leans against the counter, watching me.

"I introduced Silas to George."

She frowns. "Silas…why do I know that name?"

"Silas Wrighting, Mom."

Understanding dawns on her face, but not happiness or any semblance of joy. "I knew I recognized him. Better snap him up quick before he hops to someone else."

The cork pops free and it's my turn to frown. "What do you mean?"

She laughs, unfeeling and cold. "I used to date Trey back in high school. Thought he was 'the one' until I found out there's no such thing," she adds bitterly.

"I didn't know that." *And why would I?* We rarely talk about anything except my half-sisters. When it comes to the past, she's a closed book — has been since Dad left. Anything from before her time with George just…ceased to exist, like she buried it, never to be dug up again.

"He dumped me for someone else. I was just another in the long line of broken hearts he left behind before settling on Judy." She scowls. "Still don't know how *she* landed him."

A lead ball settles in the pit of my stomach. That all sounds achingly close to Silas' past, and my hand shakes as I pour the wine. Doubt weighs me down, even as I tell myself that I could be Silas' Judy.

But the sentiment feels lacking.

"Mark my words, Meg. All men are the same." Her face hardens, and I know she's thinking about my dad, even if she doesn't call him by name. "That boy is all cuddles and love for now, but one of these days he'll trade you in for a newer model. Then all you'll have left is a cold, empty side of the bed and a mind full of memories to keep you warm."

The bleak image has bile rising in my throat—me upstairs in the house I share with the Wrightings, but no longer having Silas in my bed. Back to the tense relationship we had before. But I push it away, knowing Mom is speaking from her own bitterness. Silas wouldn't do that to me.

Would he?

Needing something else to focus on, I quickly ask the first question that comes to mind. "Why even bother getting married then?"

Her smile has a cold edge to it. "I had to prove to your father that he made a mistake when he left me. George wanted me, and I deserved to be taken care of. Your father left me with nothing, Meg. Nothing."

"What about me?" The desperate words spill from my lips before I can stop them. *Am I really nothing?*

"Oh, Meg…" She trails off, reaching out to touch my shoulder but stopping just short of contact. Her gaze meets mine in a searching stare tinged with longing. "You look just like him, you know. You have his eyes."

For one brief moment, I glimpse the well of pain she still holds within her, and sympathy swells in me. Maybe this is it. Maybe we can talk about how my father hurt her when he left, how it all hurt me. We can connect and heal and —

"You were always such a tough cookie. So independent and resilient. I always admired that about you. It's why I knew you'd be okay, knew you could handle me dropping you off with Leah when it hurt too much to look at you."

The words sever any hope and empathy blooming in me, and they go even deeper to stab my aching heart. My own mother couldn't stand seeing me. I blink in the face of the realization, too stunned and hurt to move.

Naomi calls from the other room, "Mommy!"

Mom sighs. "Duty calls," she says before staring behind me at the stove. "You don't mind finishing the spaghetti, do you? Holler when it's ready." Without waiting for a response, she spins on her heel, saying, "I'm coming, sweetie," with a smile in her voice.

I stare after her, the familiar sight of her back as she leaves digging the wound even deeper. A hollow feeling settles over me, and I begin working on autopilot as my brain fills with static. I test a noodle to find it's done then dump the contents of the pot into a colander, watching the water drain through the holes and feeling my own energy ebb from me.

When I carry the pot to the table, I see the table isn't set either, so I return to the kitchen for plates and silverware. The oven timer buzzes, startling me from my daze. I feel fragile as I put my hand over my racing heart. I shut off the oven, wondering how I'll make it through dinner.

As I finish up, I work on rebuilding the familiar walls within me, needing to protect the bleeding mass of my shredded heart. I take the garlic bread to the table then somehow form the words to call everyone in.

Mom appears, hand in hand with both girls flanking her and the hot sting of unshed tears pricks the backs of my eyes. Silas and George walk in, having a real conversation as they sit down at one end of the table.

I take my place next to Silas, and he spares me a glance and a smile. He shifts toward me, but I give my head the most minuscule shake. Any touch right now would be too much.

A single graze might shatter me.

The free-for-all with the food is a perfect distraction from his concerning gaze. He and George keep talking in earnest about the Lions' chances at the Super Bowl this season while Mom dotes on Georgina and Naomi. I sit in silence, pushing my food around my plate and wondering what I did wrong. Why I can't be loved like everyone else. Why I'm not good enough for my mom or stepdad. Or my dad, for that matter.

I risk a glance at Silas, annoyed that even he is getting more attention from George than I ever did. Of course my boyfriend fits right in. Everyone loves him and they always have.

The hollow ache pulses within me and I feel more alone than I have in a long, long time.

When dinner is over, Silas tries to give me a hug, but I duck away from his touch. He frowns, and I shake my head. I know he wants to help, but if I let him hold me, I might explode into a million pieces and never be whole again. I can't break in front of Mom, can't let her know how her words affected me.

Because I couldn't bear it if she didn't care.

Somehow I keep it together through clean-up, then I make our excuses for heading out.

"You okay?" Silas asks when we get outside.

I study him for a long moment. Why would he choose me when my own mother doesn't want me? When my dad walked out on me without a second thought? Mom's words echo in my head as she compared him to Trey. I'll probably be just another in the line of broken hearts Silas leaves in his wake.

Forcing a smile, I shove all the doubts down and say, "Yep. Just fine." When he stares at me for an extra beat, I wave him off. "I warned you, visiting my mom isn't easy. I'll be my usual self in no time."

He doesn't seem convinced, but he also doesn't push as we walk to the car in silence. I'm grateful for the space because I need time to recover.

But the silence follows me home and the gap between us widens even more. I don't have the energy to attempt to close it, can only watch as Silas moves farther away. At what point will my baggage become too much and he'll stop understanding?

When we walk upstairs, I plead having a headache. Silas understands, granting me some much-needed alone time to work through the endless tide of doubts threatening to swallow me.

* * * *

Silas

Meg hasn't been herself since our dinner with her mom and George. I don't know what her mom said to her, but it feels like a canyon stretches between us. All the closeness we've gained is — *poof* — gone.

She seems to need her space, so I'm trying to give it to her, even though every fiber of my being screams that we need to fix this. It feels so close to what happened last time, the not talking. But I don't want to push either. I'm trying to trust that she's working through whatever happened and believe she'll come to me when she's ready.

Monday I get through my classes and walk home in the rain. I get in the door, my mood as heavy as the gray clouds, but then I see Meg, curled up on the couch. Just the sight of my gorgeous girlfriend lifts my spirits.

When she smiles at me? The tension drains away.

"Hey," I say, wiping my face on my damp sleeve.

"Hey." She shuts her book and rests her arm on the back of the couch. "You still have a game today?"

"They haven't called it off yet." I'm not sure if I'm wishing for a thunderstorm so it'll be canceled or if I want to go play in the rain. I'm torn. "Either way, I've got some time." The pause drags out between us, then I take that leap and suggest, "Maybe we could watch a *Gilmore Girls*?"

She nods, brushing a piece of hair back behind her ear.

My smile is huge as I stare at her. "Great. Just let me go change."

A few minutes later, I'm in dry clothes and tromp back downstairs where I grab a water then plop next to Meg on the couch. She has the show all queued up, and I wish we could talk first but she just pushes play.

I still count it a win when she settles close enough that our shoulders touch — more physical contact than we've had in the past two days. We watch two shows, then it's time to get ready for my game. We win, but barely, and I come back home cold and exhausted only to find Meg's door already shut.

I don't have the energy to try to change that tonight, so I grab clean, dry clothes then trudge down the hall to take a shower.

At least I'll be warm again.

* * * *

The next morning, I'm looking at the calendar while I lounge in bed and I see Meg's birthday is this weekend, September fourteenth. I can't believe I didn't realize it earlier or that Lee didn't say anything, but we've both been caught up in our new semester. Not to mention our respective relationships.

My mind begins to race with ideas. Maybe a surprise party will cheer Meg up, and close the gap between us? Two birds, and all that. I bet we can pull it off.

I hurry to text Leah. Meg always works late Tuesday night so this would be the perfect evening to get planning. We agree to meet downstairs at six, then we'll have a brainstorming session over dinner.

I can't wait.

Lee and I walk to Eat at Joe's for dinner, throwing out ideas on the way We decide we'd rather not have a huge party. Just my brothers, our girls, her friends from work, and Remy since he's still dating Kaylie. Bekah dropped Aiden and Brad, so I won't be inviting them. No need to make things awkward.

After we order, Lee takes out a to-do list and slides it toward me. "I think next we need to decide on cake and if there's a theme."

When our food comes, we've decided on chocolate cake — Meg's favorite. Lee suggested a bakery down the road and offered to pick it up. She'll call it in tomorrow, but first we need to agree what should be written on the top.

"How about 'Happy Birthday, Meg'?" I suggest, once I've finished chewing a bite of my burger.

Lee's eyelids lower halfway in a dry stare. "Original, Silas. Well done."

"C'mon, we don't need unique. That's simple and easy." I lift a shoulder. "We could have them do a white frosting with sprinkles around the edges. You know how Meg likes her colors."

"Sprinkles are your theme?"

"Either that or sharks." I grin as Leah tilts her head and a slow smile spreads over her face.

"Sharks — that's perfect."

The more I think about it, the more I agree. We spend the rest of the dinner searching for decorations and party supplies in that theme. I'm impressed with how much is available, and of course, we go all out.

We're still grinning about our finds as we walk along the sidewalk toward home.

Meg parks as we reach the driveway. "What are you two up to?" she asks with a smile as she hops out of her car.

Panic flares in me, and I glance at Lee who is just as wide-eyed. "Um," I stall, cursing myself for not having a pre-planned excuse. "We're coming back from dinner."

Surprise crosses Meg's face. "Just the two of you?"

Lee nods. "Yep. I needed his opinion on something. You know, a guy's perspective."

Meg glances at me, doubt flashing in her eyes when I nod but say nothing else. "Okay." She draws out the word, her skepticism obvious. "Well, I'm gonna go decompress. It was a long shift."

We walk inside, Lee's mouth tight as she looks between us. Meg rushes away without another word, and I sigh.

"What was that about?" Lee asks.

"Has Meg talked to you at all about dinner at her mom's?" When she shakes her head, I don't know if I feel better or worse.

Meg needs to talk to someone, that much is clear. I quickly explain what I know, Lee's smile nowhere in sight by the time I finish.

"I'm sorry, Silas." She gives me a hug and I squeeze her back, appreciating the comfort. "It'll work out, though. She probably just needs some space."

"I hope so." But the words feel hollow.

I go upstairs, wondering what more I can do. I'm not going to ruin the surprise party but I wonder what's going on in Meg's head. I know she knows better than to think there's anything more than friendship between me and Lee.

When I tap on Meg's closed door, hope bubbles within me at her quiet, "Come in."

I walk in to find her perched on her bed. I cross over to lean on the wall near her, giving her a tender smile. "How are you? How was your day?" Maybe we can end on a good note.

"Long," she says, the word clipped. "Yours?"

"Pretty good. Lee and I ate at Joe's. My burger was delicious."

She arches an eyebrow, staring at me pointedly as if waiting for more. "What'd you guys talk about?"

I glance at the floor. "Like Lee said, she needed a guy's perspective—"

"So it wasn't about me?"

My gaze snaps up to meet hers before I can think twice. I hate the doubt in her eyes, hate that I can't immediately say no. I'm not a good liar and she'd see right through it. But the silence doesn't help.

"That's what I thought." She gives me a tight smile. "Hope you two figured everything out. I need to get to bed."

"Meg, wait…"

She stands, walks to the door, and holds the edge. "Night."

I stare at her for a long moment as my shoulders slump and the distance spans between us. Then I trudge into the hallway. My woeful "Night" is cut off by her shutting the door between us.

Again.

Chapter Twenty-Four

Silas

Dad, Steven, and I meet for dinner Thursday evening. We invited the others but Shawn's working a late shift at the gym and Sebastian has a big project at his greenhouse lab that he can't get away from. The local pizza joint has a dinner buffet, so we head there for pizza, salad and soup.

Once we've loaded our plates, we sit back down at our booth and Steven cocks his head. "What gives, Silas? You've been moping around all week."

Dad frowns. "Everything okay with Meg?"

The extra weight in his question reminds me of the ring sitting safely in my drawer, and I feel further from proposing than ever. Things between us have been beyond strained and I have no idea how to fill the gap.

"I don't know," I admit, then explain about dinner at her mom's, how she needed space after. "Her birthday is this weekend, so Lee and I went out to dinner to plan a surprise for her."

Steven knows about the party since he's been invited, but we haven't had a chance to catch up about everything else. He listens intently, frowning the whole time. When I get to our short talk in her room, he holds up his hand. "You didn't say anything when she asked what you and Lee talked about?"

I duck my head. "I froze."

"Silas, she probably thinks you two went out to talk about her," Dad says gently.

"I know, but I don't know what to say without giving away the party." I lift a shoulder. "And I'm so bad at lying."

They both nod.

"At least it's only a couple days away." A sigh escapes me. "I'm hoping that once the party is here, she'll see how much she means to me."

"What are you getting her?" Steven asks.

"Not sure yet." A burst of panic zips through me at how little time I have to figure this out. Maybe I'll go shopping tomorrow after class. "I've had a few ideas, but nothing has really stood out, you know?" Again the image of the ring in my dresser flashes in my mind, but I know we're not there yet.

I want to do something big, pull out all the stops. My grandparents give us a ridiculous amount of money for holidays and birthdays each year. Since my coffee shop job supplements most of my daily spending, I save that money for fun things.

Like spoiling my girlfriend in the best way I can.

Dad strokes his chin thoughtfully. "What about taking her out someplace really nice, just the two of you? It sounds like you both could use some quality time together, and what better way to show you care about a woman than planning a whole evening for her?"

The thought takes root as I imagine us getting dressed up, having a quiet dinner filled with meaningful conversation. Maybe some dancing afterward. Then coming home and making love slowly before spending the night in each other's arms. I ache at the image, missing the feel of Meg in my embrace.

"You should go to Club 42," Steven suggests.

My eyebrows shoot up at the name. The club is upscale and exclusive, but also known for booking out weeks in advance. It would be perfect, though, just the thing to show Meg how special she is. "Maybe," I say, "if I can get a reservation sometime soon."

"Son, let me take care of that." Dad grins. "Just let me know when you want to go."

I smile back at Dad, having forgotten that he has influential friends and some pull in the community. To me, he's just Dad. "Thanks."

I feel better after talking with them, especially now that I have a plan in place. Yes, I need to work out the details, but it's a great start.

We finish our dinner in easy conversation, other than the one low point where Steven bemoans his lack of love life.

Once he's paid our bill, Dad hugs us before heading out. "Let me know which day you want to take Meg out." He pauses, meeting my eyes with a weighted gaze. "And be sure to keep me posted about any new developments."

I try not to wince, knowing Steven won't let that comment go.

After he's gone, Steven turns to me. "What did he mean by new developments?"

A quick glance at my watch tells me Meg shouldn't be home yet, since she'd planned to grab dinner with her work friends. The sidewalk isn't the place to have this conversation, so I tell Steven, "I'll tell you at home."

He frowns but doesn't press me. At our house, we both park and he meets me on the steps at the front walk, eyebrows raised expectantly. Meg's car isn't here but she could still be home any second. We'll have to hurry.

"Come on." I lead him to my room in silence, gearing up for another lecture about my impulsiveness. I'm low enough already with everything going on with Meg.

But this is Steven we're talking about. He reads me better than anyone, and I can only hope he'll get it.

Once in my room, I tap the door so it swings almost closed then I face Steven.

He's frowning. "You know you can tell me anything, right, Silas? I'm not here to judge you. I mean, I *will* tell you if I think you're being an idiot, but I'm your brother. I've got your back, no matter what."

The words reassure me enough that I nod, then I take a bolstering breath and walk over to the dresser, opening the top drawer. "You can't tell anyone about this, okay?"

* * * *

Meg

Since I ran into Lee and Silas coming back from dinner, I can't fight the rumble of questions in my mind. They keep turning over and over, like an endless load of clothes tumbling in the dryer. I just needed some space. Why did Silas take Leah to dinner? And why won't either of them talk to me about it?

The possibilities swirl in my head, an unsettling tempest of negativity. Especially when Mom's words join the mix. Then one thought surfaces, louder than the rest.

What if he's going to break up with me?

I drive home from my dinner with my friends, wallowing in the bleakness that has surrounded me all week. Bekah and Kaylie insisted on taking me out, wanting to cheer me up, but it didn't touch the hollow ache in my middle.

The one only Silas can fill.

I picture him, his handsome face, his dancing amber eyes, and a longing wells in me to see my boyfriend. A hug from him sounds amazing and maybe…maybe it'd be the right move. The first step back onto the correct path, redirecting us from this disastrous route that we're only on because of our mistakes.

My mistakes.

I trudge upstairs, noticing Silas' door is ajar. Feeling determined, I hurry toward his room just in time to hear him say, "You can't tell anyone about this, okay?"

"I know how to keep my mouth shut."

Steven's voice carries through the door, and I hold my breath. I shouldn't stay here. I should go to my room, give them some privacy, but it feels like my feet are glued to the floor. Moments pass as a drawer squeaks open, followed by a shuffling noise.

Silence settles as I hold my breath, waiting.

Steven says in a heavy tone, "Silas, are you sure?"

Silas murmurs in the affirmative as my mind races to what they could be discussing.

"Do you really think now's the best time?"

Silas scoffs. "No, I know better than that. I'm waiting, but maybe after her birthday this weekend..."

So they *are* talking about me. The air whooshes from my lungs as I lean against the wall, my stomach feeling like someone shoved a cannonball down my throat.

"Well, I won't say I'm not surprised."

The weight in Steven's words tells me this isn't something little, and it's the final confirmation I need to know that my gut was right. Silas *is* going to break up with me.

"Just, don't do this lightly, okay? She's been through a lot."

My knees buckle, and it's all I can do to stay upright. I press my hand to my mouth to stop from crying out at the pain stabbing my heart, then I ease into my room and shut the door. I sink onto my bed, staring blankly at the wall as one thought streams through my head on constant replay.

I've already lost him.

* * * *

The next morning, I stay in bed with the lights off and the covers tucked under my chin. I don't necessarily sleep, though I do doze on and off. Mostly I stare into the dim room and don't see anything.

I just hear the conversation between Steven and Silas yesterday. Being repeated over. And over.

And over.

My energy is non-existent. I can't turn off my brain or get up long enough to focus on anything else. The hours slip by and I miss both my classes, a rare occurrence. My stomach rumbles, but I ignore it, the idea of getting food too much work.

A knock sounds on my door, and even though I don't answer, Leah pokes her head in. "Meg?"

I grunt from my fetal position on the bed. She flips on the light, making me groan and shade my eyes with my hand. *Why can't she leave me alone?*

"Why didn't you go to class? Are you sick?"

"No," I mumble.

"Then what's wrong?" She shoves me over to sit on the edge of my bed.

I don't want to tell her. I'm still upset about her and Silas lying to me about why they went to dinner. "I'd rather not talk right now."

"Yeah, I can see that you're deep in one of your wallows, but that's exactly why you need to talk." She pokes my thigh through the blanket, and I glare at her. When I don't say anything further, she pops to her feet. "I'm bringing you some soup, then we're getting to the bottom of this, whether you like it or not."

"Don't you have to work?" I ask, an annoyed edge to my tone. Maybe I'll get lucky and she'll have to leave soon.

She gives me a triumphant grin. "Nope, I have the day off so I've got nothing but time. Be right back."

Then she disappears. I huff out a breath and flop to my back as I direct my glare to the ceiling. And I stay that way until she returns. The steaming cup of beef barley soup has my mouth watering. It's my favorite, and I reluctantly sit up, rearranging my pillows behind me, then I take the soup from her.

"Okay, Meg. Spill."

I do in halting bits and pieces. I start with dinner with my mom, unable to stop a few tears from trickling down my cheeks when I repeat what she said and how invisible I felt afterward. How I haven't been able to find the words to tell Silas because I haven't wanted to say any of this out loud.

Leah crawls over my legs to sit next to me, then she gently takes the soup out of my hands and sets it down before giving me a full-on hug. Before I know it, I'm sobbing in her arms as all the hurt wells up.

"I'm so sorry she said that, Meg." Lee rubs my back as I start to calm. "I know you've had some rough patches, but I'm still your best friend. I love you. I know Silas loves you, wholeheartedly. And so do the other brothers. Not in the same way as him, but you're one of us. You're not alone."

I sniffle as I sit up, her words washing over me. I blink at her as I realize I've done it again. "Shit," I mutter. "I thought I was better, that I was past shutting you guys out with my walls and my doubt..."

She takes my hand. "I think you're doing better overall. Hopefully this was just a lapse back into old habits." She gives me an encouraging squeeze, but I can't return it.

Not without explaining the rest. I take a deep breath and blurt out, "I think Silas is going to break up with me."

"What?" She lets out a little laugh then sobers when she sees I'm not joking. "Why in the world would you think that?"

I start with their dinner, haltingly explaining Silas' reaction to my question and how I know he wasn't telling the truth.

It's her turn to glare at me. "Meg, you're going to have to trust me on this one. Neither of us was talking about you in a bad way or trying to figure out you guys' relationship or whatever you think is going on. I promise you'll get to know what we talked about soon—you just need to be patient."

I'm taken aback by her stern tone, but I know her, know she's telling the truth. I feel a bit better hearing that they weren't meeting to discuss my problems. "Okay, Lee, I can do that. But that's not all."

I repeat word for word the conversation I overheard, my heart sinking as her expression falls.

"That doesn't sound good, I'll admit, but Silas loves you. I'm sure there's a simple explanation for all of it."

"I hope so."

She has her thinking face on, her mouth scrunched to one side, and I know she's trying to solve my problems. I scan the room, my eyes landing on my wall calendar and the date tomorrow is circled.

For my birthday.

"At least all of this will be over soon. One way or another." Maybe I can enjoy my day despite his deadline looming over me.

Leah purses her lips. "I think—"

I hold up my hand, knowing she's going to tell me to talk to him. But I don't want to even think about confronting him now. "Let's get through my birthday, then he and I can sort all of this out. I want to concentrate on enjoying my day."

She looks like she might protest but instead collects herself and says, "If that's what you want. How about we go out to breakfast tomorrow, my treat? You pick the place."

"Yeah, that sounds perfect." And I'm not lying. The idea of spending the morning with my best friend makes me smile. It's something to look forward to at least.

"Okay then." She gives me another hug then stands. "You promise after your birthday you'll sort this out?"

I nod then make an X on my chest with my finger. "I promise."

After she leaves, I finish my soup, but her staunch declaration keeps echoing in my mind. That Silas loves me, wholeheartedly.

I find myself reviewing these past couple of months in my head, replaying our tender moments alongside the sticky ones. Me jumping to him at the ropes course. Our dance at the wedding. Him saying he loves me after the pool party. The way he says my name every time we make love.

By the time the montage finishes, I'm one hundred percent convinced he loves me. And if he loves me, why shouldn't I put on my big girl panties and tell him exactly what I overheard?

The thought sends fear spiraling through my chest, freezing my lungs. But I force myself to draw in a breath, then slowly let it out. I let myself think over the worst that could happen.

Silas could break up with me.

The words stab at me, piercing my heart as pain trickles in and I picture my life without Silas. It would be like this last week has been, only so much worse. To never have one of his hugs or kisses again? To never hear him whisper my name while he's buried deep inside me? To never run my fingers through his hair?

The idea has my whole body shrinking away from it, my mind racing for how to prevent it. How to hold onto the man I love.

Wait. I replay my last thought as my mouth goes dry. *Love.*

I love Silas.

The fact stares me in the face, hitting me with all the subtlety of a two by four against my head. I do another quick run-through of our journey, trying to pinpoint the exact moment.

But there isn't one. So many little steps got me to this point. One tiptoe forward, then another as Silas proved himself time and again. Proved that he loved me, that he would catch me if I jumped to him. That our cable is strong enough.

And I think back to the conversation I overheard, reviewing it through the lens of his love. Steven sounded shocked, but not upset. I picture his reaction if Silas had said he was breaking up with me and Steven would have been upset, maybe even mad. He would've had a lot more to say, too.

Then I replay Silas' words. He'd been so matter-of-fact, and I know he'd never have been that calm if he'd been talking about breaking up with me. He'd have been a wreck.

The evidence piles up that I misunderstood the conversation. Guilt weighs on me that I jumped to conclusions as I throw off the covers and sit on the edge of the bed. I glance at my phone, my heart sinking when I realize that Silas is off with his soccer team today at a teambuilding event at the ropes course.

I want — no, *need* to talk to him. To tell him that I was wrong for holding him at arm's length again, for letting my mom's words send me back into that habit of doubt.

And most of all to tell him I love him.

The words resound in me again, and I know I can't wait. I tilt my head, realizing I don't have to. I can go have a grand gesture moment like in all those romance novels Silas loves so much. Determination settles over me as I hurry to get ready.

Thirty minutes later, I pull into the parking lot of Branching Out. I sit for a moment, staring at the entrance as I think of doing this in front of Remy, Brad and Aiden, not to mention the rest of the team. My palms are sweaty as I grip the steering wheel, but my resolve doesn't weaken.

I want him to know that I'm all in. So I suck in several breaths, then stride from the car to collect my wristband.

It's more crowded than the last time we were here and I have to wait for my harness, then it takes a while to find their group. Finally, I locate them with the help of a kind employee. She leaves me at the base of the course, a different one from before, and I go through the process of hooking up my cable and testing my harness before I force myself to climb the stairs, one by one.

My heart feels like it might beat out of my chest as I stand at the top of the platform, unable to believe I'm here. But the more I think about it, the more I realize how fitting this truly is.

Here is where I first realized I trusted Silas. Here is where I made my first leap to him. And here is where I'm going to prove my love by making the right move.

Unfortunately, the first person I see is Diego.

"Meg." He flashes that blinding smile. "What are you doing here?"

"Looking for Silas." I scan the course. "Do you know where he is?"

"Is everything okay?"

I nod, still searching. "Yep, just have something really important to tell him."

He points across the way. "He's over there."

The moment my gaze lands on Silas, I feel calmer. I stare for several dopey moments, soaking in the sight of my handsome boyfriend, the love of my life. His curls are more unruly today than ever, and he's smiling but it's lacking. I'm here to fix that.

"Silas!" I call. "Silas!"

His head whips up and he finds me, his gorgeous eyes widening. "Meg? What are you—?"

"I have to talk to you." I keep my focus on him as we wind our way to each other, trying to find the shortest route. It takes a bit, but we close the distance until we're only separated by a few short feet.

With a flea jump even bigger than the last course's. *Shit.*

"Meg?" Silas is grinning, his smile back in full force. "What are you doing here?"

I stare at the space between platforms, feeling the culmination of everything that has built between us over the past few months. All the obstacles we've overcome to get here play through my mind. Then I gaze into his wondering eyes.

"I'm here because I love you," I say, loud and clear.

His mouth drops open.

"Now move out of the way, mister. I'm coming over."

Disbelief and awe flood his face, but he steps back onto the central platform. I take a deep breath and launch myself across the distance, laughing when I stumble forward on the opposite side. I don't stop until I'm hugging Silas with all my might.

"Hi," I say, studying his adorable face.

"Did that really just happen?"

I nod, almost melting at the tenderness in his gaze.

"Say it again."

My lips tip up of their own accord. "I love you, Silas Wrighting. I couldn't wait another second to tell you that. I'm all in, just like you."

"Really, Meg?" His whisper is full of awe.

I lift a shoulder. "Yeah —"

I don't get to finish my sentence because he cuts me off with a searing kiss that makes my mind go blank and steals my breath. I melt against him. Even as his teammates whoop and holler, he doesn't stop.

And I hope he never will.

Chapter Twenty-Five

Silas

Meg's declaration of love resounds in my mind as I kiss her with all the pent-up longing I've held inside for the past week. Damn, I've missed this woman. When I break away, my teammates' raucous calls reach me through the heady daze I'm in, but I can't bring myself to care.

Meg loves me.

I beam, cupping her cheek. "I love you, Meg. I can't believe you're here, that you came. That you jumped to me again."

Her dark eyes hold only love and adoration. "I can't believe it took me this long to see it, and like I said, I couldn't wait another minute when I realized it."

"I'm glad you didn't."

She blinks then shifts away, her cheeks heating as if registering where we are. She glances around then ducks her head. "I'm sorry to interrupt. I should —"

"Meg." I run my hand down her arm. "You have nothing to be sorry about. I'm thrilled you came here, that this was that important to you." I lean forward until our foreheads touch. "It sure as hell is that important to me."

Her shoulders relax again and her palm comes to rest on my chest, outside of my harness.

"Besides, this is our last course. I've already done all of it, so I'm happy to leave now." I pull back to search her gaze, hoping to spend more time with her. Hoping to hear what's been going on with her. "Maybe we can talk?"

A flash of guilt crosses her face but is quickly replaced with determination, and she nods. "Yes, please."

Relief washes over me as I lead the way across the course, waving off the back slaps and teasing from my teammates. My smile never dims as we leave the course, shed our harnesses, and walk hand in hand to her car.

"I rode with Remy," I say when she glances around for my vehicle. "You okay giving me a lift?"

"Of course!"

Her full lips call to me and I walk her backward until she's pressed against the car, caged in by my body. I run my hands over her hips to rest below her ribcage, letting my gaze drift over her beautiful face to settle on her delectable mouth.

"I missed you," I whisper before I lean in for another scorching kiss.

She hums her agreement, flinging her arms around my neck and pulling me closer until our bodies are flush. My cock bobs in my shorts, desire crashing through me as that familiar passionate fire ignites between us. I moan into her mouth, unable to resist grinding against her.

She pulls back with a breathless gasp of my name, and I go still, waiting.

"Can...can we talk first?"

The pleading in her words has me reeling in the need that threatens to overtake me. "Sure, Meg," I say, ignoring the half-mast in my pants. "Whatever you need."

We get into the car, and I beam when she lays her hand palm up on the console. I love how perfectly our hands fit together as I lace my fingers through hers.

"Can we go talk while we walk the beach?"

I'll never turn down a trip to Lake Michigan. "Sounds good to me."

We spend the fifteen-minute drive with her asking me about the ropes course. I know we need to talk about more substantial things, but I give her this time, letting us ease into our usual routine of comfortable chatter. It feels good to have things relaxed between us once more.

At the beach, we kick off our shoes and walk across the light sand. The gentle breeze feels refreshing and stirs up some decent-sized waves. The water itself is darker than the last time we were here, and I marvel at Lake Michigan's many moods.

We hold hands again as we reach the water. I stay on the water's edge, letting the waves wash up to my ankles and giving her the higher, drier path.

Several moments pass in silence, then she sighs and glances at me. "I'm sorry, Si."

I give her an encouraging smile, squeezing her hand.

"I'm sorry I shut you out again. I thought I was done with walls, done with hiding, but in the moment I didn't know what else to do."

The thought strikes a chord within me, so close to how I used to feel when handling rejection or being paralyzed by a task. I tuck that away for later as she begins to tell me what happened. I can only listen in horror as she repeats what her mom said about her dad leaving her nothing.

"What about you?" I blurt out. I can't imagine how that must have hurt Meg.

"That's what I said," she says, her voice thick and her grip tightening on me.

Her mom's reply didn't help, and my heart breaks for my girlfriend, who has been through so much. I tug her to a stop then gather her into my arms, wishing I could take away all her pain.

"I'm so sorry, Meg. That sounds absolutely brutal." She sniffles against my chest and I run my hand over her back before adding, "You know I love you, right? You're part of our family, Meg. My brothers love you too, and so does Leah. You've got us, Nutmeg. You're not alone."

She sniffles again then leans back to give me a trembling smile. "I know. I forgot that for a little bit when the doubts were so loud, but Leah helped me remember."

I wipe away a stray tear from her cheek with my thumb, cradling her face and loving how she leans into my touch. "Therapy has helped me so much, and I wonder…maybe it could help you too? I used to feel helpless when I perceived rejection or when I was spiraling after being overwhelmed. Mara's helped me, given me techniques to halt those negative habits in their tracks."

"I'll think about that." Her gaze flicks back and forth as she considers. "It would be nice to have some tools to use so I stop shutting everyone out all the time."

I stroke her jawline with my thumb. "I'd like that too," I say, keeping my tone light even though it's more than true.

Her expression sobers and she steps back. "There's more, Si."

The seriousness in her words has me frowning, but I fall into step as we begin walking again.

"My mom said something else."

I frown as I listen to her mom's toxic words, hating that the woman who is supposed to be nurturing and protecting Meg has been feeding her doubts instead. Hurt pricks me as well, that Meg would believe me capable of that, but I stay quiet as she keeps talking.

"That seed of doubt was already in me, but Mom's words made it grow." Meg presses her lips together then glances at me. "Seeing you and Leah together added to that, especially when neither of you would tell me the truth."

A sigh escapes me. "You know we would never —"

She holds up her free hand. "I know, Si, I do. You'd never hurt me and you didn't get together to maliciously discuss me behind my back. I was so traumatized by my conversation with my mom that I couldn't see the truth. I'm sorry."

I squeeze her hand, still feeling hurt, but understanding that she was in a bad place.

"I do trust you. I'm not even going to ask what you guys actually talked about because I don't need to know."

The declaration is a balm to my stinging heart, but she's not done.

"It gets worse." She lets go of my hand to wring her own together, keeping her gaze on the sand in front of her.

I stare at her, wondering what else could possibly have gone wrong.

"Yesterday, I came home, planning to try to talk to you. I needed one of your hugs more than anything…"

Alarm courses through me as I line up the time to when I was showing my brother the ring.

"Your door wasn't closed all of the way, so I heard you talking to Steven."

My mouth goes dry, panic flaring in my chest at her response to my impulsive action. "I—"

But she talks over me. "That solidified the idea that you were going to break up with me."

I stop in my tracks, the words nothing like what I expected to hear. I gape at her. "Wait, what?" How did she ever get to that conclusion? I try to keep an open mind as she relays what she heard.

"So remember the head space I was in. My mom made me feel like nothing, plus her comment about me being the next in a trail of broken hearts you left behind. Then you and Leah not telling me the whole truth."

Empathy trickles in, and I reach for her hand again, to show her I'm listening. That I care. Even if I don't like it. I begin to understand, though, as she repeats the conversation from her perspective, and we walk in silence for a few moments after she finishes.

"I…" I take a deep breath then let it out slowly. "I can't believe you thought I was actually going to break up with you, Meg. That's the last thing I want, and I hoped I'd proven my commitment to you by now."

This time, she pulls me to a stop and puts her hand on my cheek. "You have, Silas. I just fell into that pit of doubt and couldn't see anything else. I'm sorry."

Confusion takes over. "How did you get from that to coming to the ropes course today?"

A brilliant smile tips her lips. "Leah pulled me out of my wallowing and made me eat some soup. But the thing that truly tipped the scale?" She loops her hands behind my neck as I wait for her answer. "You, Si. I thought back to everything you've done for me these past couple of months. How steady you've been, how attentive and caring. How you've proven time and again that I can trust you, with everything."

I begin to relax at her sincerity.

"That's when I realized that I loved you and I have for a while now. I'm sorry it's taken so long to get here, but I'm so thankful that you've stuck with me through it all. Thank you for your patience. Thank you for loving me even when I pushed you away." She leans in to brush a kiss against my lips and I melt in the face of her love.

"Meg," I breathe, overwhelmed by this amazing woman. "You deserve all of that and so much more. I'm sorry you've had so many obstacles to overcome, but you never gave up. I just hope you'll let me help you tackle any future ones. That's what partners do — work together."

Her eyes glisten as she nods. "I'd like that, Si. You're so much more than my boyfriend. You're my partner, and I promise to do my best to let you in, or get the help I need until I'm able to do that."

"That's all I ask." I bend down to press my lips to hers in a tender kiss that seals our promise.

When I straighten, I stare at my girlfriend, my partner, feeling like we're finally both on the same page. That, despite all the wrong moves, at last we're where we're meant to be.

I take her hand once more and we begin walking back in the direction we came as I turn the conversation to something lighter. Something I'm even more excited about now. "So someone has a birthday tomorrow..."

* * * *

Meg

My birthday starts off in an amazing way, with Silas waking me up at midnight to make love to me again. Since it's officially my birthday. Then I have a late breakfast with Leah, after Silas promises we'll do something this afternoon.

Even if he won't tell me what.

I can't stop smiling. I jumped to Silas and the cable held. I poured my heart out to him, and the cable held.

I finally know where I belong and it's with him. With all of them. My amazing family, tied together not all by blood but by choice. They chose me, and I chose them, and somehow that makes our bonds even stronger.

Silas taps on the partially open door to my room and I look up from my laptop, smiling in response to his handsome face.

"Homework?" he asks. "On your birthday?"

I lift a shoulder. "I'm a little behind." I hadn't felt like doing much this past week.

He nods his understanding, then leans on the wall. A mischievous glint dances in his amber eyes as he watches me. "Think you could take a little break?"

I nibble at my lip. "Maybe in like an hour?"

"Meg…" He pushes off the wall and sits next to me on the bed. "The homework can wait. Let's go celebrate you." When I hesitate again, he nudges me with his elbow. "I'll tell you what Leah and I were talking about at our dinner."

That tips the scale, and I quickly put my computer into sleep mode then pop to my feet. "What are we waiting for?"

He chuckles and takes my hand, leading me down the hall to the stairs. Where he nudges me to go first.

The moment I start down them, everyone yells, "Surprise!"

I freeze at the sight of Silas' brothers clumped together at the base of the staircase. Bekah, Kaylie and Remy are here too, all grinning at me. Several banners hang on the walls, proclaiming *Happy Birthday* with adorable sharks in party hats in the background.

Then Leah walks out of the kitchen with a blue cake, lit candles on top and starts singing, "Happy birthday to you."

The others join in as Silas steps down next to me and takes my hand. He sings softly as he tugs me to the main floor where they finish the song. Leah stands in front of me, beaming as she offers me the cake.

"Make a wish, Meg," Silas whispers in my ear.

But I don't know what more I can wish for because I have everything I need right here.

* * * *

It's been almost a week since my birthday and I haven't left the bliss bubble yet. Silas and I have stayed with one another every night, even Tuesday, although that was just to snuggle and sleep. I found a therapist and have an appointment next week with her.

But tonight, Silas is giving me my official birthday present — taking me on a date to Club 42. I have no idea how he managed to get us a Friday night reservation, but I'm thrilled. I've never been, and I can't wait to share this with him.

I go all out, shaving and moisturizing before slipping on my laciest underwear set. The red dress from Callie's wedding is next — I know how much Silas loved it. When I'm done with my hair, it hangs in loose curls, draping over my shoulders. And my makeup is on point.

When Silas taps on my door right at six, I'm ready to go. I open the door with a grin. The appreciation on his face as he stares at me sends warmth through my heart, even as desire simmers below the surface.

He surveys me with a soft smile, awe in his gaze. "You look...amazing, Meg."

So does he. He's wearing one of his tailored suits, a white button-down shirt sans tie with the top two buttons open. I want to drag him into my room by those lapels and never let him leave.

But a girl's got to eat so I simply say, "You too."

He leans in, brushing a sweet kiss on my cheek. "Happy birthday again." And he produces a present from behind his back.

"You didn't have —"

"I wanted to." The sweet gesture is accompanied by a blinding smile.

He's already thrown me a surprise party and is taking me out to this fancy restaurant. It's too much, but I'm also loving how he's spoiling me. So I rip open the paper. Once I raise the lid of the box, I squeal at the adorable stuffed shark staring back at me. I lift it up, loving how soft it is.

"He's so cute! Thank you." I launch myself at Silas for an exuberant hug.

He holds on a beat too long, and I wonder if he's also having a hard time controlling himself. The thought has me grinning as I pull away, putting some extra sway in my hips as I sashay over to my bed. I think I hear Silas groan as I lean over to put the shark right in the middle of my pillows.

His gorgeous eyes smolder as I pick up my clutch from the nightstand then stride back to him. "Shall we?" he asks, offering his arm.

I slip my arm through his, the smile never leaving my face as I let him escort me to the car and open my door. We chat the entire way there, catching up on our classes this morning and talking about Steven's date tonight. Hopefully it works out. The parking lot is pretty full, but we find an opening in the back corner.

"I could drop you off, if you'd like," Silas offers, glancing at my heels.

I laugh. "Honey, I could run circles around you in these things. A little stroll won't hurt me." But I appreciate his sweet suggestion all the same.

The sleek black building takes my breath away as I get my first glimpse of the exclusive venue. It glints in the fading sunlight, hints of metallic accents keeping it from feeling foreboding or overdone. A line of people stand behind red ropes next to the building, and I expect to go to the back of the line. But Silas guides me right to the front door, which an employee opens for us.

I'm still gaping as we walk in, following along as Silas leads me by the hand. He gives his name to the host, then we trail after them across a quiet dance floor with calm yellow light and a fleur-de-lis pattern behind the DJ station. The host leads us to a roped-off area then up some stairs to a very private booth.

"What is all this?" I ask, feeling beyond overwhelmed.

Silas raises my hand to his lips. "You deserve to start this year with something special."

I melt at the gentle brush of his kiss. "Si…I already have." Intensity flares between us as we hold each other's gaze. I started it right because I chose him, and I let him love me the way I've always wanted.

Our server greets us, startling me back to reality. We put in our drink orders and Silas gets us bruschetta for an appetizer, one of my favorites. We peruse the menu, and I try not to gape at the prices. He always says that his grandparents spoil him with way too much money for birthdays and Christmas, that he saves it for special occasions. I just don't know that I'm special enough to warrant this much fanfare.

Then I glance up and find Silas staring at me with complete adoration and I forget all about my doubt. I'm here with the man I love, and I'm going to savor every moment.

When our drinks arrive, I eagerly sip my vodka cranberry. The tart flavor bursts on my tongue, just the way I like it. We put in our order for entrees as another server brings our bruschetta.

Silas serves me a piece, and I bite in, savoring the crunch and the delicious taste. Though the tomato squirts a bit of juice on my chin. I quickly grab my napkin from my lap to dab at the mess, but when I look up, a small black velvet box sits near my plate on the table.

I jerk my chin up to stare at Silas in shock. "What's this?"

He grins and nudges it closer to me. "This is what I was talking to Steven about the other day."

I frown, wondering if he's going to ask me to marry him. We just got on solid ground and I have work I want to do on myself, not to mention school and my job. I'm just getting used to us...

"I'm not proposing, okay?" he says, as if reading my thoughts. "Just open it."

The gentle plea has me reaching for the box, and my breath catches in my throat at the sight of the gorgeous gold ring with the brilliant red gems. My lips part as I take out the ring to examine closer. "It matches my dress."

"I know how much you like red."

My mouth is dry and I have to swallow several times before I can speak. "Silas, what is this about?" I hold the ring out between us, more than confused.

He takes it from me, spinning it in his fingers as he stares at it. "I put a hold on it on a whim when Dad stopped at a jewelry store. It made me think of you."

Panic dances at the edges of my mind as I wait for his full explanation. I trust Silas, I remind myself. And if he's moving too fast, I can tell him. I know he'll respect me. The reassurance calms me slightly and I relax as I will myself to listen.

"It's what he and I fought about, my impulsiveness and how I'm not like my brothers."

The quiet admission still holds pain and I reach out to grab his hand, knowing touch comforts him.

One side of his mouth tips up. "I went back and bought it the day after you helped me with my task paralysis. You understood me on a level that I didn't realize I was craving. You saw me like no one else, and

I knew then that there was no one else I'd rather spend my life with."

I gape at him. "I hadn't even said I loved you yet."

"I know." He smirks. "I knew you'd come around."

I roll my eyes, but a smile graces my lips. He's always been cocky, in the best possible way.

"So I was showing Steven the ring when you overheard. He asked me if I was sure, about you."

My mind races to adjust the memory, to replay the words in light of him wanting to marry me, and I can't move for a long moment. "Silas, I thought you weren't proposing."

That arrogant grin grows wider as he puts the ring back in the box and shuts the lid. "I'm not. Not today, at least."

I begin to relax again.

"I showed you this for two reasons, Nutmeg. One, I wanted you to know what you overheard, to put any lingering doubts to rest for good." He tips his hand and trails his fingers along the inner part of my wrist. "And two, I want you to know just how much I mean it when I say I love you, that I'm truly not going anywhere."

The intensity in his words overwhelms me and I slip out of his grasp to lean back against the booth as I stare at him. I'm not panicking or withdrawing, though, just processing. The love I feel for him wells within me.

How did I ever get so lucky?

"So, Meg, whenever you're ready, we can take that next step." He runs his fingers over the box then slides it toward me. "How about you hold onto this until then?"

"What...what if you change your mind?" I stare at the box, the commitment he's making settling on me as another thread strengthens the cable that binds us. "Or what if I'm never ready?"

"I won't change my mind. You're it for me, the love of my life, the partner I choose to have every day—forever, if you'll let me." He grins again. "And that's why I'm giving it to you. For you to have it, knowing you can go at whatever pace you're comfortable with."

My throat is thick with the love and patience he has for me, for the understanding he's shown and the wonderful gift he just gave me. "Silas?" He arches an eyebrow and I nudge the box back toward him. "Could you hold onto it?"

His face starts to fall.

"I don't think it'll fit in my clutch." I lift up the small purse, my lips twitching as I fight my amusement.

His mouth drops when he realizes I'm not rejecting him and he pretends to glare. My delighted laughter spills out. He joins me a few moments later then feigns a huff as he shoves the ring into his pocket.

Then we share a tender smile, and I say quietly, "I'll get it back from you when we get home, okay?"

He nods and the waiter appears with our food. Every bite is delicious, every glance is heated, and when the dance floor opens, the sultry beat is just what I need to build the tension aching within me. We dance together, in perfect harmony until I can't take it anymore.

"Silas?" I ask when the song ends. He tilts his head as I toy with the curls at the back of his neck and say, "Take me home?"

"Why would I want to do that?" he asks, his voice rough and full of gravel.

"I have something I want to give you."

One eyebrow lifts as he waits for an explanation.

I lean up on my tiptoes to whisper in his ear. "Me."

* * * *

The weekend is full of bliss, sex and perfection. Monday, I zoom through my two classes then Silas and I walk to lunch afterward. We're sitting at Eat at Joe's, swapping out the ingredients in our salads, when my phone buzzes.

I lift it up, my face falling as I see the name on the screen. "It's my mom."

Silas freezes, fork in mid-air. I push the ignore button then set the phone on the table again. Hurt pierces me as I remember our last encounter, but instead of weighing me down, it ignites a spark of anger within me. I stab the rest of the red onion and toss it on Silas' plate then drench my salad with dressing.

"You okay?" he asks.

My shoulders slump, but I appreciate his concern. "No," I say slowly. "I'm not okay. I'm not okay with how my mom treats me and I'm not okay that she thinks so poorly of you that she said you're just going to toss me away. I'm not okay that she thinks nothing of me, that she gave me to Leah's family anytime she didn't want to look at me."

Silas watches me with wide eyes full of empathy and understanding.

"I'm not okay." The words feel good to say aloud, especially when I add, "But I will be."

I reach over and change the settings in my mom's contact to hide alerts. I'll deal with her when I'm ready, on my terms.

Then I grab my salad and slide it over next to Silas. He watches in confusion as I stand then poke his arm and say, "Scoot over, you. I need to snuggle with my boyfriend."

A massive grin splits his face as he makes room for me then lifts his arm as I scooch in next to him. I don't stop until I'm smooshed against his side and can rest my cheek on his chest. He squeezes me tight until I finally shift away.

"You know I love you, Nutmeg," he says, placing a kiss on top of my head. "Let me know if there's anything I can do."

I raise my chin to meet his sincere gaze. "You're already doing it."

The smile we share warms my heart. We finish our meal like that, side by side, and when we leave the restaurant I have no doubt that I will be okay. Because I have the support I need to make it through anything life wants to throw at me. I have a place that I belong, a place I've always had but was too scared to accept.

But I'm not scared anymore.

I tuck that happy thought away as I link hands with my boyfriend and ask, "What's next?"

"Whatever you want, Meg." He beams at me. "Whatever you want."

Epilogue

Seven months later
Meg

One more school year comes to a close. I can't believe April is here already, can't believe Silas and I are both on track to graduate next year.

We spent this Saturday morning lounging in bed after celebrating too late last night. I just heard the shower shut off then his door close. The idea I've been playing with for the past month surfaces again, and I pad over to my dresser to take out the ring he gave me last fall.

I slip it on my finger, holding up my hand to admire the perfect fit.

I'm in a much different—much better—place than I was last year. Therapy has helped me so much and I've learned to set boundaries for myself. And with my mom. If she doesn't abide by them, I don't see her. It hasn't been easy, but I'm finally learning that I deserve to feel safe, and I'm working through the trauma of my past.

Silas has been with me every step of the way — encouraging, loving, bolstering. I can't picture my life without him. I want him with me for every step. I want to be his.

Mrs. Silas Wrighting. The name plays in my mind, full circle from the crush I had as a teenager. I filled notebooks with the practiced signature, complete with hearts dotting the 'i's, and now here I am, about to make it a soon-to-be reality. I wait for the doubt to creep in, the panic at what planning a wedding will entail.

But it doesn't. This is the right move, and I'm more than ready for it.

* * * *

Silas

I whistle as I walk back to Meg's room, wondering what else we'll be doing today. There are still moments that I can't believe she's mine, that she loves me. I can't wait to take the next step with her, but I'm also happy being patient.

Because I know she'll come around. Eventually.

I slip into the room, not sure if she'll still be sleeping, but I find her sitting on the bed. Her smile lights up the room and I stride over to her to give her a sound kiss. "Morning, Nutmeg."

"Morning, Si."

That sinful robe is all she has on and I let my gaze drift down the V of the front to the gap over her thighs. Her hand rests on the silky fabric. I do a double-take when a hint of red glints in the sunlight.

She's wearing my ring.

I gape at her, overwhelmed by the idea that she might be ready. I need to hear her say it. "Meg…?"

Standing, she places one hand on my chest then stretches the other out so we can admire the ring gracing her finger. "It's too pretty to keep in the drawer any longer."

I search her dark eyes, hope bubbling in me like an uncorked bottle of champagne.

"I'm just waiting for the love of my life to ask me a very important question," she says, the teasing undercurrent in her words reassuring me.

I take a deep breath then drop to one knee, the words I've practiced over and over perched on my tongue. "Meg Parker, you are the one I want to spend the rest of my days with. You are the one I want to fall asleep next to and wake up beside. I want to share every high and every low with you as my wife. Will you marry me?"

She nods, blinking furiously for a moment before she gives me a wobbly smile and a tremulous, "Yes."

Leaping to my feet, I wrap my arms around her waist and lift her off her feet. She clings to my neck as I spin her in an exuberant circle, our delighted laughter filling the room. If I had my way, I'd never let go.

And now, I'll never have to.

Sign up for our newsletter and find out about all our romance book releases, eBook sales and promotions, sneak peeks and FREE romance books!

Want to see more from this author? Here's a taster for you to enjoy!

Wrighting the Wrongs: The Wrong Time
Maren Jenner

Excerpt

Steven

A flash of lightning illuminates the walls of my room as I lie on my bed, staring at the ceiling. Rain pours steadily outside, April showers at their finest. Thunder rumbles, emphasizing my dark mood and underlining my bleak thoughts. I turn on my side, tucking one hand under my arm as today's events replay. *Again.*

My youngest brother Silas just got engaged.

I should be happy for him. Hell, I *am* happy for him and his fiancée, Meg. But I'm the oldest, and I can't help wondering when it'll be my turn.

All three of my younger brothers are now paired off. Sebastian is married, Silas engaged, and Shawn is — well, he's definitely in a serious relationship with our family friend Leah. I don't resent their happiness or the fact that they've found life-long partners to share their days with.

I just wish I could find that too.

Another flash of lightning bathes the room in pale light, glinting off the high school yearbook on my night stand. My lips press into a thin line as *her* name flashes in my mind. It hurts just to think it, let alone say it. But sometimes the past won't be contained.

A montage plays before me, all featuring the same beautiful young woman — Bianca Wakley. I grip my pillow tighter, waiting for the stab of pain to fade to its usual dull ache. It's been nearly ten years since I last saw her, ten years since the night of our graduation when we had plans to elope. And she never showed.

I grind my teeth, then push myself up off the bed, unable to bear another moment of the tortured path my mind insists on wandering. A giggle sounds from above, and I fight a groan.

Ever since Shawn roped us into cleaning out the attic last year, he and Leah like to sneak up there during storms. The space is partially above my room, and the ceiling isn't soundproof. Usually, Shawn gives me a heads up.

My phone dings, and I pick it up to find a message from Shawn. Better late than never, I guess. I sigh, glancing at the clock to find it's only ten p.m., too early to be going to sleep, especially on a Friday night. Another giggle sounds.

Definitely time to relocate.

I pad out into the hallway and have to turn sideways to skirt around the ladder that takes up a good chunk of the space. I clench my jaw when Leah giggles again, and hurry to the steps as quietly as possible just in case Silas and Meg are sleeping.

The light from the kitchen stove casts a yellow glow, dim, but bright enough that I can find my way. We turn it on every night for moments like this, or in case someone wants a late-night snack. It's too dark for my mood though, so I turn on the lamp next to the couch then grab the remote and flick on the TV, hoping for a distraction.

Of course the first thing on is a commercial featuring a couple in love. Rolling my eyes, I change the source, flipping to Netflix and pulling up my profile, then I select the first rec they have, but the damage is done.

As the oldest, I've paved the way for my brothers. Firstborn, first to graduate, first to earn his bachelor's degree, first to get a job in his field. Excelling in every way except the one I long for most. I'm twenty-seven and have no one to share my accomplishments with.

My bank account is full but my heart is empty.

My job at National Lending may pay the bills, but it doesn't exactly help when it comes to meeting new people. I work in the IT department and specialize in making things run smoothly in the background. Although I appreciate not dealing with annoying calls asking me to help find a deleted email or demanding they get more space because their storage is full, it would be nice to interact with someone outside of my department.

As my youngest brother Silas so kindly pointed out—it's not like the love of my life is going to just show up on my doorstep.

Silas also suggested I try some of the different dating apps out there, but the very idea of sorting through all the potential matches is exhausting. Dating itself is exhausting, though I have tried since Bianca—with women I've met through friends or at events. But the universe seems to be against me. Things will go well, then she'll get back together with her ex. Or she'll only be in town for a visit and hate doing the long-distance thing.

Images of Bianca flit through my mind again, each one punctuated by an ache I've not been able to soothe since she disappeared. Her blonde hair, silky smooth. Those dancing blue eyes sparkling like the sun. That enticing smile I could never resist.

Thunder crashes, shaking the house, and I jerk out of the past. The home renovation show catches my eye.

I stare intently at the construction scene, a wisp of nostalgia wafting through me and one corner of my mouth tips up in an involuntary smile.

I'd needed a distraction after my high school heartbreak. When my uncle Jason said he had an opening on his construction crew, I leaped at the chance and threw myself into the job. The labor took every ounce of my concentration and strength, and I was too exhausted when I fell into bed each night to think about *her*.

A rapping noise echoes through the house, and at first I think it's the TV. But when it sounds again, I realize it's coming from the front door. Frowning, I stand, then cautiously walk over. I peek out of the window next to it.

Lightning illuminates a slight figure and she turns her head, giving me a glimpse of her face beneath her hood just before the light fades. My heart stops as my mind races to line her profile up with the one that haunts my dreams. But it can't be her.

Can it?

The knock sounds again, followed by a feminine voice calling, "Steven? Shawn? Sebastian? Silas?"

I'm frozen to the spot. She knows our names, knows who live here.

"Anyone?"

That last pleading note spurs me into action, and I yank open the door, my heart in my throat. Hope bubbles within me, though the bitterness of pain and hurt twine with its effervescence.

She steps forward, out of the rain, and the lamplight reaches her features. Her lower lip quivers as I stare into a pair of cerulean eyes I never thought I'd see again.

"Bianca?"

About the Author

Maren Jenner lives in Michigan with her supportive husband and spunky daughter. She loves writing, and when she's not working on her next book, she's got her nose in a different one. Her summers are spent on any lake she can visit, but the beaches of Lake Michigan are her favorite.

She's been writing for as long as she can remember, and it's always been her dream to become a full time author. None of this would be possible without the love and support of her family and friends, and of course, her amazing readers!

Maren loves to hear from readers. You can find her contact information, website details and author profile page at https://www.firstforromance.com

ENTWINED PUBLISHING

www.ingramcontent.com/pod-product-compliance
Lightning Source LLC
Chambersburg PA
CBHW030400030726
47497CB00002B/422